THE BACK OF BEYOND BOOK CLUB

An escapist and heart-warming romance for summer

ANGELA BRITNELL

Choc Lit
A Joffe Books company
www.choc-lit.com

First published in Great Britain in 2024

© Angela Britnell 2024

This book is a work of fiction. Names, characters, businesses, organizations, places and events are either the product of the author's imagination or are used fictitiously. Any resemblance to actual persons, living or dead, events or locales is entirely coincidental. The spelling used is British English except where fidelity to the author's rendering of accent or dialect supersedes this. The right of Angela Britnell to be identified as author of this work has been asserted in accordance with the Copyright, Designs and Patents Act 1988.

Cover art by Alexandra Allden

ISBN: 978-1781897560

To my wonderful mother who proudly told everyone about her daughter 'the author,' and passed away at the grand age of 95 while I was writing this book.

CHAPTER ONE

'I know you're in there, Melissa Martyn. And I'll break this door down before I let you go back on your promise.'

Josie's strident voice made Melissa wince.

'The others said to leave you be, but that's a steaming heap of cow manure.'

Trust Josie to tell it like it was.

Josie was Melissa's next-door neighbour and the first friend Melissa had made when she moved to Cornwall. She suspected that she had made a beeline for Josie, partly because the capable, forthright nurse's self-confidence reminded her of the American women — like her own mother — that Melissa had both admired and envied growing up. Melissa's husband, Robin, used to joke that Melissa must've been English in a previous life because she would happily tie herself in knots rather than be rude to anyone, she queued obediently, and frequently apologized for things that weren't her fault.

A pang of grief, mixed with guilt and anger, swept through her.

Strictly speaking, Melissa should refer to Robin differently these days. The problem was that calling him her "late" husband implied tardiness — something he'd considered a cardinal sin. If she said she'd "lost" him, it sounded as though she'd accidentally mislaid him. And that was patently untrue because he lay under an imposing stone in the Penworthal parish church graveyard alongside generations of the Martyn family.

'The girls will all be at Becky's by now.'

It amused Melissa that they called themselves girls, even though the youngest of the seven-strong group was in her mid-thirties and the oldest was well past retirement age. Aside from Melissa, they were all local women who'd known each other forever. Their group met regularly over daytime cups of tea and coffee, and the occasional evening glass of wine, at the Rusty Anchor pub. Despite its name, the pub, and Penworthal village itself, was a good three miles inland from Cornwall's rugged coastline.

'Melissa, please. Open up.' Josie's wheedling tone brought Melissa out of her reverie. 'Becky's baked a lemon drizzle *and* coffee and walnut. You know you've never met a cake you didn't like.'

Melissa did what she'd known was inevitable since her friend's first knock, and dragged herself off the sofa and over to the door.

'Finally.' Josie pushed in past her. 'I thought I'd have to go home for my battering ram.' Her sharp green eyes narrowed in on Melissa. 'For God's sake rake a comb through your hair and put on a bit of lipstick. As my old nan used to say, you're looking as wisht as a winnard.'

'I've no clue what that means but I'm guessing it's not a compliment.'

'It's the Cornish version of white as a ghost. "Wisht" is sickly. Pale. A "winnard" is our word for a redwing — the bird? They're often thin and weak by the time they migrate here.'

Melissa took a peep in the antique mirror hanging over the old granite fireplace. Pale — yeah, she'd give Josie that. Thin — maybe. Weak? Never. 'Give me five minutes,' she said, and hurried upstairs.

This would be the first time she'd been to the group since Robin's death last May — unbelievably, a full year ago this week. At the time she'd been too numb to protest when her parents cajoled her into returning to Tennessee with them, and the rest of the year had slipped by in a blur of nothingness. After Christmas the Rutherford family had mounted a campaign to convince her to move back to Nashville permanently, but the idea of selling *Gwartha an Dre*, which meant "top of the town" in Cornish, stirred Melissa to rediscover her backbone. She loved Robin's old family home, an unpretentious mid-nineteenth-century farmhouse built of mellow Cornish stone.

When she returned a few weeks ago, it almost ripped her heart out to see Robin's chair still positioned by the bay window, where they'd shifted it for the best view of his beloved garden when he became too frail to go outside. Thankfully Josie was with her that first day back and told Melissa — in her inimitable forthright manner — that it needed to go. Reluctantly, Melissa went along with the idea and they hauled the chair off to the nearest charity shop. Since then she'd worked on making small changes so she felt more at ease living there alone.

Melissa was drawn to the bedroom window. The glorious view out over a patchwork of fields bordered by ancient hedges, the occasional isolated farm and a spider's web of narrow lanes always soothed her soul. With an effort she forced herself to turn away and concentrate on getting ready. She'd washed her hair last night, so at least it was clean. The reflection in the mirror still had the power to shock, mainly because her hair had turned from its usual rich, vibrant brunette to a stark silver-grey within days of Robin's death. Over the last year she'd carelessly allowed the chin-length bob to grow out, and now the heavy strands brushed her shoulders. With a sigh, she dragged off the baggy black T-shirt and holey leggings she'd worn all day as she'd worked in the garden and slipped on a pale blue linen dress. Melissa dug a rose-pink lipstick out of her neglected make-up bag and, after using it for its intended purpose, added a smudge to her sunken cheeks. On impulse she grabbed a silky floral pashmina and draped it artfully around her bony shoulders. Adding that touch of her usual style boosted her confidence a couple of much-needed notches.

'Much better,' Josie grunted, when she reappeared. 'Let's go before you change your mind. Bag, keys and phone?'

The flutter of nerves in Melissa's stomach flapped like a cage of trapped birds. She was having doubts that the inaugural meeting of the group's new book club was an ideal way to ease back into circulation. The problem was that they all knew she was a voracious reader and had worked for a major New York publishing house before making the change to being her own boss as a freelance editor. There was no reasonable way out of this.

She took a couple of deep breaths and trailed after Josie.

* * *

Nathan sipped his pint of Tribute and let his mind drift while Paul carried on whinging.

'You aren't listening to a bleddy word I'm saying, are you?' his friend complained in a rumbling Cornish accent that was far broader than Nathan's own.

'Course I am. You're pissed because Becky's kicked you out of the house so she can have her girlfriends over.' An educated guess, but that was all he'd heard for the last hour, so probably accurate.

'The Back of Beyond Book Club, they're calling themselves. Ruddy nonsense. It's just an excuse to drink wine and slag off men,' Paul scoffed.

'But Mrs Taylor's in charge, isn't she? She'll make them toe the line. If they haven't read the assigned book, she'll rap them over the knuckles and order them to do a hundred lines and a book report before the next meeting.'

'You're probably right. She were an old Tartar when she taught us.' Paul chuckled. 'You know what we ought to do? Gatecrash the club. Tell them we demand equal rights. No reason why men should be excluded from their la-di-dah club.'

'Seriously? Have you even opened a book since leaving school? And I'm not counting car magazines or top-shelf stuff.'

'Not everyone gets paid to read for a living,' Paul sniped. 'Some of us pay our bills unclogging toilets and whatever for people like you.'

Nathan knew he'd been out of line, but if he tried to apologize he'd make matters worse. It would blow over. He'd known Paul since they were boys and that link wasn't easily broken. Many of their old schoolmates had moved away, and a couple of others — like poor Robin — hadn't lived to see forty. He must've looked grim because his friend's cheeks turned ruddy.

'Forget that, mate.' Paul lifted his empty glass. 'It's the beer talking. You wouldn't want to go near my place tonight anyway. *She's* coming and I know you don't want nothing to do with her.'

'Melissa?' About a fortnight ago, Nathan had overheard Josie Hancock telling everyone in the village shop that Robin's widow had returned from America. He hadn't seen Melissa since they'd clashed at his friend's funeral. Cutting her dead when she'd tried to speak to him, and stomping off home without going to the wake hadn't been his finest moment.

Paul shot him a wary look. 'You still blame her for—'

'Yeah.' In his bones Nathan was convinced that if Melissa hadn't intervened, Robin might've beaten his illness and still be here. Drinking with his friends. Playing cricket for the village. Generally being an all-round good mate. Instead, his bones were rotting in the ground and his widow had everyone's sympathy — undeserved in Nathan's opinion. He drained the remnants of his beer in one gulp. 'My round. You're right. I don't want to go anywhere near her — especially not this week.'

'A year already . . . I can't believe it.'

'Me neither,' Nathan muttered.

'You know my Becky thinks you're wrong. She said—'

'I don't care what your wife said, all right? I know what I know, and nothing's going to change my mind.'

That intransigence was totally out of character. Nathan normally lived up to his reputation as an even-tempered and open-minded man. Except when it came to Melissa. There were other reasons that went deeper than Robin's untimely death, but they stayed in the furthest recesses of his brain, which was exactly where they needed to remain. Keeping the barrier in place between himself and Robin's widow was the easiest way around that.

CHAPTER TWO

'So, what do we all think of *Jamaica Inn*?' Evelyn's steely gaze landed on Melissa.

She squirmed in her seat and cleared her throat, hoping someone else would jump in and respond, but there was silence. 'Uh, well, I guess it's definitely set in the back of beyond.' The club had coined its tongue-in-cheek name in reference to Cornwall's reputation for being so far off the beaten track geographically. 'Bodmin Moor is kind of grim and the perfect setting for the story. It's one of the main characters really, isn't it?'

'Absolutely.' Evelyn beamed at her, as if a light bulb had suddenly switched on in one of her less-engaged pupils. Before her retirement she was headteacher of the village school, and everyone in the group, apart from Melissa, had been her student at one time or another. 'Had you read any Daphne du Maurier before?'

'I'm ashamed to say I hadn't. I raced through this one yesterday because I've been too busy getting the house and garden back in shape to do much reading.' She left unsaid that she'd put it off because she hadn't expected to attend the meeting. 'I loved it though, so I'll be rereading it — slower this time — and searching out more of her books.'

'Well, I own copies of everything she ever wrote so you're welcome to borrow them anytime you like,' Evelyn offered. '*Jamaica Inn* is a classic for good reasons. The book has everything. A gripping, heart-pounding story at the core. An atmospheric setting. And of course, romance. Daphne was an incredible writer and an incredible woman. Lovely lady.'

'You knew her?'

'She certainly did,' Josie interrupted. 'Evelyn is our celebrity, although she keeps it under her hat.'

'Don't talk rubbish,' Evelyn scoffed. 'They are exaggerating hugely, Melissa. My mother was the housekeeper at Menabilly, Daphne's home over in Fowey, for many years. And before you ask, she most definitely wasn't the inspiration for the evil Mrs Danvers in *Rebecca*.' She quelled the group with a stern glare. 'The house, however, *was* the basis for *Manderley*. I was in and out of Menabilly a lot as a child and knew Daphne as Lady Browning, her married name. When she discovered I could read well beyond my years she was wonderfully kind and loaned me books from her extensive library.' She looked thoughtful. 'They do say she was often cold to her own children, but I prefer to speak as I find and she was never that way with me.'

Melissa wondered what else she didn't know about the people around her. Everyone had their secrets. She knew she did. Things that would horrify her friends if they found out.

'Anyway, we're here to discuss the book, not my brush with so-called celebrity. Who else has a contribution to make?' Evelyn's tone made it clear the subject was closed.

They all trotted out their opinions and the discussion was lively and spirited, as it always was when they got together. Until tonight, Melissa hadn't realized how much she'd missed their company.

'Time for cake.' Becky sprang up from the sofa. The jovial, well-padded woman worked part-time in a local supermarket and loved nothing better than nurturing them all with her wonderful bakes. It'd surprised Melissa to discover she and Becky were the same age, both approaching forty, and she'd come to the conclusion that her friend's air of maturity came from marrying her husband Paul straight out of school and having their four children all before she was twenty-one.

'Where's your better half tonight?' Laura asked, pushing a blonde curl away from her plump face. The nursery school assistant was the most easy-going and amiable of them all, and Melissa couldn't credit that her wide hazel eyes hid any dramatic revelations.

'Drinking in the pub, of course, need you ask.' Becky gave a good-natured shrug. 'He was meeting Nathan Kellow. I expect the two of them are making fun of us by now.'

Melissa's heart sank. There would be nothing "fun" in whatever Nathan said about *her*. She'd never understood why her husband's best friend had taken such an instant dislike to her, but it had rolled off him in waves the first time they met in the village pub. Once she'd ventured to ask Robin why Nathan had a problem with her, but he claimed to have no clue what she was talking about. After that conversation, however, she noticed Robin tended to meet Nathan on his own and rarely invited his friend to the house unless other people would be there too.

'Dr Nathan Kellow is a fine young man,' Evelyn bristled. 'He wrote his thesis on the influence of Cornwall on Daphne du Maurier's writing, so he'd hardly be mocking us. I considered asking him to join us tonight to give us his insights.'

Melissa blinked hard. She assumed it was common knowledge around Penworthal that Nathan blamed her for Robin's death — not in the criminal sense, but in a moral one. Changing the subject seemed wise. 'I was obviously dragged here under false pretences. Someone promised two sorts of cake and I haven't seen any yet!'

'I'm on it.' Becky smiled with obvious relief. 'Let's forget the book and get down to the real business of the evening.'

* * *

'I'm off, mate.' Nathan stood up. 'It's gone nine so I'm sure the book club is over by now. You should be safe to go home.'

'I s'ppose. I'll have another beer then be on my way too.'

Outside, the hit of fresh air came as a welcome relief. Maybe Nathan was getting old or jaded — or both — because these days he preferred a quiet evening with a good book and a mug of weak, sugary coffee.

He crossed the road but, instead of carrying on to his house, he came to a stop outside the church. Should he visit the place that'd been on his mind all night? Perhaps he should have brought flowers? He could hear Robin now, laughing at that ridiculous idea.

'Flowers? You out of your mind, mate? Now beer — that's another story.'

He didn't think the vicar, or old Jimmy Trevail who kept the cemetery tidy, would appreciate finding a can of Tribute on Robin's grave. The thought made Nathan smile before tears pricked the back of his eyes. He trudged past the church gate and turned down the narrow path running alongside, to the newer cemetery.

The moon cast dappled shadows on the rows of headstones and a sigh slipped out of him as he crouched down by Robin's, fashioned from a block of dark Cornish slate. Even as boys they'd been very different: Robin headstrong and confident in everything he did, in contrast to Nathan's more considered, cautious ways. But as equally disparate men the friendship endured, and he missed Robin more than he could put into words. The crunch of footsteps on the gravel path made him jerk around.

'What on earth are you doing here?' Nathan blurted out. His first thought was that Melissa could be a ghost. A curtain of silvery hair framed her face, and her huge grey-green eyes stood out from her translucent skin. Even in the semi-darkness he noticed her clothes hung off her previously healthy frame.

'In case you'd forgotten, Robin was my husband, so I've every right to be here,' Melissa said in her warm southern drawl. 'Despite what you might think.'

A streak of guilt crawled through him. Was this how his old friend would want him to treat the woman he'd loved? 'Put me right then. Explain.'

'I don't have to. Robin trusted me. You don't. I guess that's all there is to it.'

'How have you been?' The ridiculous question popped out before he could reel it back in.

'How have I been?' Her voice rose. 'How do you *think* I've been? Or are you too self-righteous to care? I don't have a clue what I did to offend you, but you made up your mind about me the minute we met and you never really changed it, did you?' She shook her head when he didn't respond. 'Thankfully my good friends aren't as narrow-minded as you.'

Nathan must've been staring because she pushed away a strand of hair flopping in front of her eyes and fixed him with a resolute look.

'I've no intention of dyeing it.'

He couldn't admit he'd been thinking how beautiful it was. Suddenly he registered the bunch of wildflowers clutched in Melissa's hand. 'I'll leave you alone. Maybe one day we—'

Nathan cut himself off before he could dig a bigger hole for himself, and strode away, kicking up gravel as he went.

CHAPTER THREE

Melissa wouldn't have thought it possible in tiny Penworthal, but she hadn't spotted Nathan Kellow's distinctive loping gait or striking auburn hair for three whole weeks. Perhaps he'd also been doing his best to stay out of *her* way. The tempting timbre of his deep, raspy voice, laced with a hint of Cornish, had made her uncomfortably aware of him that night at the cemetery. So much so that she struggled to remember the long-running antagonism marking their relationship.

'Oy, are you going to buy that loaf, Mrs Martyn, or squeeze it to death?' Vernon Bull's gruff voice reverberated around the small shop. She stared down at her hands in surprise. She'd clutched the bread so hard it resembled a wonky egg-timer.

'I'm sorry. I was miles away.' Her efforts to un-squash the sad object failed miserably so she gave up. 'It'll do for breadcrumbs.' Melissa pulled out her purse to pay, not in the least offended by the shopkeeper's grumpy manner. In fact, it made her day to be treated with the same disdain as the rest of his regular customers.

The cramped shop was packed to its old oak rafters with a motley range of groceries and household essentials, but to the annoyance of the irascible Mr Bull its primary role was the dissemination of village gossip. A short, stout man in his late sixties with improbably thick, improbably black hair that no one ever dared to snicker about — he was the Basil Fawlty of shopkeepers. But along with Pixie, the landlady of the Rusty Anchor, and a few others, he was part of the beating heart of the village. The tight-knit community did its best to support the scant number of local businesses, but the butcher's shop and a café had already been forced to close since Melissa and Robin arrived three years ago. She'd heard rumblings on both sides of the argument because Penworthal hadn't been swamped yet by a rush of incomers desperate for a slice of rural life, or at least the version of it that existed in their imaginations.

It'd bemused Robin how easily she'd settled into village life. Despite her protests to the contrary, it was fixed in his brain that the glossy, poised woman he'd met in New York was the real Melissa. That persisted even after she took him to Carter's Run, the tiny hole-in-the-wall community in rural Middle Tennessee where she grew up. In many ways Carter's Run wasn't that different from Penworthal, but Robin was still convinced that she'd be bored in the blink-and-you-miss-it village where the Martyn family had settled long before the United States was even a country.

On that first long drive down to Cornwall he'd promised that if she really hated it after a year, they'd find a way to move back to New York. She'd been more pragmatic and known deep down that was unlikely. His reckless spending had landed them deep in debt and a more frugal lifestyle was the only option. For a while Robin enjoyed the hint of celebrity that surrounded his return to Penworthal, but the low-key existence soon chafed on him. She'd sensed him longing for the challenge of new pastures and became increasingly worried that it might include her and their marriage. There had been several trips to London the year before he got ill, supposedly work-related, about which he got extremely defensive when she asked a few run-of-the-mill questions on his return. And after his death she discovered their financial troubles were worse than she'd realized. Struggling to sort it out on her own was wearying, but she hated the idea of sharing the sordid truth with anyone.

She strolled back outside and lifted her face to the sun, soaking up the warmth. They'd been enjoying bright blue, cloudless skies for the last week, although the pessimistic locals continually predicted that it must break soon, despite the fact it would be June in another week and undeniably summer time, at least in her mind. Melissa stared at the hairdresser's shop across the road, deep in thought. Her friend Tamara's younger sister owned "Tracey's", and thankfully she'd named it simply after herself rather than something cringingly cute like Shear Delight. She ran her fingers through the lank strands hanging around her shoulders. It was an extravagance she couldn't really afford but the extra dose of courage a haircut might provide would help tonight. Her friends had put together a team for the Rusty Anchor's quiz night and talked her into joining them.

She sucked in a deep breath and crossed the road. Melissa was no chicken. She knew exactly why she was going to the other side.

* * *

'C'mon, mate, we need you,' Paul begged. 'Micky's off sunning himself on a Spanish beach so we're one short.'

Nathan regretted opening the door. He'd been set to celebrate the start of the weekend with a large measure of the bottle of Laphroaig he'd treated himself to at Christmas, plus a delve into the new biography of Sir Arthur Thomas Quiller-Couch. The Cornish novelist, better known by the pseudonym "Q", who died in the mid-twentieth century, was a long-time favourite of his.

'*Proper Choughed* are top of the league,' Paul bragged. 'You won't be quizzing with a bunch of deadbeats. We could have stiffer competition tonight though because Becky and her coven decided to enter at the last minute. Surely you're not going to let the *Back of Beyond Brains* edge us out?' His voice took on a challenging edge.

Nathan refused to ask if Melissa was one of the so-called brains, but took a guess that his friend's expression wouldn't be as wary if she wasn't involved. 'All right, but just this once. I'll need to go shower and change first though.'

'No probs. The quiz doesn't start until half seven. I'll get a pint in.' Paul clasped his shoulder. 'You're a good mate.'

Nathan nodded and retreated into the house. His heart pounded uncomfortably in his chest. Logically he knew he couldn't avoid Melissa forever, and there was no reason to think they'd be forced into speaking face-to-face. None of those things helped.

Half an hour later he stepped outside. He couldn't put it off any longer. With any luck, Melissa and her cohorts would already be settled in the pub so he could slip in unnoticed.

Nathan's front gate opened onto the main street running through the centre of the village, and he stood for a moment to savour the view. Penworthal had evolved through the centuries with its mixture of old terraced workers' cottages, a few squat 1970s bungalows, one pretty Georgian house belonging to Judy, the village GP, tucked up a side lane, and a smattering of former council houses. They would never win a prettiest village competition. His gaze strayed towards the church spire, one of the tallest in Cornwall. The building's architectural heritage was a compilation too, from a wonderful Norman font to the Victorian addition of two garish stained-glass windows.

It wasn't that he didn't enjoy travelling and seeing the wider world. Italy was a particular favourite because of its culture and wonderful food, but he was always content to return home again.

The sight of two women walking towards him, arm in arm, jolted him back to earth. The evening sun picked up the bright silver of Melissa's hair and Josie Hancock's vibrant red curls. He couldn't pinpoint what was different about Melissa until the distance between them narrowed. She'd had her hair cut, pixie-style, so it feathered in around her slender neck and brought her fine bone structure to the fore.

'Good evening, ladies. I believe we're all headed to the same place.' He pointed towards the pub, trying to appear on the polite side of friendly. 'I've been arm-wrestled into joining Paul's team tonight.'

Josie fixed her perceptive eyes on Nathan. 'Good luck is all I can say — you'll need it.'

Melissa didn't say a word.

If it wasn't for letting down the team, he'd turn around right now and go back home. He hung back until the women walked on, and watched as they disappeared into the pub. Only then did he start walking again.

The Rusty Anchor lived up to its name with a collection of old ship anchors dotted over the rough whitewashed walls. Being several miles from the sea hadn't put a damper on the enthusiasm of successive landlords to add to the collection of nautical memorabilia scattered throughout the place. He'd enjoyed his first legal pint here on his eighteenth birthday, and more than a few since then.

'Oy, we're back here,' Paul shouted and waved from the team's spot at the back of the long, narrow room.

Navigating through the crowded pub was a challenge and he bumped into a chair while trying to avoid a young woman carrying a full tray of drinks. 'Sorry, I . . .' The apology dried in his throat when Melissa turned around. He could never pin down what shade her eyes were. In certain lights they shone a pale silver-grey, while in others they were a curious luminescent green. In his mind he labelled them mermaid eyes, or how he imagined a mermaid's eyes might look if such things existed outside of people's imaginations. 'Sorry, I should've watched where I was going. I'll leave you in peace to plot our downfall.'

'Oh, we've done that already,' Becky said with a chuckle. Glee ran through her voice and Nathan was the recipient of seven smug smiles.

Time to beat a retreat.

* * *

'That threw him.' Josie smirked. 'We've well and truly rattled Mr Nathan Kellow's cage — sorry, I should say, Dr Kellow. It's time *Proper Choughed* realized that being a big fish in a small pond only works until a bigger fish — or in this case the sharks of the Back of Beyond Book Club — swim in to eat them up.'

Melissa managed a weak smile. The consensus was that the men needed putting in their place and their group was the one to do it.

'Remember what they say, girls.' Evelyn wagged her finger. 'Pride before a fall. Although to be precise, the original quote from the King James bible is — Pride goeth before destruction, and an haughty spirit before a fall.'

Melissa loved the older lady. A throwback in many ways to a different age with her steel-grey hair fixed in an old-fashioned French pleat, sensible skirts paired with soft wool jumpers in winter or neat collared blouses in summer — but woe betide anyone who assumed she was stuck there. Evelyn's brain was sharp as a well-honed carving knife and she put the rest of them to shame when it came to keeping up with everything, good and bad, that was going on in the world.

Melissa attempted to join in the light-hearted banter but her mind lingered on Nathan. When they'd met earlier she'd paid far too much attention to how his shirt matched his sky-blue eyes and the way the summer evening light brought out the rich dark red of his thick, wavy hair. Robin told her once that when he and Nathan went out on the town as teenagers, his best friend always caught the girls' attention first. Nathan's awkwardness and tongue-tied manner would let him down though, especially in comparison to Robin, who never met a person he couldn't charm in a matter of minutes. Being here in the pub brought back memories of the way her stomach flipped when Robin introduced them that first night. It'd been a million miles away from how a brand-new wife should react to her husband's best friend. But Nathan's cold manner and dismissive attitude had thrown cold water on her unfortunate reaction and she'd never thought of him again that way until now. She mentally reprimanded herself. Tonight had simply been a knee-jerk reaction from a lonely woman to a handsome, presumably available man.

'Listen up, everyone.' Pixie tugged on the thick rope hanging from the gleaming brass ship's bell. 'Turn your mobiles off. Jimmy's bringing the first group of questions around and you'll have fifteen minutes to come up with your answers before you swap sheets with the team seated nearest you for marking. The first subject is — Geography.'

Before she knew it, Melissa found herself engrossed and her confidence rose when no one else knew that Pierre was the capital of South Dakota. They aced that round, swanned through the next one on Art, struggled a bit with Business and Technology but came surging back in Entertainment, thanks to Amy. It always struck Melissa as amusing that Amy, a rather serious-minded paralegal with her sleek, severe haircut, horn-rimmed glasses and tailored suits knew about all of the reality TV shows. Apparently, Amy and her partner, Tessa, watched them obsessively and the two women had even gone on an *I'm a Celebrity Get Me Out of Here* cruise earlier in the year.

Pixie marked the scores on a large whiteboard as they went, and as they entered the final two rounds their team was neck and neck with *Proper Choughed*.

'Our last category is Sport,' Pixie announced blithely.

Melissa stifled a groan. That subject was their one weak spot. Becky had absorbed some football trivia thanks to Paul, and Tamara was something of a tennis fan, but unfortunately sport was pretty much a mystery to the rest of the group. And Melissa? Unless the questions were on American football or baseball, she'd be equally useless. She glanced around and caught Nathan's eye. His rueful smile could be out of sympathy because he guessed this was their least favourite subject, or perhaps it was his nemesis as well. She recalled Robin going over to Nathan's house a few times to watch cricket so she assumed he must be keen on that at least. Melissa turned away and reached for one of the question sheets that Jimmy Trevail had piled in the middle of the table. Evelyn was in charge of writing their agreed upon answers on her sheet ready for marking.

'We're done for.' Laura grimaced as if it was a document authorizing her execution.

'What is it y'all say here? All for one . . .' The Cornish motto raised a few tentative smiles. 'We're not ready to roll over and play dead yet!' Her voice must've carried because there were a few ragged cheers and whistles. Melissa's eyes were drawn to Nathan, who inclined his head in a slight nod. A rush of heat raced up her neck and she suspected her skin was now stained a bright, unattractive shade of crimson.

'She's right,' Evelyn said staunchly. 'Let's do our best.' She frowned at the question paper. 'We might be in luck. There's a tennis one you might know, Tamara. Football for Becky.' She threw Melissa a wary look. 'I don't suppose you know—'

'The names of the two Major League baseball teams in New York?' She couldn't believe her luck. 'Sure do. The Yankees and the Mets.'

'Good girl.'

They worked on the rest of the answers until the bell rang again.

Evelyn swapped their sheets with the *Jam First Geniuses*, the team's name a nod to the Cornish way of eating scones with the jam on first, topped with a generous spoonful of clotted cream, as opposed to the Devon way which was the exact opposite. Jimmy went around the room collecting all the answers and soon Pixie rang the ship's bell again to run through the results. She started in last place and worked her way up to the final two.

'We've got a tie for first place between *Proper Choughed* and the *Back of Beyond Brains*. Both teams scored 49 out of 50 so we'll have a tie-breaker. I'll read out one randomly selected question and the first team to shout out the correct answer will be the winners.' Pixie jiggled a brown paper bag in one hand.

'Jimmy. Pick one out.' The wizened old man shoved his hand in and pulled out a strip of paper, giving a gap-toothed grin before handing it over. 'It's a sports question,' Pixie announced.

The women grimaced at each other.

'Who did the St Louis Rams beat in the 2000 Super Bowl?'

Before Melissa could open her mouth, Paul yelled from the back of the room.

'The Baltimore Ravens.' He sprang from his seat and threw a jubilant punch in the air.

'That's—'

'Wrong!' Melissa interrupted Pixie. 'It's the Tennessee Titans.'

'It certainly is — congratulations, *Back of Beyond Brains*!' Pixie grinned. 'Your prize is a free round of drinks and the undisputed honour of being Rusty Anchor quiz champions until our next go around.'

'That was brilliant,' Josie said, patting her on the back.

'Good Lord, if I hadn't got it right my family would've never let me come home again.' Melissa laughed. 'The Titans are our local team and we're all massive fans. That was the Titans' only Super Bowl appearance to date. A more challenging question would've been what was the Music City Miracle.' Everyone looked bewildered. 'In the playoffs leading up to that particular Super Bowl the Titans were playing the Buffalo Bills. Tight end Frank Wycheck tossed a lateral to Kevin Dyson for a kick-return touchdown in the final seconds of the AFC Wild Card Game. It was epic.'

'We'll take your word for it,' Evelyn said dryly.

'I'd say it's cocktail time,' Becky declared. 'Cosmopolitans all around?'

'Not for me, thanks,' Laura said. 'I've got a bit of a headache. I'll just have another orange juice.'

'You're looking a bit peaky, dear. Are you all right?' Evelyn frowned.

'I'm tired. That's all,' Laura insisted. Two telltale blobs of embarrassment lit up her cheeks. A sure sign in Melissa's book that she was lying.

'I'll get the drinks in,' Amy said.

'I'll give you a hand.' Melissa joined her and they made their way to the bar, fielding congratulations all the way.

'Well done,' Nathan's deep voice rumbled in her ear.

'Isn't it heresy for you to say that?'

'I won't tell if you don't.' His sparkling eyes did funny things to her stomach. 'Do you think—'

'Come on, Melissa. The girls will be gasping for these.' Amy pointed to the row of glasses glistening with jewel-red liquid and garnished with a twist of lime.

She gave Nathan an apologetic shrug and turned away. What was he about to say when they were interrupted?

CHAPTER FOUR

Nathan parked outside *Gwartha an Dre* and rested his hands on the steering wheel. He stared up at the solid double-fronted house whose creamy granite walls glowed in the mellow sunshine. It was a handsome building and older than his own Victorian house — a fact that always peeved his father. As a boy he'd spent many happy hours here playing with Robin, relieved to be free from his father's oppressive disapproval of anything that didn't fit Harold Kellow's narrow view of suitable activities for his two children. Robin's parents were far more easy-going and rarely interfered unless forced to. It amused him that his father had wrongly considered the intelligent, well-mannered Robin a good influence. Thankfully, he'd never found out half the things they got up to. The long bike rides the teenage boys took were considered healthy exercise and therefore acceptable, but they'd usually ended up at one of the local beaches, and not simply for a swim. Harold would've been appalled to discover that his son's best friend was expert at tapping into the underage drink and illicit drugs floating around the area. Robin was an expert at fooling people.

What on earth had he been thinking coming here? The idea that he and Melissa could find some common ground and be friends was ridiculous.

A loud bang on the car window made Nathan jump out of his skin.

'Are you spying on me?' Melissa's expression was grim.

He wound down the window and struggled to get his brain back in working order. 'I thought we might try to sort some things out between us. I should've phoned first. Sorry.'

'Are you talking about you being convinced that if it wasn't for me Robin would still be here?' She folded her arms and fixed him with an ice-cold stare.

Nathan's tongue swelled to the size of an elephant.

'I suppose you'd better come in. This isn't a conversation to have in the street.' Melissa stepped away from the car.

'Thanks.'

'You might not thank me soon.' With that pithy response she turned her back on him and headed towards the house, leaving Nathan to leap out, lock the car and sprint after her.

'I was about to fix a coffee if you want one. Milky and loaded with sugar, right?' she asked.

He nodded, before a rush of emotion tightened his throat the moment he stepped inside the door. The last time he was in the house was shortly before Robin died. On that day, Melissa tactfully stayed out of sight and left them alone to say their goodbyes. Nathan had resisted saying anything negative about her to his old friend because it was too late and he'd have hated their last words to be spoken in anger.

'Go on into the lounge. I won't be long.'

There were subtle changes to the room, from fresh pale green paint on the walls to an eye-catching selection of artistically arranged Cornish watercolours. A pang of memory tightened its grip as he spotted a light-coloured wood rocker with plump dark green linen cushions situated in place of Robin's old tan leather recliner.

'I couldn't look at it every day.' Melissa returned carrying two mugs. 'Sit down.' She placed their drinks on the coffee table and settled herself on one end of the grey leather sofa, tucking her long legs up under her. It struck him how little resemblance she bore now to the sophisticated, fashion-conscious New York career woman Robin had boasted about whisking off her feet and down the aisle. Her crumpled linen trousers, white T-shirt and red flip-flops were clearly worn for comfort rather than fashion. From what he could tell, she wore little in the way of make-up, but to him that only made her more lovely.

'Do I have dirt on my face?' She looked puzzled.

'No. Why?'

'You keep staring.'

Nathan's face burned. 'Sorry, I . . .' He couldn't explain without digging a bigger pit to fall into.

'Why don't you get on with whatever you came here to say?'

He cleared his throat. Now he finally had the opportunity to challenge her, he'd no clue where to start.

* * *

'How about *I* clear something up first and then we'll see if you've still got a problem with me?'

Melissa's heart thudded and her palms turned sweaty. She'd been taking a break from work when she glanced out of the study window and spotted Nathan's car sitting at the curb. No one else drove a car as beautiful as his 1964 light blue Aston Martin. It'd been a mystery to her that an English professor could afford to buy the archetypal James Bond car. Robin had explained that Nathan inherited the car from his father, who'd inherited it from his father, and he babied the vehicle as if it was his own child. 'You blame me for Robin deciding to stop his treatment.'

'Yes. Yes, I do.' He appeared to collect himself. 'One minute he was determined to fight his illness as hard as he could, and then out of nowhere, he gave up. He wouldn't talk about it with me and insisted you were fine with the decision.' His hands clenched into fists. 'In fact, he said you were more than fine and actually encouraged him.'

'There's some truth in that.' That touch of honesty made his blue eyes turn to steel. 'Before you rip into me — listen, please.' She took Nathan's slight shrug as a positive response. 'You'd seen the awful side-effects of the treatment and what it did to him. Draining him of any quality of life. All for the sake of a few more days or weeks ticked off the calendar.'

When Robin's diagnosis first came it had stunned them, but he'd been so positive and sure he could beat it. As time went on it became clear that wasn't going to happen. 'I was furious with him at first when he admitted he couldn't do it any longer.' She swiped at her eyes.

'I'm sorry to upset you. Look, we don't need to do this now, we—'

'Yes we do! You need to understand that I didn't want him to give up. I tried, believe you me I tried. But he couldn't do it.' She blinked away another rush of tears. 'He needed me to understand and to respect his decision. What could I do? It was Robin's choice to make. Not yours. Not mine . . .'

Melissa looked at Nathan head on, challenging him, and she watched his eyes follow a tear that continued down her cheek and dropped on her shirt.

He visibly took a deep breath and shook his head. He said quietly, 'I got this all so wrong, didn't I . . .'

'Yeah you did. It didn't matter how hard he fought, in the end the battle couldn't be won. He knew that. And yes, he brought me around in the end. He needed my permission. Needed me on his side one last time. I couldn't say no.'

Melissa couldn't bear to tell Nathan everything. Some things were too private ever to share, especially as they didn't always show Robin in a good light. She thought back to her book club meeting when she'd wondered how many of her friends were keeping secrets. No doubt the answer was, everyone.

The silence now filling the room was broken by the loud chirping of a brown sparrow outside the window.

'Why couldn't he tell *me* that?' Nathan's eyes glazed over. 'I would've understood and I wouldn't have treated you the appalling way I have done.'

'Perhaps Robin assumed you'd get it without him having to spell it out.'

'I should've listened to what Robin *didn't* say and paid attention when everyone insisted I was wrong about you.' His voice turned hoarse.

'Don't be too hard on yourself.' She managed the ghost of a smile. 'That's been my job, and I'm not sure I'm ready to give it up yet.' Nathan had no idea how torn she'd been ever since Robin first got sick. It'd put paid to any discussion of where their marriage was going and how he planned to get them out of the financial mess he'd dragged her into.

'Shall we call it a tie and be done with it? Friends?' Nathan said, and threw her a wary glance.

Melissa hesitated briefly before giving a quick nod. 'Yeah. Friends. Sounds good to me.'

During the silence that followed, Melissa watched Nathan closely. He seemed to be about to say something. He finally spoke.

'I don't suppose . . . no, it's a crazy idea.'

'Oh, spit it out, Nathan, for heaven's sake.'

He looked sheepish. 'I don't suppose you fancy getting away from things? It's a beautiful day. Perhaps going for a drive and maybe getting a coffee somewhere? The last undergraduate classes finished yesterday for the summer, but Monday is time enough for me to start marking exam papers so the weekend's my own . . .' He shook his head, frowned and looked cross with himself. 'I'm sure you've got work to do, and just because we're on friendlier terms now doesn't mean you want my company. Sorry, it was a stupid—'

'I thought you'd got past making assumptions about me? I'd like it very much. Thank you for the invite. You'll be dragging me away from a manuscript that's giving me the devil. The over-protective author treats every word like it's written in her own blood and fights me tooth and nail over any changes.'

'In that case I'll whisk you off somewhere you can forget all about the problem for a while.'

'Where were you thinking of going?'

'I don't know.' Nathan avoided her eyes. 'I wouldn't want to pick somewhere you and Robin . . .' His voice trailed away.

Inspiration hit her. This would test their tentative friendship. But what better person . . .

* * *

'Jamaica Inn?' Nathan struggled to hide his surprise. 'We can, but I hope you won't be disappointed. It's—'

'A tourist trap with a tacky museum and even worse gift shop,' Melissa said with a mischievous smile. 'At least that's how Robin described the place when he talked me out of going there. Even the book club girls warned me it's best left to the imagination.'

'If you want to capture the real atmosphere, it's better to visit on a rainy day in late November because that's the way Daphne du Maurier saw it on her first visit.' He pointed to the bright blue sky outside the window. 'It won't look very menacing today.' Nathan sensed her disappointment. 'But if that's what you want, I'm happy to oblige. It's a pretty drive over there and it'll only take us maybe forty minutes or so.'

'You're sure you're okay with going?' Her face lit up.

'Absolutely.'

'I'll go and change. I promise I won't be long. Five minutes at the most.'

Nathan held onto his smile. He was recalling how Robin always boasted that he had the only wife in existence who when she said she'd be ready in a certain time, meant exactly that. 'I'll wait for you in the car.'

Once she joined him he shook off Robin's ghost, determined not to allow any more guilty thoughts to cloud the rest of the day. On the drive across to Bodmin Moor their mutual love of literature proved an easy ground for conversation. Most of the women he'd dated — not that he placed Melissa in that category — yawned with boredom if he rambled on too long about books. That wasn't a problem today because her opinions were as decided as his own and she wasn't reticent about sharing them. It was a little disconcerting to go from resenting Melissa to enjoying her company in such a short space of time.

They were getting close to their destination when an idea popped into his head. 'I don't know if you're hungry, but we could stop and pick up a couple of pasties and some drinks and take them to Dozmary Pool to eat?'

'Dozmary Pool?' she prompted.

'It's a small lake near the inn and supposed to be where the Lady of the Lake from Arthurian legend rose up to give Excalibur, the mythical sword, to King Arthur.' He chuckled. 'That way you'd get two famous places for the price of one. If you were up for it, we could even pop into Altarnun to visit the church — home of Du Maurier's infamous vicar . . . What do you think?' Perhaps he shouldn't have asked, but it was too late now.

'I've never turned down the offer of a pasty and don't plan on starting now!' Melissa's burst of laughter made him smile. 'Let's do that.'

He nodded and felt irrationally happy inside. 'There's a petrol station just down the road on the right so we should be able to get our picnic supplies there.'

They were successful with their purchases and it wasn't long before they arrived at the lake.

Melissa pulled out her phone and started to take pictures of the serene clear blue water in front of them. 'I'll share these with my older brother, Pat. He's a long-time King Arthur nut and he'll get a real kick out of this.'

'How many brothers do you have?'

'Two. Pat's the oldest of the three of us. Bryan's the youngest. They both live back in Tennessee near our folks.' She sounded wistful.

'You're a close family?'

'Yeah. Missing them is the only downside to being here.' Melissa sat next to him on the warm grass, fanning out her soft, pale pink dress around her. 'I remember Robin telling me your parents passed away but he never mentioned if you had any other close family? You always strike me as rather solitary.' She took the pasty he offered and pulled it far enough out of the paper bag to take a bite.

'I lost my father shortly before I got my doctorate.' It'd been a bitter-sweet moment wondering if Harold Kellow might finally have been proud of him. 'I came back here afterwards to live with my mum, then she died a couple of years later. I've got one older sister, Catherine, who lives in Sussex with her husband and daughter. My niece, Chloe, is up at Oxford reading PPE. Politics, Philosophy and Economics.'

'Clever girl.'

'Yes.' He dragged out the word, unsure how much to say.

'But?'

'I deal with unhappy students all the time, who've been steered into courses by their parents, and it usually doesn't end well. Nine times out of ten they drop out. Catherine's always pushed Chloe academically and she got worse after they discovered they couldn't have any more children.' Nathan shrugged. 'Still, I'm only an old bachelor academic so what do I know about parenting?'

'For a start you sure aren't old, and with the job you do you probably understand a lot about the workings of youngsters' minds.' She sounded quite fierce. 'Just because you haven't fathered any kids yourself . . .' Melissa turned bright pink.'

'It's okay.' Without thinking, he slid his hand over to rest on top of hers. 'You're spot on. That's not something I've ever . . . it simply never happened.'. Nathan moved his hand away and picked up his pasty again. 'Jamaica Inn next stop?'

'Of course, Doctor Kellow. I bet you've got a secret soft spot for the place? As a hard-core Du Maurier fan, you must do.' Her eyes shone. 'Or is it insulting to call you a fan? Should I say you're the pre-eminent scholar of your generation on her Cornish connections and how they affected her writing?' Melissa's laughter rippled through the air. 'That's how Evelyn describes you anyway.'

'You can call me whatever you like.' A wry smile slipped out. 'I'm sure you've given me a few less salubrious names in the past.'

'Maybe.'

'Is it time for our creepy ancient pub?'

'Bring it on.'

They strolled back to the car and after driving a few minutes they spotted Jamaica Inn's famous black sign, which was notorious for creaking ominously in the high winds that blew off the moors. Nathan found a space in the car park and they both jumped out. 'Stand still for a moment.' He touched her bare forearm. 'Close your eyes and imagine yourself on horseback, soaked through to the skin and shivering with the cold because you've been lost on the moors for hours. Through the lashing rain you see the inn, lit only by the swinging lanterns carried by people out searching for you. Okay you can open them again now.' The picture he'd painted of Daphne du Maurier's first encounter with Jamaica Inn was totally at odds with the glorious sunny day. Shrieking children ran around the cobblestone patio in front of the low-pitched dark stone buildings, laughing and eating ice creams.

'Oh my God, it's magnificent. No wonder she was inspired to write such a powerful story.' Melissa's eyes shone. 'You're the exact right person to be here with — I can't wait to pick your scholarly brain. Come on, let's go.' Out of nowhere she grasped his hand and dragged him towards the inn.

The next couple of hours were a whirlwind of the best sort. He happily followed along while Melissa soaked up every inch of Jamaica Inn's history — the real, the fictional, and some that no one was quite certain of. She didn't care that the museum exhibits hadn't been altered or dusted in fifty years and featured the most un-lifelike models on the planet.

'I've devoured several more of Du Maurier's works now and loved every one so far.' Melissa gazed at the desk in front of them.

They were standing in the section of the dingy museum dedicated to the author, and Nathan was no less fascinated by the Sheraton writing desk with its heavy black typewriter, the packet of Du Maurier cigarettes (named after her father) and a bag of her favourite mints.

'You must take my picture on the spot where Joss Merlyn was "murdered" and we've got to drink a tot of smugglers' rum,' Melissa announced decisively. 'Then the gift shop. I need a tacky memento of the day.'

'Your wish is my command.' Nathan playfully bowed low with a flourish worthy of Sir Walter Raleigh laying down his cloak for Queen Elizabeth.

'You're one crazy man!' In the blink of an eye her sunniness faded. 'I had no idea. I see now why you and Robin . . .' She left the sentence unfinished.

'Let's get our glass of pseudo-smuggled rum before I treat you to a stuffed parrot and an eye patch in the gift shop.' The deliberate change of subject brought back her gentle smile.

For the rest of the day he'd do his best to ensure the past didn't intrude on the present — and as for the future? Who knew?

CHAPTER FIVE

'So, are you going to spill the beans or not?' Josie settled herself in one of Melissa's patio chairs and plonked a bottle of chilled prosecco on the table. 'Fetch the glasses. We've got fifteen minutes before we need to leave. Plenty of time for a drink and all the juicy details.'

She could hardly feign ignorance about what her friend was referring to. Josie must've spotted her leaving with Nathan on Saturday morning, so it was no coincidence that she'd been stationed outside, ostensibly watering her garden, in the evening when they returned. At the time Melissa blithely waved over to Josie before saying a swift farewell to Nathan. Luckily Josie had been on weekend duty at the hospital so she couldn't come banging on Melissa's door for information. Of course, Josie had known that today loomed — the first Monday in June and book club night. It handed her the ideal opportunity for an interrogation on a plate.

'Fine. I'll be back.' Melissa wondered how long she could drag out fetching two glasses before ordering herself not to be childish. In the sanctuary of her kitchen she selected a couple of mis-matched glass goblets, recent flea-market finds in Truro. She pulled a bag of Josie's favourite roast chicken flavour crisps from the cupboard and dumped them in a bowl.

Back outside she stopped briefly to relish the warmth of the mellow evening sun on her face. Now it was early June, the heat and humidity would start to crank up in Tennessee, one aspect of life back home she didn't miss.

'Wow, you must have something really juicy to confess.' Josie's eyes widened. 'Go on, hand them over.' She grabbed a handful of crisps and crammed them in her mouth. 'I skipped lunch so don't judge me.'

'I wouldn't dream of it.' Melissa prised out the cork to open the sparkling wine and filled their glasses to the brim. 'As for confessions, it's . . . complicated.'

'Really? The man has been standoffish since you met and bad-mouthed you around Penworthal for the last year or so. Out of nowhere he turns up outside your door in his admittedly beautiful car, turns his admittedly rather lovely smile your way and you're suddenly best friends? At least that's how it looked until you spotted me, then you practically pushed him away and ran off like a scalded cat.' Josie wasn't known as the nemesis of the student nurses at Treliske Hospital for nothing. She might not be the starched matron of years gone by, but she took her responsibilities as a Senior Staff Nurse seriously, and when she told the trainees to jump, if they were wise all they asked was how high.

Melissa took a fortifying slug of prosecco and ran through everything that had happened. The longer the story went on, the redder and hotter her face turned.

'Well, that's a turn-up for the books.' The laconic response didn't fool Melissa. She could expect this same reaction, or stronger, from her other friends when the word got around. Josie drained her wine and seized another handful of crisps. 'We'll be on carrot sticks and fresh fruit tonight. Poor Tamara is back at WeightWatchers for the umpteenth time. She swears since she turned forty all she has to do is look at food to blow up like a blimp. I suppose it doesn't help that she works in the pub with Pixie, who's like a stick insect. I can't believe she's worried to death about attracting another man before she's too old for anyone to give her a second glance.' She shook her head. 'I don't know why she wants to bother. Her ex-husband rivalled mine on the jerk scale. Left her to bring up Toby on her own, he did, and she's done an awesome job. You won't find a kinder, smarter young man anywhere. He's one of my best trainee nurses.'

'You've never said much about your ex.' That gentle probe from Melissa only elicited a shrug from her friend. Josie was open and candid about everything apart from her romantic life. Apparently, she'd been briefly married to a doctor years ago but that ended in divorce. Since Melissa had known her, she'd never even been on a date, and brushed off any enquiries on the subject by saying she was married to her job.

Her sharp eyes swept over Melissa. 'I was worried about you when you came back from the States. You looked like the Ghost of Christmas Past. You've perked up now though.' A throaty laugh broke out. 'Could that be anything to do with a certain literature professor?'

Melissa ignored the pointed question and picked up their empty glasses. 'I'll put these in the kitchen and fetch my book.' The group's theme for the year was female authors with a Cornish connection — either personally or in their writing. This month's choice was Agatha Christie's *Peril at End House*, a Hercule Poirot mystery set in the fictional Cornish town of St Loo.

'You do that.' Josie's satisfied smile made her nervous.

* * *

Today had been a long, hard slog at work, where Nathan had divided his time between marking exam papers and meeting with a young man who would be one of his post-graduate students in September.

Nathan checked his watch. Paul would bang on the door in a minute to ask why he wasn't at the pub as he'd promised. It was book club night again, so his friend was at a loose end, but Nathan wasn't in the mood for company. Of course, if it was Melissa asking that would be a different story. He was still trying to make sense of whatever changed between them on Friday, and kept wondering what might've happened if Josie hadn't appeared. All weekend he'd gone back and forth in his mind about whether to call Melissa again, but in the end he did nothing. Robin would call that typical of him. His old friend routinely teased him about being useless with women.

'You're oblivious to the fact they're interested even when it's right under your nose and practically handed to you on a plate. By the time you get the hint it's too late and they've hooked up with a man who's more on the ball. How do you think I got Melissa? I snatched her from under the nose of some lame musician chap. Had a ring on her finger and down the aisle before the idiot knew what hit him. Or her!'

That didn't sound a solid basis for a relationship to Nathan, but what would he know? The longest any of his girlfriends had hung around so far was nine months. At that point Harriet, a very charming and attractive lawyer, had suggested moving in with him. Whenever they were out shopping she would look pointedly in jewellers' windows and the pressure freaked him out. He ignored her unsubtle hints and very soon that was the last he saw of Harriet.

His phone jangled to life with a version of "Trelawney", the unofficial Cornish anthem, sung by the Fisherman's Friends, the famous local folk music group.

'Hey, Chloe, what are you after?'

'Why should I be after anything? Can't a girl call her favourite uncle without him thinking she's begging for money or whatever?' His niece's protest went over his head. Chloe normally only got in touch when her parents turned down her latest request and she wanted him to intervene.

'What won't your long-suffering parents let you do now? Take a year out to explore Thailand with your Australian boyfriend? Or is the eco-warrior who wanted the two of you to live up a tree in the rainforest back in favour and intent on whisking you off to the Amazon jungle?'

'They're both history,' she said blithely.

Nathan bit his tongue. There'd been furious rows over the two men in question, with his over-dramatic niece swearing blind in each case that her life was being ruined by people who didn't understand the meaning of true love.

'It's nothing like that, I swear. I'm at a loose end for the summer and you're rattling around in Nana and Poppy's big house on your own, so I thought you'd appreciate some company. Mummy suggested it.'

He doubted that very much because Catherine thought he was far too sympathetic to his students' points of view. If Oxford allowed parents to shadow their children around the university, his sister would be first to sign up.

'Honestly. You can ask her yourself. She's right here.'

Before Nathan had a chance to reply, Catherine's voice trilled down the phone.

'We think it's an amazing plan, Nat, dear. The unappreciative girl has turned down all my suggestions.'

He could imagine the sort of worthy projects his sister had lined up, all chosen to look good to her daughter's Oxford tutors.

'There must be plenty of summer jobs going in Cornwall? Surely you can fix Chloe up with something?'

Beneath his sister's crisp tone, he picked up an undercurrent of frustration. The quiet summer he had planned receded into the distance.

'Maybe.'

'Please, Nat.' Now his sister was flat out begging and a trickle of guilt headed straight to his gut. Catherine had always been there for him. She was the only one who'd stood up to their father when he tried to force Nathan into following in his footsteps to study engineering instead of — in Harold Kellow's words — wasting his time with a useless subject like English literature. Strictly speaking, she was also half-owner of their family home so he could hardly turn down the request for her daughter to spend some time here.

'Okay,' he conceded, and Chloe's loud shriek in the background almost made his eardrums explode.

'We'll put her on a train tomorrow.'

'Great.' Nathan tried to inject some enthusiasm into his voice. 'I'm working from home tomorrow, catching up on paperwork, so I can pick her up from Truro any time after about three o'clock.'

'You're the best, Uncle Nat.' His niece had reclaimed the phone. 'I can cook for us.'

Now he'd be forced to endure the latest crackpot food fad. Thanks to his students he was painfully aware that their eating habits changed weekly according to the latest viral craze sweeping TikTok. He'd better head to the pub for one of Pixie's homemade pasties while he had the chance.

* * *

If Melissa was a better person she'd feel guilty. A minuscule part of her did genuinely feel sorry for Laura, but at least her friend's dilemma took the heat off her. She'd been prepared for Josie to take great pleasure in spreading the news of her friendlier relationship with Nathan, but Evelyn snatched away the opportunity. In full headteacher mode, she'd homed in on Laura sitting in the corner of Tamara's well-worn brown leather sofa as if that might make her invisible. Normally pink-cheeked and smiley, she was deathly pale and seemed to hover on the verge of tears.

'You look terrible, dear, so don't bother telling us you're fine.' Evelyn's tone softened. 'You know they say that a trouble shared is a trouble halved. Or in this case shared by six good friends, which must be even better.'

'I'm pregnant,' she whispered.

Melissa was about to offer her congratulations when she became conscious of an awkward silence filling the room. True, Laura was in her early forties, but these days it wasn't unusual to give birth later, and as a long-time nursery school assistant she clearly loved children so why was everyone so shocked?

'But we all thought—'

'Me too.'

'Have you seen Judy yet?'

'No!' Laura's voice wobbled. 'I'm not going to the doctor. Not yet.'

Evelyn fixed an unwavering stare on her hapless friend, one Melissa felt sure had put the fear of God in thousands of pupils over the years. 'Sticking your head in the sand won't help. You're not an ostrich. You know what Judy told you last—'

'Don't say it.' Laura's wild eyes swept the room. 'Any of you. This is my last chance.'

Josie's covert glance told Melissa she'd explain everything later.

'Does Barry know?'

'No! He'll tell me to . . . you know.' A sob caught in her throat. 'He's always insisted I was more important to him than any baby.' Laura's chin lifted. 'Well, that's not true for me.' The defiance running through her voice dared them to contradict her.

'Right, well that's it then. You know we're here for you so if you want our help you only have to say.' For once Evelyn looked every one of her seventy-three years. 'I think we'll have the delicious fresh fruit and yogurt dip Tamara's prepared before we discuss the book tonight for a change.'

Now Melissa caught Josie's eye and they fought against laughing. Chocolate cake and wine would hit the spot far better.

The evening slid back into routine. There was a lot of lively chatter about the book — a more light-hearted story than last month's offering. The typically glamorous Christie setting was on the so-called Cornish Riviera and loaded with the fashions and elegant Art Deco architecture of the era. One spirited debate ensued about whether the faithful representation of Hercule Poirot by David Suchet, or Kenneth Branagh's more modern interpretation, would bring the story to the screen best. In the end the verdict was that no one matched up to Suchet, and that Kenneth's moustache was simply too ridiculous. Josie was particularly vociferous, and it amused everyone when she let slip that she'd always had a book crush on the little Belgian detective.

By nine o'clock the group started to break up and Josie nabbed Melissa on the way out.

'How about a detour to the chip shop? I'm starving.'

Melissa's stomach rumbled on cue, answering for her.

'Let's take them to my place,' Josie offered. 'I've got a bottle of cheap plonk in the fridge. I warn you now, it's Vernon Bull's weekly special and guaranteed to strip the enamel off our teeth.' They strolled down the narrow path together and Josie glanced back over her shoulder, to make sure they weren't being overheard. 'I'll tell you about poor Laura and you can update me on your literary lothario.'

The last part would be a short conversation. Nathan hadn't been in touch, and she'd chickened out of contacting him. Perhaps clearing the air between them had been enough for him . . . She linked arms with Josie and smiled. 'Lead me to the chippy.'

CHAPTER SIX

Nathan sighed as he picked up a trail of abandoned clothes on his way down the stairs. If only they were a sign that he'd torn off a woman's clothes last night because they couldn't wait to get their hands on each other, but no such luck. The items belonged to Chloe, who took the meaning of the word "untidy" to a whole new level. When he'd complained about the state she left the kitchen in — how anyone could use that many dishes to cook one plate of scrambled eggs on toast was beyond him — she called him a fussy old woman.

'Uncle Nat, will you do me a really big favour?' Chloe skipped down to join him. 'I need a lift to Newquay. Some of my friends from uni are down for the weekend and there's a beach party tonight. You don't have to worry about picking me up — I'll make my own way back tomorrow.'

The last five days had given Nathan a frightening insight into what it must be like to be a parent. At the university he was responsible for his students to a certain degree, but this was different. He needed to find Chloe a job, and soon. Something, anything, to keep her occupied and out of trouble. As yet, he hadn't got to the bottom of why she'd been so keen to come to Cornwall. For a girl who could talk until the cows came home, she'd skilfully avoided his questions about how her courses were going and whether she'd settled into university life. The antenna he'd developed around his own students told him something was very wrong.

'I suppose that'll be all right.'

She snatched her clothes away with a cheery smile. 'Thanks. I won't be long.'

Nathan made a beeline for the kitchen to make himself a coffee and read the paper. He suspected his niece's version of "not long" would be more elastic than Melissa's. Sure enough, he was on his second cup and had finished the crossword before Chloe bounced in wearing a skimpy red T-shirt and minuscule denim shorts. Her long blonde hair swung in a tight high ponytail and her bright blue eyes had regained their usual sparkle.

'I'm ready.'

He grabbed his keys and followed her outside.

'Come on, slowpoke!' Chloe dragged him to the car.

'Take this.' Nathan pulled a couple of twenty-pound notes from his wallet. 'Put it somewhere safe in case you need a taxi home.'

'You're the best.' She popped a kiss on his cheek then playfully wiped off a smudge of scarlet lipstick.

Nathan heard footsteps in the road and glanced up to lock eyes with Melissa, who'd stopped outside his gate. Before he could call her over and introduce her to Chloe, she lifted her hand in a brief wave and strode off again. Had she been on her way to see him or was that simply wishful thinking on his part?

'Hey, don't look so miserable. I've just seriously boosted your reputation around here.' Chloe giggled. 'The word will soon spread that Nathan Kellow has a well fit girlfriend young enough to be his daughter. No more Mr Dull and Boring.'

He forced out a weak smile and unlocked the car. 'You can tell me on the way where you want to be dropped off.'

Traffic would be slow but not as bad as in another month or so. Once the schools finished, Cornwall would be neck-deep in visitors, and the roads in and around Newquay and all the other popular spots almost impassable.

After he'd deposited Chloe he'd come back home and straighten up his house before enjoying a few hours of peace and quiet. *Really? That's the best you can come up with?* Mr Dull and Boring. Admittedly, Chloe was of the age when anyone over thirty was ancient, but did others see him that way too? Just turned forty. An academic. Single. On the plus side, he still had all his hair and could fit into clothes bought twenty years ago. Nathan grimaced. Chloe would kill herself laughing, because who held onto clothes that long?

This was ridiculous. He'd take himself off for a good hike on the moors. A sharp dose of the brisk winds that whipped around the stark granite landscape year-round should blow away his grouchy mood.

* * *

No doubt there was a perfectly logical explanation for why an extremely nubile young woman was kissing Nathan Kellow outside his house, and if there wasn't, so what? It was none of her business. Josie would tell her off and call her an idiot for running away rather than saying hello. Her friend hadn't held back the other night when they'd swapped confidences over their deliciously greasy fish and chips.

Josie had told her about Laura's sad string of miscarriages. After the last one five years ago, Judy, the local GP, had given her a stern warning that another pregnancy could kill her. As far as the girls knew, Laura had bowed to her husband's plea that they stop trying, and the assumption was that Barry had had the snip. She understood why everyone was scared for Laura, but also felt deeply for the woman, who couldn't let go of the slim possibility that this time might be different. One of Melissa and Robin's areas of disagreement — and there'd been many — had been whether or not to try for a baby. He'd been adamant that he wanted more time with her on their own, while she'd felt the ominous tick of her biological clock. By the time he received his diagnosis she'd given up pressing him on the subject because their marriage was on shaky ground anyway.

Her best friend's candour the other night had extended to Nathan, and Josie warned Melissa that he was considered a dyed-in-the-wool bachelor. Girlfriends came and went but everyone who knew him assumed he was too set in his ways to want a radical lifestyle change. Melissa met her friend's plain talk with some of her own, making it clear she wasn't looking for another husband. She did concede that occasionally she felt lonely and had started to enjoy Nathan's company. When she turned the tables on Josie, however, that didn't go down well and an enquiry about whether her friend was lonely too was answered with dead silence.

Now she'd had her plan to casually drop in to see Nathan thwarted, Melissa felt restless. None of the work she had on tap was urgent, and it'd only depress her to brood over the spreadsheet that detailed the sad state of her finances. She'd made significant progress in clearing Robin's debts, but it was an uphill struggle and there was no light at the end of the tunnel yet. This would be a good day to finish her *Jamaica Inn* pilgrimage and visit Altarnun. They'd taken so long at Jamaica Inn itself the other day that there hadn't been time to go there as well. It didn't take long to get ready and head out to the car. When Robin first brought her to Cornwall it was easy to slip into the habit of letting him drive everywhere they went. He'd grown up with the tortuous narrow lanes flanked by steep overgrown hedges and didn't have a heart attack every time they met something coming the other way. She'd lost count of the number of times she'd screamed and covered her face with her hands when a huge tractor appeared around a sharp bend. If she'd wanted to go out on her own and Robin was busy, she'd discovered the highs, and lows, of Cornish public transport. She'd enjoyed exploring the local area in the small green buses with their noisy pneumatic brakes and meeting her fellow passengers. Her American accent guaranteed an interested audience and it was rare to arrive at her destination without having swapped life stories with at least one other traveller. But when Robin became ill Melissa was forced to learn to cope with the Cornish roads.

Occasionally now she would still catch the bus but more often than not the convenience of having her own transport won out.

In less time than the satnav predicted, she arrived at Jamaica Inn, quite proud of herself. Altarnun was only ten minutes away but she decided to stop and treat herself to a coffee first. After she parked and fetched a drink from the restaurant, Melissa returned outside to sit in the sunshine. A gasp burst out of her and the cardboard cup slipped out of her hand, hit the table and splashed hot coffee all over her. There couldn't be another car in Cornwall to match Nathan's, especially as the driver that clambered out was the spitting image of him. She dabbed ineffectually at her white T-shirt with a paper napkin.

'Melissa?' Nathan strode towards her. 'What're you doing here?'

'I could ask you the same thing.'

He gestured to his sturdy walking boots. 'I came for a hike. I'm going to Rough Tor and Brown Willy.' A sheepish grin worked its way across his face when he caught her staring at his baggy below-the-knee khaki shorts. 'These were my dad's. There's nothing wrong with them except—'

'They're older than you are and make you look like one of the eccentric English hikers I see stomping about all over the place.' She pointed to his bare head. 'At least you aren't wearing one of those awful shapeless hats like Dr Livingstone in the jungle.'

Avoiding her eyes, he shoved a hand into one of his many pockets and pulled out one of the ugly hats she'd been referring to. 'They're handy for sun or rain.'

'I'll take your word for it.'

'I assume you're here to buy more over-priced rubbish in the gift shop and commune with Joss Merlyn's ghost?'

'No! I only stopped for a coffee.' She grimaced at her stained shirt. 'Not very successfully. That's your fault.'

'Mine?'

'Yeah, I was so surprised to see you I spilled my drink everywhere. I'm on my way to Altarnun.'

'Why don't you let me buy you another drink when I fetch my own?'

'Sure.'

Nathan headed inside and the welcome reprieve allowed Melissa's nerves a chance to settle.

* * *

Nathan couldn't analyse how he felt about bumping into Melissa. After spotting her outside his house this morning, he hadn't been able to settle. He'd hoped to walk off his strange mood and maybe — if he got up the nerve — go to see her this evening. Now he was in a quandary. Did they have a friendly coffee and go their separate ways? He could hardly ask her to join him on his hike wearing a pretty floral skirt and lightweight sandals, and she wasn't likely to suggest he went to Altarnun with her when he resembled a vagrant.

'Two coffees, mate.' The brawny man behind the counter pushed the cups across and turned to serve the next customer.

Before going back outside he dived into the gift shop and made a purchase he hoped might redeem him in Melissa's eyes. The sight of her pulling her damp shirt away from her chest and angling her body towards the sun to dry out the brown stains made his mouth turn dry. Naturally she chose that precise moment to catch him staring.

'I . . . er, bought you this as an apology along with the coffee.' He set down their cups and offered her the brown paper bag in his other hand. 'I guessed your size. You can change it in the gift shop if it's not right.'

'My size?' After cautiously pulling out the black and gold T-shirt, she studied the writing on the front. '*Smugglers do it in the dark.* Really?'

'Yep, they really do. It's essential for their line of work.' When her smile broadened, Nathan felt like a miner striking gold. He pulled out the chair next to her and sat down. 'I'm sorry I didn't call.'

'Me too,' she admitted. 'Look, it's a lovely day, so unless you're hell-bent on trudging over the moors, why don't you join me?'

'Dressed like this?'

'Yeah. I don't care. Anyone who sees us will write me off as a crazy American who's into everything old and British — including its eccentrics.' A hot blush lit up her honeyed skin. 'Unless there's a reason we shouldn't . . .'

Nathan caught what she was trying to hint at. 'The girl you saw outside my house is my niece, Chloe.' He rattled off an abbreviated version of why he'd been landed with taking care of her for the summer.

'I should've come over to say hi. I'm not sure why I didn't.'

The idea she might've been the tiniest bit jealous was ridiculous but made him unreasonably happy anyway.

'I'll go change into my awesome new shirt and then we'll track down where the evil vicar came from. From what I've read, the church itself is neat.'

'It is. It's known as the Cathedral of the Moors, although it's officially the Church of St Nonna, she was the mother of Saint David.' Nathan expanded on the history of the building from its twelfth-century Norman roots to the present fifteenth-century building built from unquarried local moorstone. He stopped himself. 'Sorry. I didn't mean to slip into university professor mode.'

'Don't apologize. I'm interested.' She stretched her hand across and rested her long, slender fingers on top of his hand, the warmth of her soft skin seeping through his own.

Nathan had never tried skydiving but went into free-fall. The ground rushed up to meet him and he wondered if he'd survive the landing.

CHAPTER SEVEN

'Can't you sleep either?' Josie shouted across the fence separating their two gardens. 'Come over.'

'I'll be right there,' Melissa yelled back. They were in the middle of June now but the nights were still blissfully cool, at least to her. She'd heard other people complaining of struggling to sleep because of the heat, but with a window open and a decent breeze blowing through, she was fine. Except for tonight. She joined her friend on the bench in front of Josie's living room window, situated in the perfect spot to enjoy the view over the surrounding countryside. Lilac Cottage should be renamed Gingerbread Cottage, in her opinion, because it reminded her of the Hansel and Gretel story with its fairytale gabled roof, leaded windows and scented, rambling roses arched over the gnarled oak front door. Originally it was a farm worker's cottage that had belonged to the Martyns, but Josie had bought it after Robin's parents died.

'I'm always knackered at the end of a string of four-night shifts, but getting to sleep the first night is almost impossible. I purposely stayed busy all day too and avoided taking a nap.' Josie puffed out a weary sigh. 'I know there are logical, scientific reasons for that, but it isn't much consolation when it's 2 a.m. and I'm staring at the ceiling.' She lifted the mug in her hand. 'I'm hoping this will do the trick, but it tastes vile.' Josie screwed up her face.

'Dare I ask what's in it?'

'Valerian, organic chamomile, passionflower, liquorice, cardamom and cinnamon. I'll make you one if you like?'

'Thanks, but I'll pass.'

'Right answer and very wise. So why can't you sleep? Are you missing Robin, or Nathan?'

'Wow! Put it a bit more directly why don't you?'

Josie had the grace to look ashamed. She'd warned Melissa when they first met that people either appreciated her directness or they didn't. Most of the time Melissa did. 'Sorry, I killed my marriage by being too blunt. You'd think I'd have learned my lesson.' A hint of amusement bloomed in her round face. 'We'd only been married a couple of months when I put my foot in it one night. We finished making love and he asked if it'd been good for me. I was honest and told him it really hadn't been.'

Melissa tried, and failed, to stifle a giggle.

'I thought I was helping by going on to explain what turned me on and what didn't, but he was grossly insulted.'

'He obviously had a fragile ego.'

'Fragile? You must be joking. He's a doctor and they generally don't do "fragile egos".' A shadow crossed her friend's face and Melissa wondered what Josie wasn't saying.

'Did you know Nathan's niece is working in Vernon's shop?' Josie changed the subject. 'Mrs Bull has gone to Blackpool to take care of her sister who's recovering from a stroke and Vernon spread the word he needed a temporary assistant. Nathan leapt on it. She can't get into much trouble under Vernon's eagle eyes, but the little madam doesn't look at all happy judging by her miserable face when I was there.'

'I haven't been in the village for a few days. I've been snowed under with work.' She'd taken on an extra project because of the generous pay involved, but was regretting it already.

'So why the sleepless night? Are you fretting over dotting the Is and crossing the Ts for your latest bestselling author?'

'No, although he is a pain in the neck.' Melissa sighed. 'Nathan's taking me out for dinner tonight. I told him about reading *Ross Poldark* for book club in July so we're going to Charlestown where some of the filming was done.'

'What's the problem then? That sounds thoughtful of him.' Her gaze intensified. 'Are you overwhelmed with guilt because he was Robin's best friend?'

Tears welled in Melissa's eyes and her throat closed.

'Hey, I'm sorry. Really.' Josie hugged her. 'I'm an insensitive idiot sometimes.'

'Never.' She managed a faint smile. 'It's Robin's birthday today.' She stared down at her hands. 'I thought Nathan might've remembered.'

'He's a man! How many men do you know who remember birthdays, other than maybe their wives', parents' or children's? And that's a stretch for most of them. My parents have been married almost sixty years and I still remind Dad every year about Mum's birthday and their anniversary.'

'I should've just told Nathan, shouldn't I?'

'Being frank and honest has a lot going for it. He's not a mind-reader.'

Melissa straightened her shoulders. 'I'll give him a call later.'

'He's a good man, Melissa. He'll understand. You go on home. I'll sit here a while longer.'

She could tell something was troubling her friend, but Melissa reluctantly walked away.

* * *

Nathan manfully tried to cover up his disappointment. He'd heard the wobble in her voice when she explained why she needed to cancel their dinner plans tonight. When he'd booked their table at the iconic Pier House hotel, which had recently reopened after a devastating fire, he'd specified an outside table with a view over the harbour. In his imagination they would've lingered over their meal long enough to watch the sun set over the sea.

'Could we go another night?' she asked.

'Of course.'

'I'm coming down to the village later to take flowers to Robin's grave. I . . .' Her voice trailed away.

'What were you going to say?'

'It's nothing. Best forgotten.'

'I thought we were friends now. Feel free to say whatever you like to me.'

'Okay.' She still sounded unsure. 'I almost invited myself to your house for a coffee afterwards. How out of line would that be?'

She deserved his honesty, but would she appreciate it? 'I'd have been out of line too because I would've said yes, please.'

'Oh, Nathan.'

The silence stretched out between them. 'I've an idea that's so proper even Jane Austen couldn't object. If you did pop in for coffee — or a glass of wine if you'd prefer — you can meet my wayward niece properly. At the moment she's in the middle of a six-hour shift stacking shelves, and I'm sure when she's through the poor kid could do with someone more interesting to chat to than her grumpy old uncle.' Nathan sensed her hesitation. 'Am I being thoughtless now? You won't be in the mood for her non-stop chatter.'

'No, Nathan it wasn't that at all. Stop being so hard on yourself. I'd love to take you up on your offer and I can't wait to meet the infamous Chloe.'

'Infamous?'

'The village is having a field day talking about her. A glamorous blonde with attitude ringing up the fishfingers and cans of baked beans makes going to Vernon's dingy shop far more interesting.'

'She's got attitude all right.'

'I'll see you later, and thanks again.'

'Whatever for?'

'Being you, Nathan. That's all.' Melissa ended the call, leaving him dumbstruck.

* * *

'So there we go, Robin.' Melissa rested her hand on his name, etched into the slab of dark Cornish slate he'd chosen himself. With a sharp pang of memory she recalled the day at the stonemason's yard when he'd been forced to lean on her arm for the short walk from the car. Any lingering animosity between them had disappeared by that stage. 'You know full well I would've had banners and balloons hanging up all over the place so everyone in Penworthal knew you were forty today. And I'd have baked one of my chocolate cakes that you loved so much. You used to say I should market them here to show the Brits how a cake should taste!' She pushed back up on her feet and brushed the dust off her dress. Robin had bought the bright lemon sundress for her in Rome because he thought it the perfect foil for her brunette hair. Now, against her silver hair, it was draining, but she'd worn it anyway.

She walked away with a heavy heart and hesitated when she arrived back at the road. It seemed utterly wrong to go to Nathan now, and knowing his niece would be there made no difference. The needle on her guilt-meter was swinging like mad. Her phone beeped with an incoming text and Melissa read it with a smile.

If you've changed your mind I understand, but you'll miss out on the jug of Pimm's and Chloe's hair-raising stories.

With a new lightness in her step, she set off again. She'd walked past Nathan's lovely old red brick house many times but never been inside. At some point the family must've taken down part of the wall to make a short drive on one side to park a car, but the old front entrance remained. Melissa opened the intricate black wrought-iron gate and stopped to admire the house close up. It was typically Victorian with a steep gabled roof, fancy finials and terracotta detailing, a style seen all over the country here. The tiled path she stood on led straight to the deeply recessed front door, set between two bay windows. The door's jewel-like stained-glass panels still drew the eye, despite it almost being two centuries since it was installed.

Before she could press the polished brass bell, Nathan flung open the door and Melissa loved that he couldn't hide his relief, and pleasure, at seeing her.

'We're out in the back garden. Chloe's bought stuff to jazz up my patio. According to her it was only suitable for old people drinking tea and moaning about their health.' Nathan raised an eyebrow. 'I hope you're a fan of fairy lights. I've been informed that they aren't reserved for Christmas trees these days.'

She suppressed the urge to laugh. There was something delightfully old-fashioned about this man, with his classic car, his passion for books, his good quality but deeply unfashionable clothes and slight air of bemusement at the vagaries of modern life. Robin had been the complete opposite — always a fan of the latest technology, the trendiest clothes and paranoid about getting old. Melissa suspected it was those differences that'd kept him and Nathan as best friends for so long.

Nathan's vivid blue eyes — a match for Paul Newman's any day — fixed on her. She struggled to recall what he'd been saying before her mind drifted off. 'Of course I love fairy lights.' Tactfully she didn't add that she'd draped a strand of pink flamingo lights over hers and Robin's bed once. They only stayed there briefly because he thought they were ridiculous and insisted she took them down again. 'Lead me to the Pimm's.'

'Yes, ma'am. Isn't that what they say in your part of the world?'

A peal of laughter burst out of her. 'I'm glad you teach English literature and not Faulkner or Robert Penn Warren. Your poor students' ears would bleed listening to that atrocious mangling of a Southern accent.' Unconsciously linking her arm through his, she became acutely aware of the heat emanating from his body pressed up against her side as they walked together around the side of the house.

'Hurry up, Uncle Nat. I'm dying to meet your girlfriend!' A youthful voice rang out.

A whoosh of heat zoomed up Melissa's neck but her embarrassment was nothing compared to Nathan's, whose beet-red face could've powered the National Grid.

'I didn't tell her . . . I'd never . . .' The poor man stumbled over his words.

'I know that.' For a fleeting second their eyes locked. Was the idea of her being his girlfriend no more abhorrent to him than it was to her?

* * *

Nathan untangled himself from Melissa and strode off, desperate to put some physical distance between them. He'd felt a pull of attraction since day one, but her? He wasn't the most intuitive man where women were concerned, so was he mistaking the signs? Embarrassment was one thing, and well-deserved after Chloe's blunder, but the flare of light in Melissa's luminous eyes and the throbbing pulse in her slender neck when they'd been standing close were something else.

He swiped one of the glasses Chloe held out and drained half of it straight down. Melissa strolled in to join them. How did she do it? There was nothing in her calm, smiling visage to hint that she'd been anything less than her usual serene self a few minutes ago.

'Hiya, you must be Chloe.' She beamed at his niece. 'I've been hearing a lot about you.'

'All bad, I'm sure. The good people of Penworthal are so easy to shock it's sad.' Chloe rolled her eyes. 'Here you go.' She thrust a drink at Melissa. 'Sit down and dish the dirt on Uncle Nat. He can't be as boring as he makes out if he managed to hook you.' Her gaze swept over Melissa's dress. 'Italian? You're a step up from the only other girlfriend I've seen him with.' She rattled on. 'Mousy little thing she was who didn't say a word.'

'Harriet wasn't mousy in the least and from what I remember you didn't give her a chance to get a word in edgeways,' Nathan chipped in. 'By the way, before you start spreading lies around the village while you're restocking the baked beans, Melissa and I are—'

'Good friends,' Melissa said firmly. 'Your uncle was best friends with my husband, who died last year. I came back here to live about two months ago and Nathan's been an absolute rock.'

He stared down at the grass. That was tying the truth up in knots like a German pretzel.

'Whatever. If you say so.' Chloe shrugged. 'Uncle Nat, why don't you fetch the spicy nuts and hummus and vegetable platter from the kitchen, yeah?' She took Melissa's hand. 'We're going to have a girly chat.'

Over by the door he turned and, with a sinking heart, watched the two women with their heads together, laughing and talking away like long-time friends.

CHAPTER EIGHT

'Hiya, stranger.' Melissa set down her book, heart pounding. She'd taken to reading outside in the garden most evenings after dinner to make the most of the continuing good weather. She peered at Nathan over the top of her new purple-framed reading glasses. Truth be told, she'd needed them for several years but put it off out of sheer vanity. To her mind one of the greatest inventions of the twenty-first century was the e-reader with its awesome font-size-changing ability. But since joining the book club she was reading more paperbacks so she'd bowed to the inevitable. 'Lemonade?' She pointed to the pink flamingo-shaped glass jug.

'Are you going to pour it over my head?'

'If that's your preference.'

'I was a dick, okay?' Nathan grimaced. 'Excuse my language, but there's no other way to phrase it.'

'You're excused — for the cuss word that is — but not for your infantile behaviour when I came over. Not yet anyway.' She'd waited all through the weekend and all day yesterday for an apology. 'What got into you?'

He shoved his hands deep in the pockets of a marginally smarter pair of linen shorts than he'd been wearing the other day.

'*You're* the one who invited *me* for a drink. Instead of laughing it off when your niece got the wrong end of the stick about us, you got the hump because . . . you gonna tell me why?'

Two pinpoints of bright red stood out on his cheeks. 'You and Chloe didn't need me there.'

'Oh, Nathan! Listen to how childish that sounds. Would you rather we'd hated each other on first sight and been bitchy to each other?'

'Of course not, but—'

'But nothing,' she snapped. 'Chloe needed someone to talk to and I fitted the bill because I don't have any preconceived ideas about her.' Without betraying the girl's confidence she couldn't say anything more.

A frown settled between his eyes. 'Is she in some sort of trouble I should know about? Anything her parents should be aware of?'

Melissa mentally tossed a coin and came down on the side of keeping her mouth shut. At least for now.

'I'm not asking you to break a promise, but I am responsible for her at the moment.'

'She needs a little time to work a few things through.' That was the most she could give him. 'I'm pretty sure she'll be okay. Trust me.'

'I do.' Nathan's voice turned husky. 'I was rude to dump the snacks on the table and disappear. What more can I say?'

She pointed to the chair. 'Sit down so you're not towering over me like a vulture preparing to swoop on a fresh carcass.'

'Not the most flattering description.' The glint in his eyes was unmistakable. Nathan glanced back over his shoulder. 'I hope Josie hasn't got the binoculars trained on us. I'm never sure if she approves or disapproves.'

'Of what?'

'Us. I mean . . . Oh God, Melissa, I don't know what I mean.' He slumped in the chair and heaved a weary sigh. 'Before you returned and stirred things up my life was quiet, predictable.'

'Boring?'

'Maybe.' The concession came through gritted teeth.

'And you were okay with that?' Melissa waited. She'd no idea why she was pushing him. Wouldn't it be wiser to let it slide by?

* * *

For a man whose life revolved around words, he struggled to answer. It was easier to get a handle on other people's than his own. Melissa wouldn't be the first woman to find him frustrating on that score, and it could be one reason why he'd hurtled past his fortieth birthday earlier in the year with no partner or family. Not even a pet. He picked up the lemonade she'd poured for him and took a couple of long swallows before setting the glass back down.

'It's often a problem for people like us.'

His head jerked up. 'What do you mean?'

'To a large extent we both spend our days in worlds that other people have created, and sometimes that means we neglect our own.' A sigh slipped out of her. 'At least that's how Robin phrased it when he was madder than usual with me one day for not listening properly when he was talking to me. Again.' She shrugged. 'At least that's how he saw it. That was an ongoing gripe with him.'

Nathan squirmed in the chair. Any discussion of her marriage made him uncomfortable.

'We can't avoid mentioning him, you know.' Melissa's silky drawl ran over his skin.

His increasingly strong feelings for his best friend's wife were disturbing. Though that should be late best friend and widow. More words to trip them up.

'Chloe would agree with Robin. One hundred per cent.' He managed the ghost of a smile. 'Not that I'm going to take life advice from a barely twenty-year-old!'

'That might be going *too* far.'

They both burst out laughing.

'That's better,' she declared.

'It is.'

'This might sound a bit new-age or American but I've been trying to be more mindful. Taking time each day to simply be.' Her smile faded again. 'Don't take this wrong because I wouldn't have done anything differently, but when Robin was ill my own needs naturally fell to the bottom of the priority list. Now I'm trying to take better care of me. That might be selfish—'

'It certainly isn't! You looked awful when I first saw you after you came back . . .' He clamped his lips shut. Too late. Distress filled her beautiful grey-green eyes. 'I'm really sorry. I never meant to upset you.'

'You didn't.' A hint of colour returned to her face. 'Well, maybe you did a little, but that's not your fault. You're right. I *did* look terrible. I was far too thin. My hair was a mess and I was a mess inside too.'

'You'd lost the man you loved.'

'Oh, Nathan, I . . .' Melissa's voice trailed away. 'Let's change the subject. It's too serious and I don't want to put a downer on this lovely summer evening.'

'Neither do I.' Behind her words he recognized another layer to the story, one she wasn't ready to tell and he might not be ready to hear. The way words were arranged on the page or the inflection in someone's voice changed everything. It was something he emphasized to his students that they needed to explore — the way an author chose to create the story and the meanings they might, or might not, be trying to convey. 'So, how about Friday night for dinner? We can walk around Charlestown first to follow in Ross Poldark's footsteps. Are you enjoying the book, by the way?'

'I finished it in one sitting and absolutely loved it!' She looked sheepish. 'I bought the rest of the series and raced through the next two. Winston Graham is an incredible writer.' Melissa omitted the fact she'd picked up the books in one of the charity shops to save money.

'He certainly is. His mastery of character descriptions and scene-setting is absolute. Of course, I'm sure *your* admiration has nothing to do with Ross Poldark being every woman's dream.'

'Not at all.' A fierce blush lit her up. 'He'd make a terrible husband.'

'But an exciting lover?' Nathan probed. 'In literature, and from my own experience in real life, that often seems more important than trust, integrity and friendship. That's why men like me — the regular kind as opposed to the daring and reckless — get overlooked.'

'And who's to say a woman can't have every—'

'Yoo, hoo. Sorry if I'm interrupting.' Josie breezed up the path, wearing her crisp navy-blue uniform. 'I need to see you.' She frowned at Nathan.

'I'll leave you to it.' He pushed the chair back and stood up.

'Hang on a sec.' Melissa's hand shot out to grab his arm. 'You didn't wait for my answer. Friday would be great.'

Josie's blatant curiosity was unmissable. Melissa would doubtless be interrogated, when he left.

While the going was good, he made his escape.

* * *

'I need advice.' Josie dropped into the chair Nathan had vacated. Her gaze shifted to the tray in the middle of the table. 'Cold lemonade would hit the spot too.'

Did Nathan not realize what a catch he was . . . ?

'Earth to Melissa.' Josie waved both hands in her face. 'Sometime today on both requests would be awesome.'

'Sorry.' Melissa's poor grey cells tried to play catch-up and she poured the last of the lemonade into the remaining glass. Her psychic abilities must've been on top form when she brought enough out for both of her unexpected guests. 'There you go. But advice? I can't believe *you're* asking *me* for that. It's usually the other way around.'

'Yes, well. Needs must. I'm in a dilemma — an ethical one — and I don't know how to handle it.' She gulped her lemonade. 'I shouldn't even tell you any of this.'

'Then don't if you'll regret it tomorrow.'

'How about I ask you a hypothetical question?'

'Okay.'

'Let's assume you found out some information that puts a good friend at risk if they *don't* know this particular thing. But you can't tell them without risking your job.' Josie leaned forward. 'What would you do?'

'Oh God, this reminds me of that dumb TV show where people are faced with a moral dilemma and must make a choice. But they don't know all the people involved are paid actors.' Melissa thought hard. 'I'd talk to the friend and try to find out in a roundabout way if they know about this . . . situation.'

'I'm almost certain they don't.' Josie's colour deepened. 'I should've kept my mouth shut. Forget it.'

'If what you're talking about is connected to our group, wouldn't you be better off discussing it with one of the others rather than me? Y'all have known each other for yonks.'

'That's the problem, and why I chose you. We know the ins and outs of each other's lives too intimately in some ways.'

'I'm real sorry, but I don't know what else to say.'

'It'll be out before long anyway, I expect. One way or another.'

'At least you won't be responsible.'

'Won't I?'

She understood only too well about guilt and responsibility. 'Is this friend in real danger?'

'I hope not.' Josie shrugged.

They sank into silence.

'Take my mind off all that and give me some juicy gossip to spread around,' Josie pleaded. 'Was Dr Kellow here to renew his ardent pleas for your affection?'

It was impossible not to laugh at Josie's weak attempt to mimic Jane Austen. Later, she'd ponder some more as to what their conversation had really been about.

CHAPTER NINE

'Calm down, Catherine, and start again.' Nathan grimaced at the grandfather clock ticking sonorously in the corner of the hall. If his father was alive, he'd correct his son and point out it was more correctly a longcase clock. One of the many lectures he'd received from Harold Kellow had taught him that the name "grandfather" was only coined by the Victorians after a well-known song of the time. His father had been overly proud of the seventeenth-century clock by renowned horologist, Charles Frodsham, which he'd inherited from his grandfather.

Right now, all Nathan cared about was that if his sister didn't hurry up, he'd be late picking up Melissa. As he listened, he confirmed he had his wallet and keys, and headed towards the door. With one foot out over the step, he stopped, uncertain he'd heard Catherine correctly. 'Are you telling me Chloe has been sent down from Oxford for not attending classes and blowing off her exams? And she didn't tell you?' His dinner date receded into the distance. 'Look, I need to make a quick phone call to cancel some plans but I promise it won't take long. I'll ring you back.'

Melissa deserved better than a cowardly text, but hearing the unmistakable pleasure in her voice when she answered made him feel worse. By the time he'd stammered out an apology and heard her crisp insistence that it was fine, followed by the depressing silence of a disconnected phone, he was in a foul mood. Trudging back into the living room he poured himself a large measure of whisky. Not the good stuff because it'd be a sacrilege to drink his expensive Laphroaig without savouring it.

'Uncle Nat, what're you still doing here?' Chloe stumbled through the door, dragging a dishevelled young man with a straggly beard and idiotic smile behind her. They were drunk, and reeking of marijuana. It didn't take a genius to guess they'd been planning to take advantage of his absence.

'I might ask you the same question. While you're at it, perhaps you'll explain why I've had your mum on the phone in tears? She says Oxford—'

'How the fuck did she find out?' Chloe shook off her companion and pushed him towards the sofa.

'I don't know. I find the news incredibly hard to believe.'

'Well, yeah, it's true, and so what? I'm done with that bunch of stuck-up, arrogant—' Chloe's hand flew up to her mouth and she pushed out past him to the hall. The toilet door slammed and the unmistakable sound of retching echoed through the house.

Nathan debated whether to check on her but decided she was old enough to leave to her own devices. His priority now was attempting to reassure his sister. Chloe's companion was snoring noisily already, so he retreated to his study at the back of the house.

'You took your time,' Catherine complained.

'Sorry. Now, tell me everything you know.' He settled in his father's old wingback chair by the black cast-iron fireplace, allowing it to cocoon him like an old friend. Nathan had never understood people who replaced furniture when it was at its most comfortable. So what if the dark green leather was cracked and faded? He'd changed almost nothing since returning here to live, his frugal father's philosophy of not buying new when the old was still functional ingrained in him too.

'This morning I opened a letter from the university addressed to Chloe—'

'Accidentally?'

'Not exactly,' Catherine conceded. 'I don't need a lecture about respecting her privacy either, thank you very much. Unless you're hiding a secret child somewhere, you aren't a parent so you wouldn't understand.'

Nathan didn't argue.

'We've been worried about her. We could tell she was hiding something because she never wants to talk about her studies or anything connected with uni.'

From his experience, secretiveness and not opening up to their parents was par for the course where most students Chloe's age were concerned. They were trialling adult life to see how it fitted them. The desire for independence at that stage was a positive trait in his book. None of which his sister wanted to hear.

'Read it out to me.' Nathan's heart sank as she did so. There seemed no doubt the proper procedures had been gone through, and this was simply an official notification following the college's decision.

'Will you talk to her, Nathan, and see what you can find out? She was so happy there. I can't imagine what's gone wrong.' Her anguish poured down the phone.

'Chloe's out at the moment.' The truth would rub salt in his sister's raw wounds. He knew of a million and one things that could've gone wrong, from his niece crumbling in the high-pressure academic environment to a disastrous love affair. Things that an older person could cope with often overwhelmed the young. Far too frequently he'd seen the brightest students falter and drop out. 'I'll talk to her in the morning, but don't get your hopes up. I doubt she'll confide in me.'

'But she might. It must be preying on her mind so maybe she'll be grateful for the opportunity to tell someone.' Catherine was clutching at straws. 'You'll ring me tomorrow?'

'Yes, of course I will. Even if she won't talk, I'll call you.' He desperately searched for some other consoling words. 'She'll be okay, you know. Things will work out.'

'I don't need your platitudes. We both know her chances of a decent career are negligible if she abandons university. She'll be stuck filling shelves in your village shop and end up marrying a road-sweeper and have half a dozen kids before she's thirty.'

It would send Catherine off the deep end if he pointed out that that scenario might make his niece a damn sight happier.

'Good night.'

He'd disappointed three women tonight — quite a record.

* * *

Melissa hesitated outside the Rusty Anchor. If she wanted to treat herself to a drink and a meal, why shouldn't she? The sweep of annoyance that'd sent her marching down here had dissipated. Although Nathan hadn't shared any details about what was up with Chloe, she was pretty sure it was connected to his niece's secret confession the other day that she'd been thrown out of university. That didn't lessen her disappointment about tonight's abandoned dinner date, but he needed to put his family first. If any of the Rutherford clan was in trouble, she'd be the first to drop everything and help them. The four-thousand-mile distance made no difference to their tight connection.

A wall of heat and crowds of people greeted her the moment she stepped inside. *Damn.* Quiz night. How could she have forgotten? Before she had the chance to sneak out again, Amy shrieked her name over the crowd, jumped up and down and waved her arms around.

'Over here!'

Now she'd be forced to endure a barrage of probing questions about why she wasn't out with Nathan. She'd been inundated with un-asked-for advice yesterday when a few of them met up for coffee. Everything from what she should wear to whether she should sleep with him yet. The consensus on the two points was: her flattering cerise dress, and no. The girls never hesitated to speak their minds.

She wended her way through and locked eyes with a surprised Josie. A quick glance around told her Laura was absent. 'Anyone need a drink?' The offer had to be made but hopefully most of the group were already situated so she could avoid too much strain on her dwindling bank balance.

'Yes please, and some crisps.' Josie sprang up. 'I'll come with you.' Her friend smiled, grasped Melissa's arm and steered her away. 'What the bloody hell are you doing here? If that man stood you up, I'll cut off his man parts.'

'He didn't stand me up.' Melissa ran through the brief exchange she had with Nathan. 'Now you know as much as I do.' A lie, but a necessary one.

'Mmm. Well, I'm not impressed. I'm sure whatever is up with that little madam could've waited until the morning. She's probably broken a fingernail or dropped a tin of peas on her toe.'

She understood where her friend was coming from because if she didn't know better, she'd assume the same. Her weak attempt to defend Nathan made Josie scoff.

'We're glad to see you anyway. Laura cried off with a lame excuse about needing to cut out thirty-six pictures of Stonehenge for Midsummer's Day on Monday. Monday, for heaven's sake! She's got all weekend.'

'I hope she's okay.'

'You two ordering or just taking up space?' Vernon Bull glowered and held up his empty beer glass.

She'd asked Josie once how the perpetually grouchy man ended up running a shop and discovered that four generations of the Bull family had owned the Penworthal Stores, so he looked on it as a sort of sacred duty.

'Are you offering to treat us, Mr Bull?' Josie teased.

'Wimmen. Always after a man's money.' He pushed past them and shoved his glass at Pixie.

'I'm after your money too, Vernon.' Pixie grinned. 'That'll be three pounds ninety-five.'

'Bleedin' daylight robbery,' he moaned, and tossed a handful of coins on the bar.

Once they were served and returned to their table, Melissa started to relax. She'd make the best of a bad job. No. Not a bad job. An evening spent with her friends was something to celebrate, not moan about. *Why was everyone staring at her?*

'So, are you going to tell us why you're here instead of out with our handsome professor?' Evelyn never beat about the bush.

Josie gave a resigned shrug, as if to say "what did you expect?"

For the second time Melissa explained what'd happened and received a rash of scathing reactions. This wasn't fair on Nathan but she'd no choice. He wouldn't appreciate her spreading Chloe's story around the village.

'Now that's out of the way, are y'all ready to wax *Proper Choughed* again?' Melissa said, with fire in her voice. 'They don't have their prize asset tonight with Nathan absent. I've never met Micky Broad but I can't believe he's good enough to tip the balance back in their favour.'

Tomorrow, she'd go to Nathan's and see if she could help. If he'd let her.

CHAPTER TEN

'Oh, it's you. You'd better come in.' Nathan dragged a hand over his uncombed hair. Melissa's unsmiling face registered, making him realize how rude that must've sounded. 'I'm sorry. I didn't mean to—'

'Be an ass? Make me sorry I bothered to trudge down here in the rain to see you?'

'Yeah, all of that. Come inside, please, and let me give you a towel to dry off.' If he was stupid enough to ask why she wasn't wearing a mac or carrying an umbrella when it was tipping down, that would make things worse.

'Fine.'

Melissa stepped forward and they bumped into each other when he didn't move out of the way in time. Automatically reaching out to steady her, Nathan unconsciously wrapped his arms around her. His senses were teased by the scent of fresh raindrops mixed with her distinctive perfume, reminiscent of peaches with an added punch of spice. The thin grey sweatpants he'd slept in were no match for the effect of her warm, damp body pressed against his. Nathan did his best to extricate himself from their embrace before he embarrassed them both any further. Melissa glanced up at him through her long dark eyelashes, cheeks flushed and the pulse in her neck throbbing.

'I might've guessed you'd call in the cavalry.' Chloe's voice dripped sarcasm. She posed halfway down the stairs like a movie star. That is, if movie stars appeared in front of their fans with waxy skin, dark rings under their eyes and devoid of make-up. 'Well, I'm not talking to *her* either. I'll wake Josh and we'll get out of your hair.' Her disparaging gaze swept over them. 'You can go back to groping each other now. At your ages you should be past PDAs.' She swept off, leaving them staring awkwardly at each other.

'What on earth is a PDA when it's at home?'

'A Public Display of Affection. Only allowed if you're under thirty apparently.' Melissa's lilting drawl made him smile. 'That's better.'

'What is?'

She touched a finger to his lips. 'You've no idea what an amazing smile you have, do you?' Her greyish-green eyes turned bright silver, and he melted where he stood. 'Ross Poldark has nothing on you.'

'Rubbish.'

'You promised me a towel.'

'Of course.' At least he'd caught up with the washing yesterday so had a stack of clean towels to hand. He ran upstairs and returned to thrust a soft white towel at her. 'There you go. Tea? Coffee?'

'Coffee would be great. You sure have an interesting house. It's the first time I've been inside.'

'It can't be . . .' Nathan's voice failed him and for a moment he couldn't look at her.

'This floor is stunning.' She admired the multi-coloured tiles patterning the entrance hall.

'They're original to the house. Almost everything is, really. It's early Victorian and built in 1842.' When he was young, his father's near-obsession with keeping the house the same as when *his* great-grandfather had had it designed and built to his specifications irritated Nathan. As an adult it'd grown on him.

'It's very you.'

'Is that a good thing?' He squirmed under her intense scrutiny.

'Maybe. It depends if you've kept it unmodernized by choice or default?' Melissa shrugged. 'Don't get me wrong. There's lots to love about Victorian style, but it's a little heavy for my taste.'

This is what made her a good editor. No doubt she asked the same pertinent questions to improve an author's manuscript. Nathan glanced around, seeing the brown paint, ornate dark-red wallpaper and heavy dark furniture through her eyes.

'My parents — well, my father really, and Mum never crossed him — never knowingly wasted money. If something still worked and served its original purpose, that was good enough for him.'

'I get that. My grandparents were the same way.'

Raised voices drifted out from the living room so he deftly steered her towards the kitchen.

'You look beat.' Melissa touched his arm. 'Sit down and I'll fix our drinks.'

He should protest, but he was weary to his core after lying awake most of the night worrying about Chloe. Nathan flopped down and watched her find what she needed with no help from him. After she set down a mug of his favourite weak, sugary coffee and he took a few sips, he started to revive. Most of the women he knew would feel the need to fill the silence with chatter, but not Melissa. He'd noticed that quality in her before — yet another reason Robin had been a lucky man. A grimace twisted his face as he regretted that thought sneaking into his head.

'Didn't I make it right?'

'No. It's perfect,' Nathan stammered. 'It wasn't that. I . . .'

'Tell me about Chloe. If you want to, that is?' She looked wary. 'I assume this is about Oxford? Are you mad at me for not saying anything?'

'Mad at you? Absolutely not. She told you in confidence and I respect that.' He sensed her relief. 'My sister might not agree, but she doesn't need to know.'

'Yeah, that's probably for the best. I haven't met her but—'

'Oh, Catherine would indeed rain down the full power of her wrath on you. Undeserved, of course, but that wouldn't worry her.' Nathan cracked a smile. 'I'm not top of her popularity list either, so don't worry.'

'Why not? You've taken her daughter in after all and are doing your best.'

'Not sure she sees it that way. I've always been a bit . . . less than enthusiastic, shall we say, when she's pushed Chloe academically.'

'Yeah, things come back to haunt us, don't they?' He took a guess that the wistfulness in her voice was about a whole lot more than his niece's current troubles. 'Is there anything I can do to help?'

'I'd value your opinion on how I should deal with all this.'

'Are you sure? Sometimes my authors regret asking the same sort of question.' Melissa's eyes shone with a challenge he couldn't resist.

'Absolutely. Go for it.'

* * *

'First, let me put it out there that I was an idiot and got a bit put out after you let me down last night. It was juvenile and selfish. Once I thought about it like an adult, I totally got why you needed to stay here. I went to the quiz night and complained a bit to my friends, but only because I couldn't be honest about *why* you'd cancelled without blabbing about Chloe and Oxford. I'm afraid it dented their high opinion of you a tad.' A spark of amusement brightened his tired eyes. 'It's not funny.'

Nathan squeezed her hand. 'The *Back of Beyond Brains* are the least of my worries today. You're here now, and if it's any consolation I was mad last night too. At myself, and at Chloe and her parents for dropping me in the middle of this mess. I'm rather set in my ways and appallingly self-centred, so maybe I need shaking up occasionally.' His gaze lingered on her. 'I'd hoped our dinner last night would . . . Forget that, my timing's lousy.'

'It's hard to forget something you've only heard half of,' she complained. Flashes of heat highlighted his sculpted face. *God, he really was incredibly handsome.* The thought of him reading Edmund Spenser's sixteenth-century poem *The Faerie Queene* aloud to her in his gorgeous rumbling voice, tinged with a Cornish accent, made her swoon. In a take-off of her favourite movie version of *Sense and Sensibility*, he'd be Alan Rickman playing the part of Colonel Brandon to her own beguiling Marianne.

'What's going through your mind now?'

'Something that shouldn't.' That made his smile deepen. 'Let's concentrate on sorting out what you're going to do about Chloe.'

'Yes, let's.' He lifted her hand to his cheek, pressing it against his warm, lightly stubbled skin. 'But later . . .'

'Chloe.' Melissa tried to sound stern and shifted away from his distracting touch. 'You can't force her to talk.' She thought some more. 'I'm guessing your sister's on the verge of high-tailing it down here?'

'That's what she threatened when I spoke to her earlier. I begged for more time to hopefully make progress with Chloe. There'll be ructions if she turns up now because she and Chloe have always clashed. They're two determined women and they'll both dig their heels in.' He shook his head. 'Her dad won't be any help either. Anything for an easy life is Johnny's motto.'

'Have you told Chloe about your latest chat with her mom?'

'No, but I will now she's sent lover boy away.'

'For what it's worth, my advice is to keep your mouth shut. Let her believe Catherine is heading for Cornwall right now. That might persuade her to open up because she'll be desperate to get you on her side.'

'I suppose it might work.'

The lack of conviction in his voice didn't bother her. In her professional life she was used to talking authors around to her point of view. She frequently used all the tact in her arsenal to explain to a client that although their five-page description of a character's house was an amazing piece of literature, it would send most of their readers to sleep. Phrasing was everything.

'Will you stay while I give it a try?' he pleaded.

It'd be easy to succumb, but wrong. 'I'd better not. Chloe might give the impression she's indifferent, but you notice she isn't broadcasting the fact she's been turfed out of college. That's a hopeful sign.'

'It is?'

'Yeah. It means she cares. Until you can pry out of her what's at the root of the problem, you'll get nowhere.' Her bluntness made him wince, so it was time for the softer touch. She'd discovered with her clients that it wasn't difficult to dial back on her attitude, but if she started off easy it was far harder to tighten the screws.

'You're right and I'll give it a try. Thanks.'

'You're welcome. You know where I am if Chloe wants someone else to bounce her thoughts off.' Melissa stood up.

'I do, and I'll pass on your offer.'

'Thanks for the towel.'

'It's still tipping it down out there. Let me give you a ride home.'

'No, you've got work to do. Lend me an umbrella and I'll be good.'

'Are you sure?'

'Yeah, absolutely. Call me later and let me know how you get on.' She hesitated. 'If you can get away, I'll be around for the rest of the day so you're welcome to stop by.'

'I'd love to, but—'

'You can't promise. I get it. I'm not asking you to.'

They strolled back out to the hall together.

'If you don't care about looking deeply unfashionable, you're welcome to wear this.' Nathan unhitched a long dark mac from the antique Indian mahogany coat stand carved in the form of an elephant by the front door. 'It's mine so it'll swamp you but at least it'll keep you dry.'

She stuck her arms in as he held the coat open for her and a shiver ran down her spine when he smoothed out the shoulders and spun her around to face him. Slowly he buttoned the coat up and lifted the hood over her head.

'There. You're good to go now.'

But I don't want to. It was time to leave before she did, or said, something stupid.

* * *

'Are you hungry?' Nathan kept his back to Chloe while he stirred the scrambled eggs. He'd skipped breakfast but experienced a renewed burst of energy and appetite after Melissa's visit. 'There's plenty here. The bacon's cooked already.' He pointed to a plate piled high with his favourite fried-almost-to-a-cinder bacon. 'Help yourself.'

Chloe grabbed a couple of rashers and crammed them into her mouth. The edges of her mutinous expression softened.

'Is your . . . friend gone?' he asked.

'Yes. Is yours?'

He ignored the hint of sarcasm and retrieved the bread from the toaster. After generously buttering the toast he set it on their two plates before taking the eggs off the heat and sharing them out. Nathan set their food on the table, along with some cutlery, and sat down. 'Eat up before it gets cold.' His niece dragged out a chair and joined him. Before picking up her knife and fork she shook enough ketchup over her eggs to make it resemble a crime scene.

'I spoke to your mum earlier.'

'She's bloody coming here, isn't she? Well, I'm not staying. I'll eat then go pack my things.'

'Running away won't solve anything, Chloe, love. You've tried that already by coming here but it hasn't worked terribly well, has it?' He pressed on. 'How long did you think you could keep it a secret? Were you going to go back to Oxford in September as if everything was normal? Did you expect to keep it up for the next two years? Invite your parents to graduation as if nothing was wrong?' She turned pale. 'It's time to face up to what's happened and deal with it like the grown-up you claim to be.'

She glared at him.

'If you weren't happy at uni why didn't you confide in your tutor or your parents?' This was way out of his comfort zone. He couldn't wrap his arms around Chloe and reassure her everything would be fine like he did when she was eight years old and in floods of tears because her teacher picked her to be a sheep in the school nativity play instead of an angel.

'They wouldn't understand.' Frustration oozed out of her. 'The tutors think Oxford is the be all and end all of everything, and so do Mum and Dad.' Her voice broke. 'I hate letting them all down but I can't do it any longer.' She crumpled in front of him and huge wrenching sobs broke out of her, tearing his heart in two.

Melissa's advice had been sound, but being brought face to face with the consequences now was harrowing. He worried he wasn't up to the task.

CHAPTER ELEVEN

Melissa opened one eye and peered at her bedside clock, heart racing like a beating drum. Who the hell was banging on her door at two o'clock on a Sunday morning? If it was rowdy teenagers making asses of themselves, she'd give them a piece of her mind. She'd only crawled into bed around midnight after waiting in vain for Nathan to turn up. Hopefully his non-appearance was a good sign and he'd winkled the truth out of Chloe. The banging continued so she dragged herself out of bed and tugged on her bathrobe.

Downstairs she turned on the porch light and flung open the door. 'Bugger off and pester someone— Laura?' Melissa swallowed hard.

Pale, red-eyed, and with trembling hands clutched protectively over her stomach, her friend looked dreadful. 'Come in.' She led her unexpected visitor into the lounge. 'Tea?' It amused her that she'd picked up the quintessential English habit of offering the national hot drink for any emergency.

'Please,' Laura whispered.

'I'll put the kettle on and give Josie a call. I'm pretty sure she's not on shift tonight so we can get her to check you over.'

'She's not home. I went there first.'

Melissa was puzzled. Josie hadn't mentioned going out, and especially not overnight. They'd got into the habit of letting the other one know if they had plans, sort of their own mutual protection society. 'Oh, right. Well, if you give me his number, I'll ring your husband. He'll be worried.'

'No!' Horror transformed Laura's face from tired to frantic. 'You can't do that!'

Something was going on. Melissa guessed he'd found out about the baby and they'd had a row. 'Should I get the doctor then? You don't look well.'

Another violent head shake.

'Right.' What the hell was she going to do? 'Let's have our tea. Milk and sugar?'

Laura shuddered. 'Black, please. Decaf, if you have it.'

Out in the kitchen her mind raced while she made their drinks, but no new bright idea popped up. Her friend was gazing admiringly around the room when she returned.

'You've got it nice here. The colours are so restful.' Laura perched on the sofa.

'Thanks.' Melissa set their two mugs on the table and waited.

'Look, I'm sorry. This was a mistake. I shouldn't have bothered you, especially this late. I should go.'

'You're not going anywhere, honey. Not until you tell me what's up.'

'I can't. I don't know you well enough. Don't get me wrong, but Josie would've understood.' Her agitated fingers picked at a sliver of loose skin on her left thumb.

'I'm a good listener.' She studied Laura's weary countenance and guessed she hadn't slept properly in weeks. 'Or I've got a spare room you can rest in?' Temptation flitted across her friend's face. 'No strings.'

'I wouldn't mind laying down for a little while. If you're sure you really don't mind?'

'Of course not. Do you want to finish your tea?'

'I'll take it up with me.'

Upstairs, she noticed Laura's eyes widen when she showed her the bathroom. Robin had talked her into having it remodelled, pushing aside her objections that it was an extravagance they couldn't afford. Originally converted from a large bedroom by Robin's parents, it now boasted a generous walk-in glass-walled shower, a claw foot jacuzzi bathtub and double sinks set in honey-coloured marble. She opened a heated cupboard by the door. 'Help yourself to towels if you want a bath or shower.' Laura didn't say a word as they moved on to the bedroom. 'I'm next door if you need anything, so don't hesitate to come in. Okay? How about I get you a nightdress or—'

'I don't need anything. I'll be fine. You're so kind.' Laura's voice wobbled and her eyes welled up.

'Hey, that's what friends are for.' Back in her own bed she lay flat on her back, staring at the ceiling.

Should she ignore Laura's determined refusal and call Judy anyway? The local doctor had been wonderful when Melissa saw her shortly after coming back to Penworthal. She'd been desperate to cure her newly acquired insomnia and more used to American doctors who were often only too willing to hand out prescriptions like candy. She was taken by surprise when Judy told her frankly that pills weren't the answer. Instead, she encouraged Melissa to take regular exercise, eat properly, and most of all to be kind and patient with herself. Things had slowly improved and now she managed a good seven hours rest most nights. She reached for her phone and hovered over the contacts list but her conscience wouldn't let her dial Judy's number. As a compromise she texted Josie instead, but the reply that popped in a few moments later did nothing to calm her frazzled nerves.

I was afraid of this. Tied up right now or I'd come. Keep her there until 8 if you can. Sorry.

There'd be no sleep tonight.

* * *

Nathan flung open the kitchen windows. Only his stubborn sister would insist on cooking a full Sunday roast when the temperature was soaring towards thirty degrees, without the hint of a breeze blowing in from the coast. Melissa was no doubt laughing her head off to hear everyone moaning about the heat. Yesterday she informed him that Tennessee had been baking in thirty-seven-degree heat, with a miserable dose of humidity thrown in, for the last ten days. But he'd wisely kept his mouth shut when Catherine offered to cook. He'd sensed her craving for routine. It was either that or fall apart, not an option for someone who preferred to be in control of every aspect of her life.

It'd been a tough phone call yesterday, when he rang to break the news about why her only child had thrown in a promising academic future.

She can't cope with everyone's expectations anymore? What nonsense! Stupid girl doesn't realize how lucky she is. We've given her the best of everything, she's had every opportunity handed to her on a plate, she's got nothing to complain about.

Nathan hadn't dared to suggest that if they'd asked Chloe what *she* wanted occasionally, and actually listened to her answers, they might not be in this dilemma now. Catherine had slammed the phone down on him and three hours later she and Johnny arrived on his doorstep. His sister's bad mood had worsened after being stuck in traffic and sweltering in a car whose air-conditioning had inconveniently decided to break down. To make things worse, it was a Saturday, which in the summer meant long tailbacks on the A30, the main road for holidaymakers pouring into Cornwall.

The first massive row came as soon as Catherine and Chloe came face to face. His niece stormed off for several hours, leaving the three of them to hang around the house making awkward conversation until she reappeared. Cue row number two. By the time they went to bed, Nathan felt he'd been wrung out and hung up to dry like a freshly washed sheet.

He slipped out the back door and retreated to the far end of the garden. It'd been too late to disturb Melissa last night, but now he was desperate to hear her voice and get another dose of common-sense advice. Disappointment flooded through him when she didn't answer, but before he was halfway back up the path his phone buzzed.

'Hiya, you called?'

'Yes, do you have a few minutes free? It's rather a long story.'

Melissa sighed. 'I wish. It's a bit . . . chaotic here too, and another long story.'

'Later?'

'Yeah. At yours or mine?'

They couldn't rely on getting any privacy here. 'Yours. I'll bring the wine, and a shoulder to cry on if you need one.' Nathan chuckled. 'Mind you, I might need one in return.'

'Happy to oblige. I've two fairly respectable ones.'

Before he could add anything more, Catherine started yelling his name to tell him dinner was ready. 'Sorry, I'll have to go. There's a plate of roast beef with all the trimmings waiting for me.'

'In this weather? I can't believe you cooked all that today.'

'Me? No way. My sister and brother-in-law are here and there's a three-line-whip for attendance at the dinner table.'

'Ah. I'm guessing that's part of the long story?'

'Oh yes. See you later.'

'I'm looking forward to it already.'

Nathan strolled towards Catherine with a smile playing on his lips. His sister hovered on the back step and her furrowed expression reminded him uncannily of their mother.

Johnny joined them and the worry lines on his forehead were even deeper than they had been. 'Chloe's gone off with some lad on the back of his motorbike.' His eyes turned watery. 'She swears she's not coming back until we're gone.'

'In that case we'll wait her out.' Catherine's lips pursed. 'Let's go and eat or my Yorkshire puddings will sink.'

CHAPTER TWELVE

Melissa couldn't decide which one of her friends looked worse. Laura, hunched over the kitchen table with her hands pressed over her ears, pale and silent. Or Josie, toying with the same cup of tea she'd been staring at for hours. Her neighbour's lank hair, unwashed face and crumpled dress spoke to a night spent God knows where — that little story hadn't been shared yet. All she knew was that Josie had turned up shortly after eight this morning, looking, as her own mother would say, like death warmed over. A little while ago Melissa had offered to make some sandwiches for their lunch but no one was interested.

'Bloody come out here and face me, you faithless cow.' Barry Day's gruff voice boomed through the house. By his slurred tone it wasn't hard to guess he'd been propping up the bar in the pub since opening time. If he banged the front door much harder he'd break it down.

'Should we call the police?' She got two determined head shakes in response. 'We've got to do *something*.'

'I'll have to talk to him,' Laura whispered.

'Not yet you don't,' Josie said. 'Not until he calms down.'

'Right, I'm going out,' Melissa declared.

'But—'

'But nothing.'

'You're right.' Josie sounded less than pleased about that. 'I'd better come with you. Safety in numbers and all that.' She turned to Laura. 'Why don't you go back up to the bedroom? We'll bring Barry in here and try to sober him up and quiet him down. Then maybe the two of you can talk.'

Melissa had the gut feeling her friend knew more than she was letting on, because Laura's revelation, shortly after Josie arrived, that Barry wasn't the father of the baby she was expecting didn't appear to shock her. So far they hadn't discovered who *was* the father.

'Okay.' Laura left them, and everything about her sagging posture pointed to defeat and helplessness.

'So, are you going to tell me what's up? With Laura. You. Everything.' The blunt challenge made Josie wince.

'Later.'

She already had one "later" lined up with Nathan. They'd have to form an orderly queue. 'Come on then and introduce me to the delightful Barry.'

'Oh, I forgot you don't know him.' Josie frowned. 'He's not a bad man. A bit black and white, if you know what I mean. He loves Laura to bits though, and worships the ground she walks on.'

Melissa hated that expression. Why was it always said in such a positive way? The idea of any man putting her on a pedestal, with all the expectations that came with it, gave her the creeps.

Out in the hall she inhaled a deep breath and opened the door.

'About bloody time. Where is she?' The wild-eyed man pushed past Melissa, but Josie's hand shot out to grab his arm and stop him going any further. Dealing with out-of-control patients must be good training for this sort of situation because her friend hadn't hesitated to tackle the six-foot-plus, brawny man spewing anger.

'Come and have a coffee, Barry,' Josie suggested. 'Laura won't talk to you if you're pissed.'

'Get out of my way. I don't need some interfering nurse sticking her nose in my marriage.' In a feeble attempt to push Josie away, he lost his balance and slid down in a heap on the floor clutching his head in his hands.

'Go and put the kettle on, Melissa. I'll see to him.'

She willingly fled to the kitchen, turned on the kettle and rested her shaking hands on the counter while it came to a boil.

For the next half hour they poured strong black coffee into Barry until he pushed back the chair and glared at them both.

'So, is one of you two going to tell me who's got my wife up the duff? I'll lay into the git good and proper.' His gaze hardened when neither of them answered. 'Don't you give a toss that having another baby could kill her?'

She sneaked a surreptitious glance at Josie, but her friend sat motionless and silent. 'I don't know anything, Mr Day,' Melissa said. 'Has Laura admitted to having an affair?'

'Doesn't fucking need to, does she? I had the bloody snip after the last baby we lost because I didn't want to lose my Laura. I love that woman more than life itself.' He rubbed a trembling hand over his red swollen eyes. '*You* know I'm telling the truth.' Barry aimed that at Josie. 'I bet you saw my medical records and told her and that's why she's done this.'

'I never did!'

Was this what she'd been referring to obliquely the other day when she mentioned an ethical conflict at work? The puzzle pieces were slotting into place.

'Occasionally the surgery can reverse itself.' That suggestion from Josie ripped a coarse laugh out of Barry. 'It's rare but it does happen.'

'Yeah, and we all know pigs fly so you'd better bloody watch out for their shit dropping from the sky.' He heaved himself off the chair. 'I'm tired. Tell her to come back home when she's ready so we can talk on our own without any well-meaning busybodies interfering. And in case you're worried, I won't hurt her. I'd never do that.' He trudged out of the room and seconds later the front door slammed shut behind him.

'What do we do now?' Melissa asked. '*Did* Laura confide in you—'

'No, I didn't.' Laura reappeared in the doorway. 'Barry needs to hear it first.' She touched her stomach. 'Be careful what you wish for, girls. Sometimes getting what you want isn't worth it. I've been a fool.'

'Do you want a lift home?'

'No thanks. I'll walk.' The trace of a smile lifted her tired features. 'I'll probably catch up with my hungover husband along the way.'

Left alone with her friend, Melissa stared at Josie. Neither of them spoke.

* * *

A refreshing breeze had taken the sting out of the earlier oppressive heat, so Nathan's stroll through the quiet village and up the hill to Melissa's house did him good. Chloe was still AWOL so Catherine and Johnny were camped out in his sister's old bedroom for the second night in a row. His sister wasn't pleased when he told them he had plans for the evening, but he'd stuck to his guns, given them the television remote control and the gin bottle and left them to it.

As soon as Melissa answered the door he held out a chilled bottle of wine and a packet of her favourite cheese straws. 'I come bearing gifts.'

'All I needed was to see you, but I'll happily take these as a bonus.' She snatched the gifts away with a giggle.

'You look . . .' He lost his nerve and fell silent.

'Old? Wrinkled? Fat? Thin? Don't leave it there or I'll lay awake tonight wondering what you were going to say.'

Nathan stared into her bright eyes. Sometimes they resembled the sea in winter, but on other occasions — like now — the curious mixture of green and grey sparkled like a newly minted coin. 'I was thinking how beautiful you are.'

There was no going back. 'The bright pink dress is stunning against your silver hair.' His face burned. 'Maybe if I was Wordsworth, Shelley or Keats I'd be able to write poetry about you but I'm not. I'll probably keep stumbling over inappropriate things to say and hope that you'll forgive me.'

'We are a pair, aren't we?' A hint of sadness sneaked into her voice. 'They go on about teenage angst and how terrible it is but I reckon it's got nothing on what people our age go through.' Her smile inched back. 'Not that I'd want to be sixteen again with all the crap that goes with it. I'll take how we are. Here. Now.'

'Me too.' Saying the least amount possible struck him as wise. These days the more he opened his mouth, the worse it tended to turn out.

'Come in.' She seized hold of him with her free arm and propelled him into the hall. 'Shall we have our drinks inside or out?'

'Out. It's cooled off and feels good now.'

'I forgot you Brits can't deal with a bit of heat.' Melissa chuckled. 'Grab a couple of glasses on our way through the kitchen please.' She skipped off, leaving him to play catch up.

Once they were settled on her patio, neither of them spoke right away. He was content to watch her sip the fragrant wine with a grateful sigh and fall on the snacks like a stray dog who hadn't eaten in a week.

'Some of us didn't stuff ourselves full of roast beef at lunchtime, you know,' she said through a mouthful of cheese straw. 'In fact, lunch didn't happen at all from my recollection.'

'Sorry. If it's any consolation I only ate a few mouthfuls of mine. Enough to stop Catherine getting mad . . . although "mad" is pretty much her default setting at the moment.'

'Chloe?'

'Oh yeah. Do you want every excruciating detail or just the highlights?'

'The edited version will do. I need time to tell my tale of woe as well before you trot off back home.'

It hovered in his throat, but thankfully didn't make it as far as his tongue, that he didn't *have* to go anywhere. Nathan dragged his concentration back to the ongoing saga of Chloe and ran through it all in chronological order.

'Wow, what a mess. I feel for the poor kid. I don't know how you'll get your sister to understand the situation from Chloe's point of view. I totally get parents wanting the best for their kids, but it's gotta be what's right for the child.'

'Absolutely.' Nathan leaned forward. 'I thought she might waver when I reminded her that she stood up for me when our father tried to push me into following his footsteps and studying engineering.'

'I can't see that for a minute.'

'I would've been hopeless and failed miserably. Of course, that's what he thought I'd done anyway.' Bitterness invaded his voice.

'That's a shame. I'm fortunate because our parents always encouraged us to follow *our* own dreams, not *theirs*.' She smiled. 'All three of us are completely different.'

'I'd love to hear more about your family one day.'

'Get me started on the Rutherfords and you'll wish you hadn't asked.' Melissa's laughter faded away. 'So back to Chloe. Do you know what she's really interested in doing?'

'No, and I'm not sure she does either. That's why I'm torn. I'd hate to see her give up Oxford and live to regret it.'

'It's a tough one.'

Nathan topped up their glasses and sat back. 'Now it's your turn. Tell me all.'

A frown wrinkled her brow and she reached for another cheese straw, nibbling it thoughtfully.

'Whatever you say won't go any further, I promise. I hope you trust me enough to believe that.'

'Yeah, I do.'

Whatever he'd been expecting wasn't the sad tale that tumbled out. He barely knew Laura and Barry Day, but they'd always struck him as a close and loving couple. She was well-loved at the nursery school and everyone turned to

Barry for their electrical work because he was reliable and conscientious.

'Let me get this straight. You're telling me Laura squirrelled away money from her wages to pay for a sperm donor in a last-ditch effort to try for a baby? That's madness.'

'She was desperate. Haven't you ever wanted something so badly you did crazy stuff to get it?'

'Not really.' At least not yet, but I'm on the verge of it, he thought. 'And she didn't know Barry had . . . you know . . .'

'Oh, Nathan. Are you too squeamish to say the word "vasectomy"?'

His face burned. 'In my case the subject hasn't really arisen.'

'Arisen?' Melissa burst into giggles. 'Appalling word choice there, Mr English Professor.'

They laughed themselves silly and it was ages before they collected themselves again.

'Getting back to the subject in hand. No, she didn't know. Laura was on the pill, or at least Barry thought she was, and he always used condoms as well to be doubly sure.'

'I still don't get why he didn't tell her the truth in the first place?'

'Because after her last miscarriage he suggested he had the op but she was fiercely against the idea.' Melissa's eyes shone with tears. 'He loved her so much he couldn't bear the idea of losing her. This way he thought they were safe from the possibility of her getting pregnant again.'

'Instead of which it made her desperate and there's a strong possibility it's ruined their marriage. That's sad.'

'It sure is.'

'Do you think they can—'

'Put things right?' Melissa shrugged. 'I honestly don't know. Josie's determined to take part of the blame because she's convinced that if she'd warned Laura on the quiet it might've helped. I don't see it myself.'

'Neither do I. Plus she could've lost her job. Not a great career move.'

'There's something else going on with Josie, but she's being very tight-lipped, which isn't like her.' She picked up the empty wine bottle. 'I've another in the fridge?'

Before he could trot out a sensible answer, the last rays of sun picked up a flash of desire in her eyes that must have been reflected in his own. Reaching for her hand, she squeezed his in return.

After that, Nathan couldn't help himself.

CHAPTER THIRTEEN

Melissa startled when something brushed against her bare thigh. She sneaked a glance and, as she'd suspected, it wasn't a *something*, but rather a warm hand belonging to *someone*. Someone by the name of Nathan Kellow, who shouldn't be laying naked in what used to be Robin's spot in the bed. A groan slipped out of her as the events of last night flooded back.

Nathan sprang up as if someone had shot him. 'Oh God.' He stared at her, wild-eyed with shock. 'Did we . . .' He couldn't even finish the sentence. Mortified wasn't a strong enough description for the horror suffusing his face.

'Several times from my recollection,' she said. 'I assume you regret it?' Melissa swallowed hard. She could read his conflicted feelings only too well. Was it unreasonable to feel peeved, even though she was equally torn? There wasn't a woman on the planet who wanted to believe that the man in bed with them wished himself a million miles away. But realistically? Before last night she'd assumed that if she reached a place in the grieving process where she was ready to consider having a relationship with another man, it would be exactly that — considered. It might start as friendship, move to close companionship and then maybe, just maybe, become physical. What it wouldn't be was exploding fireworks, ripping at each other's clothes, too desperate the first time to make it as far as the bedroom. If it wasn't for the possibility of Josie spotting them, they would've made love right there on the patio.

The wild, reckless side of her wanted to push Nathan back down on the bed and have her wicked way with him again. She and Robin were always good in bed together, and he had been a considerate and thoughtful lover. But Nathan? Oh Lord, was all she could say. He'd done things with her that Melissa was pretty sure were illegal in many parts of the world, every one of which she'd thoroughly enjoyed and would happily beg him to do again.

'No! But I should do.' He shoved a hand through his tousled hair. '*That's* the problem.' Nathan's searing blue eyes bored into her. 'I won't ask what got into us last night because I know what it was on my part — years of denying how I feel about you.' The play of his muscles rippling across broad shoulders and toned arms aroused her all over again. Melissa glanced away in an effort to control herself, but *where* her gaze strayed didn't help one iota. One part of Nathan's body clearly wasn't the least regretful about the part it played in the proceedings. In fact, it was up for more. 'Stop that.' Nathan tugged the sheet over him. 'There's no hope of having a serious discussion with you drooling over a man's natural and unavoidable reaction to seeing a beautiful woman inches away from him.'

'I was *not* drooling.'

'If you say so.' A frown beetled his eyebrows. 'Where does this leave us now? It's taken all this time for us to be friends. Have we—'

'Spoiled that?' Suddenly conscious of her nakedness, Melissa wriggled under the sheet too. 'I hope not. But—'

'You don't want to do this again. I can't blame you. I've screwed things up, haven't I?' He sounded resigned.

'In case you didn't notice, you hardly did it on your own,' she bridled. 'I did take part — and made a pretty damn significant contribution, I'd say.'

Nathan's face turned beet-red. 'You're twisting my words.'

'It's what editors often do to clarify a particular scene.'

He picked up his phone and checked the time. 'Good grief. It's nearly nine o'clock. Catherine and Johnny will wonder where the hell I've got to. That's all I need. Inquisition by Torquemada's protégé. No wonder Chloe did a runner. My dear sister doesn't need medieval torture racks to extract information, trust me.'

It amused her to see him turn to jelly, reduced to being a five-year-old again and at the mercy of his older sibling.

'I guess you'd better get dressed and run off then.' Melissa couldn't resist throwing the sheet off and stretched out with her head on the pillow, arching her body provocatively. 'Don't worry. I'll be fine.'

'You're more than "fine",' he growled.

For a moment she was afraid his conscience would win the battle for control, then his hand shot out to palm her breast. He leaned over to blow gently on her hot skin, arousing everywhere his breath touched.

'So, are we gonna be friends with benefits then?' Melissa gasped as he trailed his fingers lower.

'Works for me.'

'In that case, hurry up and give me some of those benefits to kick-start the day.'

'Did you know you're extremely bossy in bed?' He cocked her a sideways grin. 'That's not a complaint, by the way. It turns me on.'

'I hadn't noticed.' This time there was nothing accidental about the path of her gaze. 'You gonna do something about it?' With no hesitation, he shifted on top of her, pinned her down and slid into her as if coming home after a long absence. Last night she was thankful for staying on the pill after Robin died. It hadn't been because she thought she'd have sex again anytime soon, but for the benefits it'd given her since she was a teenager and plagued by painful irregular periods. Nathan was candid enough about his own recent sexual history to convince her they'd be safe without any added protection. After all, he certainly hadn't come prepared, and even if she and Robin had ever relied on condoms, it would've seemed tacky to use them with another man. Especially Nathan.

Refusing to think about anything but the pleasure stirring inside her, Melissa gave herself up to him.

* * *

'I don't need to ask what *you've* been up to, little brother.' Catherine's scathing observation made him cringe. 'Your bed wasn't slept in. You're wearing the same clothes you went out in last night, only now they're crumpled and your shirt has a button missing. Did the merry widow tear it off in the heat of passion?'

Nathan wished he had the nerve to admit that's what she *did* do, in a throwaway manner, as if it was no big deal. But it *was* a big deal. A huge, gigantic, massively big deal. Being with Melissa in the most encompassing sense of the word was mind-blowing. Even in his most erotic dreams — and there'd been more than a few of those involving her — it was never that incredible. Reality, at its finest, always trumped fiction.

'And yes, when Chloe wasn't shouting at me she took great pleasure in spilling the beans about Mrs Melissa Martyn.' Pity crept into his sister's sharp eyes. 'I've always suspected you had a thing for her.'

That made him sound pathetic. Needy. Grateful for the leftovers of his best friend's life. Nathan pushed his clenched fists into his thighs so he didn't punch the nearest wall.

'Catherine, that's enough,' Johnny interrupted. 'It's none of your business — or mine — who Nathan sleeps with. You're always harping on about how you wish he'd find a nice woman, so what's your problem?'

Emotion tightened his throat. Johnny, standing up for him? That was a turnaround he hadn't expected.

'I don't want him hurt, that's all.' His sister turned pink. 'She's a relatively young woman and no doubt she's missing the . . . intimacy of her marriage.'

'You mean sex.' Nathan's bold assertion made Catherine's awkwardness deepen. He hadn't forgotten her stumbling attempt to explain the birds and the bees when he was about twelve. Their parents had dumped the task on her when they were too embarrassed to do it themselves. The clinical exercise his sister described ended with her shoving a sex education book at him, along with a packet of condoms. By the time he finally lost his virginity they were well past their expiration date.

'Yes.' Catherine's chin tilted up, and she folded her arms. 'We both know you haven't been in a serious relationship in years, and you aren't the sort of man to sleep around and—'

'You *know* nothing of the sort,' he protested. 'I could be the village Casanova and have a whole string of women at my beck and call for all you know.' Heat prickled his neck. 'As it happens I don't, but that's not the point.' There was no point trying to defend Melissa's motives in jumping into bed with him last night because he wasn't sure of them, or his own. But as Johnny pointed out, that was his and Melissa's business. No one else's. No doubt her gaggle of girlfriends would join Catherine in issuing warnings from the other side of the fence, as it were. 'Anyway, haven't you got more important things than my sex life to worry about, like Chloe maybe?' Catherine visibly shrank as his barb hit home. Damn words again. Whoever came up with the idiotic saying about sticks and stones was a fool. Broken bones usually healed, but the crucifying effect of words could linger for a lifetime. 'I'm sorry. I shouldn't have said that.'

'No, you shouldn't, Nathan.' Johnny glowered.

Some good might come out of all this if his brother-in-law grew a backbone at last. It made sense that a marriage between two in-charge, opinionated people would almost certainly be doomed, but doormats were another story, and he'd watched his sister wipe her feet on her uncomplaining husband far too many times.

'I wandered over to the shop this morning for the newspaper,' Johnny said. 'Mr Bull isn't happy with Chloe. She's let him down by not turning up for work the last couple of days.' He shook his head. 'He did tell me something interesting though. When I described the young man who whisked her away on his motorbike, he said it sounded like a Toby Pascoe. Do you know him?'

'Well, that wasn't who she brought back here the other day, but yeah I know Toby.' He rushed to correct himself. 'Well, I know his mother, Tamara. There's a group of village women who are close friends, including Melissa, and Tamara is one of them. Her husband left them years ago so she's brought Toby up alone. He's a smart kid and studying to be a nurse, at Truro College and Treliske Hospital.'

'That's all well and good, but where can we find him?' Catherine asked.

'They live in Chapel Street and Tamara works at the Rusty Anchor pub.'

'What are we waiting for?' His sister's impatience grew. 'Let's go. His mother must know where he's gone. We'll try the pub first.'

Nathan didn't point out the obvious, that *she* didn't know where Chloe was. 'Tamara might not be working today.' If they tracked her down, it could prove an interesting confrontation because Tamara was another outspoken woman, the same as his sister. If she got the impression they were criticizing her son, the claws would come out.

'We won't know until we ask, will we? I presume they serve morning coffee?'

'Yes, but I'll need to shower and change before we go out.'

'Don't forget to shave,' she ordered. 'You look like a derelict.'

'He's not sixteen,' Johnny protested. 'You can't talk to him that way!'

Nathan didn't point out that she'd always done so. Their parents had been pleased to pass off some of the responsibility for their youngest child, whose arrival was something of a surprise ten years after his sister's birth.

'Ring Melissa,' Catherine ordered. 'She can join us there. It's time we met her.'

There were all sorts of arguments he could come out with, but the easiest option was to pull out his phone and do as he'd been instructed. If Melissa wanted — or needed — to say no, it let him off the hook. Nathan was unsure how he felt when Melissa enthusiastically agreed to the suggestion.

'Sure, I'd love to meet them. Is the uber-scary Catherine going to warn me off toying with her baby brother?' Her earthy laughter relaxed him. If she wasn't bothered, why should he be?

'Oh God, look at the grin on his face.' Catherine shook her head. 'She's got him well and truly hooked.'

'Good for him,' Johnny said earnestly.

'I'll go and shower.' Making himself scarce seemed the wisest move. His sister was right, but unlike most fish he had no desire to wriggle off the line.

CHAPTER FOURTEEN

Melissa hadn't been this nervous since her wedding day, which was not the image she needed lodged in her mind right now. The brief whispered telephone conversation she'd managed with Nathan while he got dressed after his shower was long enough to discover the main motivation for this morning's expedition. As far as his sister was concerned, the chance to size Melissa up was a bonus. She considered calling Tamara to put her on alert but decided against it. If her duplicity was discovered it would put Catherine's back up, and unnecessarily so, because Tamara would undoubtedly give as good as she got if Nathan's sister turned shirty.

She was in the middle of locking the door when Josie yelled over the garden fence.

'Have you got a minute? It's about Laura.'

Wandering across the garden, Melissa idly noticed that her roses needed deadheading. 'I've been worried about her too, but I'm really sorry, I don't have long now for a chat.' She ran through where she was going, and why.

'I nearly went to see Laura last night but I was afraid I'd make things worse.' Josie said.

'This is not your fault. If Laura and Barry had been honest with each other none of this would've happened.'

Melissa's guilty conscience gave her a swift kick up the backside. Her own marriage had hardly been the perfect example of complete honesty. If it had been, then among other things, she wouldn't be robbing Peter to pay Paul when it came to her bills. Every day another one popped in, and sometimes she wondered how much longer she'd be able to keep it all under wraps.

'Maybe, but it was obvious how unhappy Laura was and I did nothing. None of us did. We were her friends and we should've tried harder to help.'

'But y'all thought it was sadness over her miscarriages and what could you do about that, apart from being there if she wanted to talk?'

'I suppose.' There was no conviction in her voice. 'Anyway, you need to get going. Things must be progressing well with you two if Nathan's roping you in to help sort his family problems.' A weak smile inched over her tired face.

'Maybe.'

'OMG! You wicked thing! You've done the dirty with our hot professor, haven't you?' Josie squealed. 'I was going to say I want every detail but maybe I don't. It would only make me jealous . . . Oh, don't get the wrong end of the stick, I'm not after Nathan but . . . ignore me, it's that time of the month. Cramps. Night duty tonight too.'

Melissa still hadn't discovered if a man had been involved when Laura turned up in the middle of the night and Josie was nowhere to be found. For a while now she'd got the impression that her friend's bright countenance and pragmatic disposition hid a deep sense of loneliness.

'If you're back before I've got to leave for work, we'll catch up then. If not, it'll wait.'

'Are you sure?'

Josie nodded fiercely. 'I'm happy for you and Nathan.'

'Bye then.' Melissa pushed away everything else for now and strode off down the road, enjoying the warm sunshine on her face. After last week's rain the summer weather had kicked back in, making the ten-minute walk into Penworthal a pleasant one. Along the way she stopped to say hello to a couple of people and check out their flourishing gardens. The pub came into sight, bathed in sunshine under a bright blue sky. It made the worn paint look shabby-chic rather than neglected, an impression helped along by the baskets of bright, gloriously scented flowers hanging either side of the oak door.

Taking a deep breath, she plastered on a smile and stepped inside. The first voice she heard was Nathan's, rising over the low chatter from the smattering of Monday morning patrons.

'Ladies, please. Let's keep it down.'

He was standing in front of the bar holding two women apart with his hands. Tamara's muscular arms, toned from lifting beer barrels and the surfing she loved to do every summer, were folded over her ample chest. She was glaring fiercely at her adversary. The woman with Nathan's elegant bone structure and tall, commanding build must be the infamous Catherine. As Nathan turned and spotted her, relief softened his worried expression. Josie's comment about being happy for them flooded back and Melissa smiled broadly and headed straight for him.

* * *

'Ah, there you are, darling.' The affectionate words popped out before he could consider their possible effect. Curious stares blossomed on the faces around them. In his pleasure at seeing her come to the rescue, it had slipped his mind that their brand-new relationship was unknown around the village. Now they'd zoomed to the top of Penworthal's gossip list. 'We're just about to have coffee and Tamara's joining us . . . I hope?' He held his breath as the barmaid's scowl darkened. Melissa sidled up to Tamara and murmured something in her ear.

'I'll take my break now, Pixie, if that's all right?' Tamara muttered. The landlady's rapid agreement didn't surprise him. A cat-fight in her respectable pub wasn't good for business. 'I'll fetch our coffees.'

'You okay?' Melissa came to him. 'You lied when you said you're a boring man who leads a predictable life.' Her smooth, low drawl worked its usual magic. 'Aren't you going to introduce us?' She nodded towards Catherine and Johnny.

'Of course.' He grimaced as Catherine offered the briskest of handshakes before scrutinizing Melissa from head to toe. But his smile crept back in when his girlfriend/lover/partner — the definition was sketchy in his mind — treated his sister to a similar inspection in return without missing a beat.

'It's awesome to finally meet you, Catherine, or do you go by Cathy or Cat maybe?' A hint of mischief played around the corners of her mouth.

'Certainly not! I feel terrifically sorry for poor Princess Catherine, who must tolerate being referred to as Kate Middleton still.' His sister narrowed her eyes. 'I would never put up with that.'

'Right, Catherine it is then.' Melissa turned to face Nathan's brother-in-law. 'So, should I call you Jonathan?'

'Good Lord no!' Johnny guffawed. 'I was christened John, but I've been Johnny ever since school.'

'Unfortunately.' Catherine's jaw tightened.

'Let's sit over here.' Tamara emerged from the kitchen with a loaded tray and led them to a large round table away from anyone else.

After a few minutes of shuffling and whispered discussions everyone was settled and had a drink in front of them.

'So, are you going to tell us where your son typically hides out?' Catherine had asked that same question multiple times since their arrival at the pub.

'Now look here, I've already told you my son is twenty-one next week. Your precious daughter is twenty after all. According to the law, they're adults.' She jabbed a finger perilously close to Catherine's face. 'He don't have to tell me where he's going or who he's going there with.' Her expression softened. 'I get that you're worried, but if it's any consolation Toby's a good boy. He's never been in any trouble and he's looked out for me ever since his dad cleared off. Chloe won't come to any harm if she's with him.'

'She'd better not.'

Nathan felt his sister's pain. No matter what mistakes she might have made, no one could deny how fervently she loved Chloe.

'Calm yourself down and try one of these clotted cream shortbread fingers.' Tamara pushed a plate towards his sister. 'I make all the sweets here and they're a new recipe I'm experimenting with.'

He fully expected Catherine to refuse because she always insisted the only way she managed to maintain her slender figure was by never eating between meals. Instead, she reached for one of the biscuits and took a large bite.

'Oh my goodness, these are incredible. So light and buttery. I've never been any good at baking.' A tinge of red bloomed in her narrow cheeks. 'I'm sorry if I've been rather abrupt. I'm incredibly worried about Chloe, but mostly for reasons other than her being with your son — or not, as the case may be.'

Melissa threw him a bemused smile. He'd told her once that his strong-willed sibling never apologized or admitted to failing at anything.

'It appears that Chloe dropped out of Oxford without telling us and now she's been sent down. She insists she won't go back and I don't even know if they'd give her another chance anyway. We'll have to contact them and plead with the authorities on her behalf.'

'Are you sure that's a good idea?' Tamara frowned. 'My Toby would throw a fit if I interfered like that.'

When Nathan had said the same thing his sister hadn't taken it well.

'We haven't decided yet, have we, Johnny?'

'No, you haven't, dear.'

Judging by Melissa's red face and Tamara's sudden coughing fit he wasn't the only one suppressing the urge to laugh.

'If you're staying around the village a bit longer, why don't you come along to the pub quiz on Friday evening?

You'd be an asset to the *Back of Beyond Brains*.' Tamara's suggestion made his sister's eyebrows shoot up.

'A pub quiz?' She sounded like the imperious Lady Bracknell in *The Importance of Being Earnest* speaking dismissively about Jack being found as a baby in a handbag.

Tamara nodded at Johnny. 'I'm sure Nathan's team would appreciate an extra brain too.'

'They're not *my* team,' he protested. 'I subbed in when Micky Broad was out, that's all.'

'From what I hear they're desperate to get their crown back, so I'm pretty sure Paul will be begging for your help again.'

'Doesn't matter. I'd be useless anyway.' Johnny turned bright pink.

Melissa kicked Nathan's shin under the table and he rubbed his sore leg while trying to speak.

'You certainly wouldn't. You'd be a huge asset, especially if we get questions on rugby or steam railways.' He clasped his brother-in-law's shoulder. 'I'll tell Paul we're both in if they want us! Don't worry, none of us are *Mastermind* material.'

'Right, well now we're sorted I need to get back to work.' Tamara stood up. Her smile faltered at Catherine. 'You're okay?'

'Yes. You told me what I needed to hear, unlike some people, who let me get away with it far too often.' Nathan squirmed as her gaze landed on him and Johnny. 'I'm not surprised Chloe left. I drove her away.' She murmured the heart-breaking words under her breath. Visibly pulling herself together, she turned her attention on Melissa. 'We'd be delighted if you're free to come and have lunch with us tomorrow? Would twelve o'clock suit you?'

'I'd love to. Thank you.' Melissa smiled over at Nathan. 'I could do with your help to put up a new blind in my sunroom if you don't have anything better to do?'

'If you've finished your coffee we can go now.' His swift agreement set off a round of smirks. Seizing her hand, he practically dragged her out of the pub. 'Blind-fitting? Was that the best you could come up with?' He slipped an arm around her waist.

'I could hardly say I wanted to get in your pants again, could I?' Melissa chuckled. 'And yeah, I'm being British and referring to your underwear as opposed to an American pair of trousers.'

'So what instances of British English as opposed to American English tripped up you and . . .' He wished he'd kept his mouth shut.

'We can't avoid mentioning Robin.' She jerked on his hand to stop him in the middle of the road. 'He was a huge part of both of our lives.'

'I know that, but it seems crass when all that's filling my mind is making love with you.' Damn words again. Her dead husband. His best friend. Robin's ghost stood between them whether they liked it or not.

Melissa wound her fingers around his neck and stared into his eyes.

'One day we'll talk more about Robin. There are things I want . . . need you to know, but not today.' She pressed her fingers against his lips. 'And not because we're off to have toe-tingling sex either. It's too soon.'

He squashed his reservations and grinned back at her. 'Let's see if I can make those toes tingle again.'

'I've no doubt you will. You're a dark horse, Nathan Kellow. Underneath that aura of academic other-worldliness you're flat out sexy and very dangerous. Did no one ever tell you that before?'

'No, but that's probably because everything's different with you. If I *am* any of those things it's because you make me that way.' That made her blush. 'I think we should hurry up to your place and sort out that blind!'

CHAPTER FIFTEEN

Melissa waved until Nathan's car disappeared out of sight, missing him already. After coming to "fix her blind" yesterday he'd never left. Following a messy lunch in bed they'd forced themselves to get dressed and paid a delayed visit to Charlestown. Nathan showed incredible patience as she retraced Ross Poldark's footsteps around the charming harbour with its authentic tall ships and cluster of pastel-painted cottages. He even indulged her love of all things piratical with a visit to the museum.

'I thought that man was never going to leave.' Josie hurried up the path. 'You must have the poor soul bewitched.'

Melissa ignored the jibe. 'Coffee?'

'Oh God, yes. I'm fit to drop. I haven't had the energy to change out of my uniform yet.' The creased scrubs, dark rings under her eyes and tired rasp to her voice spoke of a long night.

They wandered into the house together.

'I've got cinnamon rolls too, with cream cheese icing.'

'I don't care if you only made them to impress a certain man, I'm happy to take the dregs.' The bite to her words brought Melissa up short.

'I made them a couple of days ago before I knew Nathan was coming.'

'I'm sure he came all right. Probably more than once.' Josie gave a knowing wink.

'No comment. If I was in the States, I'd plead the Fifth. That's the constitutional amendment that says you can't be forced to speak and possibly incriminate yourself in a court of law.'

In the kitchen she refilled the coffee machine, and the familiar intoxicating aroma soon filled the room. She'd learned to drink tea like a native but that didn't lessen her love for her lifelong caffeinated hot beverage of choice. Not Nathan's milky, sweet version either, but black and strong enough to justify frequent visits to the dental hygienist to preserve her white teeth. After a quick zap in the microwave she placed one over-sized roll on each plate. 'There you go. Eat that. Food of the gods.'

Josie stabbed the fork into hers and practically inhaled several mouthfuls before taking a break. 'I don't care how unhealthy a breakfast this is, I could happily eat it every morning.' She patted her well-padded hips. 'Of course, these would be even heftier and I'd have to put my name on the waiting list for a heart bypass.' After a swig of coffee she heaved a sigh. 'Have you seen Laura?'

'No. I've been too wrapped up in other things. I'm sorry.'

'Don't beat yourself up. You deserve some fun.' A flicker of amusement brightened Josie's tired eyes. 'I'm certainly not having any so you might as well get enough for us both.' She shook her head. 'Listen to me. Self-righteous prig.'

'You aren't still fretting about the mess Laura got herself into, I hope? I might sound unsympathetic saying this but at the end of the day that's what she did.'

'I bumped into Barry in the shop on my way home and he looked rough as rats. According to him they had a right old ding-dong and Laura packed a bag and went to stay with her mum in Redruth. He's wiped his hands of her and says if she wants to kill herself that's her business.' She leaned forward. 'I think we need to go after her.'

'And say what?' Melissa had received a heap of well-intentioned advice after Robin died, and rejected ninety-nine per cent of it. 'Laura's made her choice. We may not agree with it, but it's hers to make.'

'What about Barry?'

'Again. That's her choice. And how he reacts? That's his. We shouldn't interfere.' Josie looked mutinous. 'Sorry, but that's how I feel. Now I need to get ready for lunch with the dragon lady.' Melissa ran through everything that had happened at the pub the day before, including her summons to lunch at Nathan's house.

Her friend's eyes narrowed. 'You're a funny woman sometimes. Quiet and meek on the surface, but you know your own mind and aren't afraid to speak out when pushed.'

Melissa took that as a compliment.

'We'll see what the rest of the group thinks about Laura later.' Josie sounded as if she was throwing out a challenge.

'I guess we will.'

'I'd better get some sleep or my one functioning brain cell won't be on duty tonight.' Josie pushed the chair back and stood up. 'Good luck with the Royal Command Performance.'

Time to polish her tiara.

* * *

'This is delicious.' Nathan scooped up another forkful of Melissa's homemade bourbon chocolate pecan pie. 'I'm not much of a pudding eater really but—'

'You interfering cow! I told you to keep your nose out of my business.' Chloe burst into the dining room followed by a tow-headed young man Nathan recognized as Toby Pascoe. She stalked around to her mother and stationed herself by Catherine's chair.

A peaceful meal had been too much to ask for.

'Chloe Elizabeth, don't you dare talk to your mother that way.' Johnny's sharp admonition came out of nowhere. 'If you can mind your manners, you're welcome to join us for lunch.' He nodded at Toby. 'And your friend too, of course, after you introduce him to us. Otherwise, you can wait elsewhere until we're finished.'

Nathan caught Melissa's eye and winked. She was certainly seeing the warts-and-all side of his family today.

'Sit down, Chloe dear. Please,' Catherine begged. 'There's plenty of food left. We've had poached salmon, salad and new potatoes, if that's okay for you both? I'll fetch it from the kitchen.' Her face tightened. 'And Melissa made a wonderful American pie you really must try for pudding.'

'I'll fetch more chairs.' After Nathan did that they soon had the new arrivals settled and the atmosphere felt less like an erupting volcano. Tamara hadn't exaggerated her son's qualities. Toby *was* polite and well-mannered and he worked hard to smooth over the upset caused by their unexpected arrival.

'Have you been away somewhere nice, Chloe?' Johnny asked, as if this whole scenario was nothing out of the ordinary.

'Uh, yeah. Toby's friend Seth is working in the gardens on St Michael's Mount for the summer, so we stayed with him.' Her eyes shone. 'It's awesome there. Really sick.'

The innocuous chatter continued until they all finished eating and his sister brought in a pot of coffee.

'My mum texted and told us you were looking for us,' Toby explained. 'Chloe . . . wasn't happy when she heard about your plan to contact her old college.'

"Not happy" probably didn't come close to covering his niece's reaction judging by her earlier outburst.

'We haven't taken any action yet.' Catherine's assurance made Chloe roll her eyes. 'We hoped you'd come back so we could convince you to get in touch with your tutor yourself and plead for a second chance.' Her voice faltered. 'This is your future we're talking about, Chloe. Don't throw it away in a fit of pique.'

'We've talked. Lots.' Toby reached for Chloe's hand. 'She's giving the matter a lot of thought, but I'm afraid you need to be patient while she makes up her mind.'

'I'm happy to intervene if you'd like me to broach things with the university,' Nathan offered. 'I have a few contacts there.'

'Thanks, Uncle Nat.' Chloe sounded a shade less belligerent. 'I'll think about it. Promise.' She turned to her parents. 'You don't have to hang around, you know. You can go on home.'

Catherine and Johnny flinched as if she'd hit them.

'They can't run off now until at least Saturday because they've been roped into joining Friday night's pub quiz. On opposing teams.' Nathan managed a smile. 'Melissa and I will be showing off our lack of knowledge too, so perhaps you and Toby would like to come and support us all?'

'We might if we've nothing better to do.' That grudging agreement was more than he'd expected.

'The first thing you need to do though is apologize to Mr Bull.' Johnny looked stern. 'You let him down and that's not on, you know.'

'Fine.' Chloe rolled her eyes. 'I'll go over to the shop now and grovel if it'll stop you nagging.' She turned to Toby. 'Are you coming?' Nathan caught a hint of trepidation under the layer of bravado.

'I'll walk over there with you and wait outside.'

Nathan expected his niece to blow up, but she shrugged and flounced out of the room. Toby flashed a sheepish smile around the table, thanked them for lunch and hurried after Chloe.

'She might've met her match in that young man.' Johnny beamed at Nathan. 'I think that deserves a brandy, old chap.'

'Excellent idea.'

'One. That's your limit.' Catherine wagged her finger. 'We may be on opposing teams for this quiz but I'm not having you let us down so we're going to do some swotting up this afternoon.'

'Well said.' Melissa tossed a smirk Nathan's way.

He'd worried whether the two women would get on, but an alliance between them could be a far worse prospect.

CHAPTER SIXTEEN

'Whatever that man's doing to you, make sure you keep him doing it.' Josie smirked. 'You look incredible.'

'Don't exaggerate.' Melissa blushed. 'I've caught the sun some with working out in the yard, that's all. I'm pretty sure I've put on a few pounds too because I'm eating better, and—'

'Stop making excuses and admit that our Nathan is good for you. It's a well-known medical fact that regular sex releases loads of feel-good endorphins.' She rolled her eyes. 'At least that's what they told us at nursing school.'

They walked on down the road.

'Aren't there any interesting, cute doctors or male nurses at work? According to every TV programme I've ever seen set in a hospital, the staff spend as much time flirting and having hot sex in linen closets as they do tending patients.'

'I wish that were true,' Josie grumbled. 'Fifteen years ago I got my fair share of offers, but be realistic. If it wasn't for Nathan wouldn't you be invisible too? Most men our age make plays for younger women. The only moves I've had made on me recently have come from married men looking for a bit on the side, divorced ones with loads of kids and huge alimony payments, or the sad rejects still living at home with their mums.'

Melissa still hadn't found out where her friend had been the night Laura turned up, but decided this wasn't the time to ask.

'Oh well, here we are.' Josie sighed at the pub as if it were to blame for the ills in her life. 'Don't get me wrong. I love my girlfriends. I love this village and my job. But sometimes I think . . . more would be great.'

'Next time you're off, let's go out for the day. We'll have a good natter and see what we can come up with to liven things up for you.'

'Sure.' By Josie's resigned tone it was clear she didn't expect Melissa to follow through, or if she did that it wouldn't do any good. 'Come on. Let's slay *Proper Choughed* again.'

The usual hubbub of chatter greeted them as they wended their way through the crush of people. Pixie had thrown open all the windows to let a welcome breeze blow through. Melissa's gaze sought out Nathan and his face lit up at the sight of her.

'For God's sake, go kiss the man before the two of you incinerate.'

'I'll see him later. We've got a job to do.' She'd suggested to Robin once that they came to a quiz night but he swore she'd be bored out of her mind. It was almost as if he hadn't wanted her to get too involved with the village. There'd been layers to him she'd never understood, and now would never have the chance.

The evening always followed the same format, so at precisely eight o'clock Pixie announced the half-time break. The fifteen-minute interval helped keep bar profits up and gave people a chance to make a quick dash to the toilets.

'I'm going to the lavatory,' Catherine announced. 'Would you all care for another drink? I'll get them.'

It surprised her how easily Nathan's sister had fitted into the group, and she'd proved quite an asset already by answering several questions no one else knew.

'We'll have to make sure your visits here coincide with quiz night again!' Evelyn said.

No sooner had Catherine left than Josie brought up the subject of Laura. Melissa almost felt sorry for her when one by one everyone expressed the view that it was best to wait and see what happened. So far Laura had politely rebuffed everyone who'd attempted to get in contact.

'People can't be forced to accept help, Josie love,' Evelyn said softly. 'New teachers soon find out they can't force education into children's heads. You're a wonderful nurse and it's in your genes to want to help people. To heal. Make them better. But you've learned the hard way in your professional life that it isn't always possible. It's more challenging in your personal life, though, isn't it?'

Josie nodded, her eyes glistening.

'Let's get prepared for round two.' She nodded at Melissa. 'Help Catherine with the drinks, there's a dear.'

Naturally she did as she was told, but her concern for her friend grew. Josie wouldn't let this go.

* * *

All eyes were on him when Nathan ended the call.

It'd surprised him when Chloe appeared at last night's quiz, with Toby in tow. When neither of her parents were hovering around he'd succeeded in taking her aside to find out if she'd given the possibility of contacting Oxford any further thought, while making it clear he would support her either way. His niece's reply had been resolute. She was willing to talk to her tutor, but very much doubted it would change her mind. Nathan had insisted she told her parents that when they got back home, another miserable conversation. Catherine's face had fallen and she'd stared down at her clenched hands, uncharacteristically silent. It fell to Johnny, his eyes glassy with tears, to force out that all they wanted was for their daughter to be happy.

'Dr Azar Shah is happy to meet with you on Monday morning at ten, Chloe.' Using his influence to circumvent a few official procedures, Nathan had contacted one of his own old professors who'd put him in direct touch with Chloe's tutor.

'Thank you — I think.' Chloe sounded wary.

'She only wants to hear the full story and see whether there's any way to help you continue with your degree.' He shrugged. 'If there isn't, perhaps she'll help you figure out what you *do* want to do next. You're young and you've plenty of time to try different options.'

'I haven't heard a thank you to your uncle yet, Chloe,' Catherine chided.

His niece had the grace to look shamefaced. They'd had a tough few days since she'd returned, and Toby had been a rock throughout it all. Nathan surely wasn't the only one hoping the relationship would survive long term.

'I don't need thanks. You're my family and I love you. All I ask is that you listen to Dr Shah with an open mind.'

'I will. I promise.'

'Why don't we all ride home together?' Johnny suggested. 'We can run you up to Oxford then on Monday.'

'No thanks. You go on.' Chloe straightened her shoulders. 'I'm scheduled to work today and tomorrow and I don't want to let Mr Bull down again. Toby's offered to drive me home after work on Sunday and go with me to see Dr Shah.'

Nathan caught Catherine's eye and hoped she'd heed the silent warning to agree with her daughter's plan.

'I suppose that will be all right.' The concession sounded forced. 'Come on, Johnny, let's finish packing. If we get away in good time and the traffic isn't too dreadful, we'll be home in time for the Jenkins' bridge party tonight.'

'Of course, dear.'

He guessed his brother-in-law wasn't thrilled at the prospect, but had already stood up to his wife more over the last week than in the last twenty-five years of their marriage. After they left, Chloe threw her arms around him.

'You're awesome, Uncle Nat. If it wasn't for you . . .' Her eyes brimmed with tears.

Talk about silver linings. This whole sad business had brought them all closer. He and Catherine were very different characters and a decade apart in age so they'd slowly drifted apart after their parents died, their relationship reduced to very occasional meetings and dutiful phone calls for birthdays and Christmas.

'You'd better hurry up and get changed. Those shelves won't stack themselves.' Her grimace made him laugh. The biggest humiliation for his fashion-conscious niece was Vernon Bull's insistence that she wore an unflattering blue nylon overall. At first he'd doubted that his niece would stick to the job but she'd proved him wrong. Vernon Bull didn't put up with any of Chloe's dramatic nonsense and expected value for money from his employee.

'You're done for the summer, yeah?' Chloe asked.

'Thank goodness. I finished up the last of my paperwork at the weekend so I'm through.'

'You'll have plenty of time for romancing Melissa then.' She ran off, laughing like a train, and giggled all the way up the stairs.

The clock ticked from over in the corner and Catherine's imperious voice drifted down the stairs giving Johnny orders. Dust motes danced in the sunlight filtering in through the stained-glass panels in the front door. A flutter of nerves exploded in Nathan's stomach. He felt himself hovering on the verge of something big. Something that could change the direction of his life. If he was too impatient he'd ruin everything, possibly forever.

* * *

Tonight's dinner date with Nathan deserved a dress, but she'd be sensible and pair it with flat sandals. She'd learned her lesson on that score after turning her ankle on the cobblestone streets of Truro in six-inch stilettos. Then she was still foolishly trying to live up to Robin's image of her as a sophisticated career woman, instead of the regular Southern girl she'd always been at heart.

They'd be setting off to Newlyn in a while, a small fishing village in the far west of the county. When she and Nathan were talking books again — a frequent topic of conversation — he'd wanted to hear about next month's book club selection. He'd cracked a joke about enjoying the book club vicariously through her and admitted he'd reread all the Poldark books after her enthusiasm was too infectious for him to resist. The book club were due to discuss *Ross Poldark* at the July meeting in a few days, but she'd already bought the club's August selection, *Snapped in Cornwall*, after spotting it on sale at a local garden centre. It was the first in Janie Bolitho's Rose Trevelyan mysteries, and Amy's choice because it was set in Newlyn where she'd grown up. Naturally Nathan had read them all before; in fact she'd yet to find anything related to Cornwall that he *hadn't* read. He'd praised the writing and homed in especially on its wonderfully described settings. They'd agreed it was a shame the author died at a relatively young age.

While she brushed her hair, Melissa's mind drifted to Chloe. The young woman had seemed subdued when she popped into the shop for a few things this morning. There must be a lot weighing on her mind if she wasn't up to dishing out sarcastic comments along with the loaves of bread and tins of carrots.

She slipped into the dress she'd found in one of the local charity shops and decided that being forced to budget more stringently wasn't all bad. When she'd first realized the extent of Robin's debts it had taken her breath away. Melissa used to berate herself for not insisting on being an equal partner in the marriage until she concluded that was a waste of effort. Instead, she channelled her energy into drawing up a plan to tackle the problem and work slowly through the list of people who needed to be repaid. But every time she appeared to make some progress another debtor crawled out of the woodwork, pushing her back a step.

Pushing away those depressing thoughts she studied her reflection in the mirror and twirled like a ballerina so the vibrant purple silk swirled around her thighs. Before her hair changed so dramatically, she'd considered it an old woman's colour but now found it immensely flattering. It looked particularly good tonight against her newly acquired tan. Melissa hummed as she selected the slender silver necklace and bold silver hoop earrings that had been her mother's Christmas gifts last year. She glanced at her wedding rings. After she made love with Nathan for the first time, she almost took them off, but in the end left them alone. He'd be too considerate of her feelings to ever suggest she did so, but did it bother him to see her wearing them still? There were a lot more conversations they should probably have, but she was afraid to initiate any of them in case they spoiled something wonderful. Her mood was sombre as she made her way downstairs.

She sank down on the sofa and covered her face with her hands, bursting into tears.

'What on earth's wrong, love?'

Melissa couldn't wrap her head around why Nathan was crouching down in front of her, his face white. She glanced at the clock and saw it was gone seven. He must've wondered why she didn't answer the door when he arrived and used his own key, the one she'd given him last week.

'Are you ill?' He pulled her hands away so he could see her tear-stained face. 'Talk to me, please.'

'I'm fine.' Emotion clogged her throat. 'Well, not fine, obviously.' A weak smile inched out. 'I guess women don't usually break down in hysterics at the thought of a date with you?'

'It's a first.' Nathan's mouth tweaked up at the corners. 'As far as I know anyway. I've been cancelled a few times so maybe this explains it? They were freaked out?' He shifted off the floor to sit beside her and slid his comforting arm around her. 'If I've done something wrong, I'll try my best to put it right. I can't bear seeing you upset.' The gruff rasp in his voice tore at her.

'It's not you—'

'Oh please, not that old chestnut.' His deep blue eyes filled with hurt. 'We're better than this. More honest. Aren't we?'

She eased away. 'I wonder if we're going too fast? If we'd stayed as friends . . . I know I wanted the "benefits" part as much as you but maybe that's a mistake.'

'We can't turn back the clock. Robin died, and there's not a damn thing we can do about that. You and I have found something amazing we didn't expect, and I've no regrets about that.' He splayed his large hands on his thighs. 'If you do, I'm sorry.'

'That's not what I meant.' Embarrassment made her face burn. 'Not exactly. Do you know what kicked this all off?' She stuck out her left hand and gestured to the rings. 'These did.' The poor man looked puzzled, and even after the whole story tumbled out of her he still seemed confused.

'But I would never ask you to do such a thing.'

'I know that!' Melissa's annoyance at herself bubbled over. 'I've spoiled everything, especially as I really think I might be ready to remove them now anyway . . .' She swiped at the tears dripping down her cheeks but Nathan pulled a clean white handkerchief from his pocket and gently wiped her face. Even amid the maelstrom of emotions she found it amusing that he didn't use paper tissues like everyone else.

'No, you haven't spoiled anything.'

'But how can we—'

He touched his finger to her lips. 'Shush, sweetheart. Why don't you go and freshen up? I'm forced to say that even on you, raccoon eyes aren't the most flattering look. When you're ready we'll go out to dinner as planned. I can't have you being less than top of the class at next month's book club. Every successful editor knows it's essential to immerse yourself in a story to get the most from it.'

Part of her wanted to object and say it was no good brushing things aside in the hope they'd sort themselves out. Send him away. But as she touched his freshly shaved cheek and inhaled his intoxicating musky scent, part cologne and part pure Nathan, she couldn't do it.

'Trust me,' he growled, 'we'll get through this. Now, I don't know about you but I'm starving. The disgusting green smoothie Chloe fed me for lunch left a hollow gap where my stomach used to be.'

'No doubt there was kale in it.' She rolled her eyes. 'These days anything without kale isn't considered food.' They both laughed, and a gleam of satisfaction burned in his eyes. 'Five minutes,' she said. 'I won't be any longer, I promise.'

Nathan's brilliant, heart-stopping smile emerged. 'I know you won't.'

She ran upstairs, scrubbed off her make-up and abandoned the idea of reapplying it. Nathan liked — far more than liked — her exactly as she was.

With a far lighter heart she left the house and locked the door firmly behind them.

* * *

Nathan could happily watch her for hours, although she'd die laughing if he was foolish enough to admit it. The balmy summer evening meant they'd been able to wander around Newlyn's cobblestone streets and harbour at will. Melissa had treated him to a mischievous smile when he started to recite the history of the town, which still had one of the largest fishing fleets in the UK and a thriving art scene.

'Yeah, sorry, but I'll stop you there because I know most of that already, Professor. When I started digging deeper into Rose Trevelyan's character in the book, I discovered the link between her love of painting in the open air and Newlyn's artistic reputation as the centre of the British plein air movement, started in the late 1800s by Stanhope Forbes and Walter Langley.'

The trait of curiosity running right through her, like the place name in a stick of rock, thrilled him. It was the same as when one of his students was keen to delve deeper than the course work demanded. In his view the wealthiest, most "successful" people were to be pitied if they'd lost the precious gift of being interested in the world around them.

After a late supper in one of the harbourside pubs they'd got lucky and found an empty bench on the quay. The brass plaque behind their backs attested to the lovely memory that this used to be the favourite view of a lady called Dot Hunkin. Now they were enjoying their ice creams while watching a variety of boats bobbing around the harbour. Melissa was fascinated when he pointed out beam trawlers, crabbers and small open boats used for hand-line mackerel fishing. She'd refused dessert in the pub and insisted it should be enshrined in law that no one could sit by the sea in Cornwall without eating a "ninety-nine", a wafer cone loaded with swirls of vanilla soft-serve ice cream with a chocolate flake stuck in the top. She ate like a greedy five-year-old — flake first then huge licks of ice cream, her tongue flicking in and out like a lizard. Now she'd moved on to the final step and was nibbling the bottom of the cone to suck out the remainder of the ice cream with no regard to the drips inching down her chin.

'You're an unbelievably neat eater.' She stared at him accusingly. 'You don't have a spot of ice cream on you anywhere!'

How was he supposed to respond to that?

'Relax. I'm jealous, that's all.' A sigh puffed out of her. 'My mom tried to teach me good manners but I was something of a lost cause. Pat and Bryan always competed to see who could eat the most and the fastest. They had regular burping and farting competitions too, and because I was determined to beat them at everything, I'm afraid I joined in.'

'You've obviously tamed your baser tendencies since then.'

'We all have to grow up sometime,' Melissa mused. Heat rose up her neck to flood her cheeks. 'Oh God, don't look at me that way.'

'What way?'

'The way that makes me want to . . .'

'Go on,' Nathan growled.

'I reckon I've another blind that needs fixing.'

'Are you sure?' A stronger man would claim that her friendship was enough for him and the "benefits" weren't important. But he refused to lie.

She took his face in her hands, lowered her mouth to his and trailed her tongue over his lips. Sugar. Warm hints of vanilla. Silky chocolate.

'You need to bleddy well get a room, mate.' A ruddy-faced old man stopped walking past to grin at them. 'She'll eat you for supper, boy, if you sit 'ere much longer.'

'Sounds good to me,' Nathan cheerfully replied. He grabbed Melissa's hand and pulled them both to their feet. 'Time to go home.'

Halfway to the car she tugged him down a narrow alley between two old cottages.

'I appreciate you're keen to get your hands on me but—'

'Shush.' She poked her head back out. 'It *is* her. I thought so. Look.' Melissa pointed to a couple waiting in the queue at a fish and chip van. 'It's Laura. And that's definitely not Barry.'

From their sideways view, the bulge of her pregnant belly under a skimpy red dress was evident. Laura was smiling and leaning against the man's shoulder and in return he kissed her cheek.

'Josie will be appalled.'

Nathan struggled for something positive to say. 'She looks happy enough, and she's still pregnant, so that's good news.'

'But we've all been worried sick about her.'

'We can't live other people's lives for them. She's a grown woman.'

'Do you reckon that story about paying for a sperm donor was just that — a story?'

'Possibly.'

Melissa scoffed. 'Tomorrow, I might manage to be happy for her but tonight it's more than a bit sickening.'

'Do you want to go over and say hello?' Indecision flitted across her face, then she shook her head. He continued,

'We could snap a picture of them as proof. Call it research. *Snapped in Cornwall* — get it?'

'You're hopeless, Dr Kellow.' She whipped out her phone and fired off a couple of shots.

'It's rumoured I'm excellent at fixing blinds though.'

'Prove it.' The fire in her eyes stirred him and a groan escaped his lips. Her triumphant expression told him all he needed to know.

'Willingly.'

CHAPTER SEVENTEEN

'Look! Can you believe it?' Melissa passed her phone around. Her friends' expressions showed she wasn't the only one shocked by Laura's behaviour. Josie was missing from the book club tonight because she'd supposedly been called into work at the last minute to cover a gap in the schedule. Melissa didn't believe that story for a moment because she'd seen her friend running out to her car, not in her uniform but wearing smart pale blue trousers and a white silk shirt. Josie had been uncharacteristically quiet earlier when Melissa had shown her the picture of Laura and the mystery man. Her only comment was that she'd taken Evelyn's advice regarding Laura and felt better for it.

'Should we tell Barry?' Amy ventured.

'Absolutely not!' Evelyn shook her head. 'I thought I knew Laura well, but we all have our secrets and clearly she has hers.' Her brow furrowed. 'I do wish she hadn't found it necessary to lie to us though. At least we know she's well, and if she doesn't want to contact her husband that's her prerogative.'

'But he's so miserable, poor sod. It doesn't seem fair.' Amy wasn't giving up.

'Life isn't. You're old enough to know that.' Evelyn picked up her copy of *Ross Poldark*. 'Are we all ready?' Her arch tone suggested they'd better be. Amy sagged back in the chair, took a swig of wine and scowled.

Melissa listened closely so she could remember as many of the comments as possible to repeat to Nathan tomorrow. Both the literary ones and the less literary sort revolving around the handsome Aidan Turner. The consensus was that the multi-faceted character of Ross made for a fascinating read, but in real life he'd be difficult to live with. Robin was often that way too, and his strong opinions and mercurial character had often frustrated her. Before his illness she'd come to the sad conclusion that their marriage wouldn't make it for the long haul. Although she'd dropped Nathan several hints in that direction, he didn't know for certain. It struck a chord, especially with her, because being with Nathan *was* easy. Melissa kept expecting the ball to drop and she'd discover Nathan's clay feet. Could anything really be this good?

'Melissa, stop dreaming about sweaty, shirtless men scything and tell us — as a non-Cornish reader — what you think of the book.' Tamara poked her elbow.

'The book?'

A burst of unrestrained laughter ran around the room and Melissa joined in. This was her tribe. Her friends. If she couldn't take a joke from them, it was a sad day. After they all calmed down, she managed to cobble together a few intelligible sentences. The book had impressed her. The author's writing was superb. If you weren't familiar with Cornwall when you started reading then by the time you finished you'd be booking a holiday to experience its beauty and wildness for yourself.

'Of course, for the sake of reaching a deeper understanding of the story I might have to look for a scything instructor,' she quipped.

'We'll fix you up with Abe Trebilcock.' Becky chuckled. 'I saw a fake picture of a pot-bellied Aidan Turner out scything once and it was called "Poldark — The Pasty Years". I'm pretty sure it was modelled on Abe.'

'At least Nathan won't get jealous,' Tamara chimed in.

It'd been futile to think they could keep their blossoming relationship under wraps. No doubt Josie had already described in minute detail all the comings and goings she'd observed.

'Time to eat,' Amy said firmly. 'I found an almond cake recipe that's a nod to the scene where Ross offers Verity ale and almond cake. We've also got heavy cake, which they served at Julia's christening, and of course we have saffron buns. The traditional Cornish staple.'

Melissa would have preferred a moist fudgy brownie but would happily sample all three offerings.

When everyone congregated in the kitchen, Evelyn pulled her to one side.

'What's going on with Josie?'

'I wish I knew. She's being very close-mouthed and you know that's not like her.'

'Has she ever mentioned . . .' Evelyn shook her head. 'No, it can't be that again.'

'What? Tell me.'

'I'm not sure I should.'

Melissa held her breath and prayed her friend's conscience wouldn't win out.

* * *

Catherine was sobbing so hard he could barely make out his sister's words. He said to clarify, 'So am I getting this right — Chloe's tutor offered her another chance but she won't take it?'

'Yes! Oh, Nathan, I could kill her. She's a foolish, foolish girl. She'll regret this one day.'

When they lost first their father, and later their mother too, Catherine had barely shed a tear. Not because she hadn't loved them deeply, but the disciplined emotions she'd learned from their father hadn't allowed her to unbend. But when it came to her only child, Catherine's heart was a marshmallow.

All he could do was cross his fingers that his sister was wrong, and Chloe's decision wouldn't come back to haunt her.

'I'm sorry it didn't work out how you'd hoped, Cath.' No one else dared shorten her name, but in his case it lingered from when he was a small boy and couldn't pronounce her full name. Nowadays he only resorted to it when they were alone together, which meant very rarely. 'Is Chloe coming back to Cornwall?'

'Oh yes. When I tried to pin her down about what her plans are, she blew me off and said she wasn't sure yet.' He sensed her hesitate. 'You don't mind, do you?'

'Of course not.'

'Toby's driving them both down tomorrow. Your slave driver in the shop wants her back at work first thing Wednesday morning.'

'Keeping busy will be good for her, Cath, and I think she secretly rather enjoys it. She loves shocking the customers but most of them have a soft spot for her.'

'You sound like Johnny,' she huffed. 'He's been very bossy recently. Can you believe he says we've spoiled her and all these problems are what he calls a reality check. Terribly American expression, but there you are.'

Nathan got the impression he was being blamed for that, through Melissa. 'I'd better go now, I—'

'You're turning into a lap dog. I suppose *she's* beckoned you with her little finger.'

'You like Melissa!'

'She's pleasant enough.'

'Oh, Cath, don't be such a prig. Your Hyacinth Bucket act won't work on me.' The vintage comedy with the ultra-snobbish main character beloved of so many people had been one of their mother's favourite programmes. He often suspected that was because she considered his perfectionist father to be the male equivalent.

'I can't please anyone these days! Perhaps I should leave you all to it and see how you manage then.'

'I didn't mean—' Nathan realized he was talking to himself because she'd hung up on him. He shoved his hands through his hair and sighed. Melissa would put things in perspective. She must be back from book club by now, so he'd grab a bottle of wine and go see her. Before he made it to the fridge his phone pinged and the sight of her name on the text made him smile. He wasn't the only impatient one.

Sorry but something's come up. Rain check for tomorrow?

Of course he couldn't do anything other than reply in the affirmative. A few minutes later he sat in his father's worn-out old chair with a glass of whisky in his hand, brooding.

* * *

Melissa was hopeless at deception. Robin always claimed she was the most guileless person he'd ever met, and it was only later that she came to realize it wasn't intended as a compliment. But that same quality was something her most successful clients appreciated. Not that she was never unkind, but if she spotted something in their writing that could be improved it'd be quietly pointed out along with concrete suggestions about making changes. On the other hand, when she praised them, they knew she meant it and wasn't simply saying so to boost their fragile egos.

If she lurked around the garden with a pair of secateurs until Josie returned, her sharp-eyed friend would pick up on the ploy in one second, but phoning or going to the door would be harder. After all, what could she say? *Oh, I thought you'd like to hear about book club, and please tell me you haven't hooked back up with your ex-husband who's messed you around time and time again?*

It'd shocked her when Evelyn whispered the story under her breath earlier this evening. Melissa knew about Josie's brief marriage, but what her friend never shared was that despite the man's multiple infidelities, she'd hooked up with him again several times when he was between relationships.

'The silly girl can't stay away from him. I thought after the last episode that I know of — which was several years ago — he burned her badly enough that she'd never go near him again. Of course, we don't *know* it's what she's doing now, but if she is hiding something I bet it's to do with that prick Christopher Deacon. Excuse my language.'

Evelyn wasn't a prude, but she was always very correct in her speech and circumspect when it came to gossip. Dr Deacon clearly pushed her buttons in a major way.

The sound of a car roaring up the hill and stopping in the road startled her. Melissa saw an expensive red Lamborghini parked on the curb between her own house and Josie's. Next thing, her neighbour climbed out along with a tall, fair-haired man. There was no choice but to brazen it out.

'Hiya.' She strolled down towards them. 'You missed a good book club meeting.' Josie turned bright pink. 'I'll catch you up later.'

'Thanks,' Josie muttered. 'This is—'

'Doctor Christopher Deacon.' His hand shot out and clasped Melissa's in a firm grip. After holding on a shade too long he let go and a glimmer of satisfaction lurked in his dark eyes. The man's lean figure, designer suit and artful two-day stubble spoke of a man supremely conscious of his striking good looks. She suspected it was something he used to full advantage whenever possible but couldn't understand why her eminently sensible friend kept falling for it. 'You must be Melissa. The American widow.'

The languid mocking tones put her back up. 'That's right. I'll leave you to enjoy the rest of your evening. Good night.' Melissa stalked off, seething inside. She told herself that Josie wouldn't have described her in that smirking way, but the sour taste lingered in her mouth. Everyone had secrets, so why had she assumed Josie's wouldn't be this big? Sadness washed over her and she regretted putting Nathan off. Tomorrow seemed a long way away.

CHAPTER EIGHTEEN

'Didn't you invite her?' Nathan whispered in Melissa's ear. He gestured towards Josie's house, where its occupant was digging furiously in one of the flowerbeds.

'No.' Melissa pushed back a lock of hair and flipped a hamburger before moving on to the next. He had offered to help cook but she'd shaken her head and put the spatula firmly out of reach. According to her, everything she'd eaten at a British barbecue was either woefully overcooked or raw. 'She's avoided me for three whole days now.'

'Perhaps she doesn't know what to say.'

'I won't have my Independence Day party spoiled by a woman I thought was my friend. An honest one.'

The garden was packed with her book club group and other friends from the village. By the loud laughter and raucous chatter, everyone was enjoying themselves.

Nathan suspected that Melissa had decided on this last-minute gathering in part to spite her neighbour. That wasn't like her, although he'd been wise enough not to point it out.

'Doctor Know-It-All isn't around today, I see,' she scoffed. 'They've gone out together each of the last few days but he's either working or lost interest again already.'

'Maybe he's changed.'

Melissa tossed him a look that said he must be naive to believe that. She set the cooked burgers off to one side to stay warm and banged a spoon against a metal tray to get people's attention. 'Let's eat,' she yelled. 'Come and fix your burgers over here. This is the first time I've celebrated the Fourth of July with a bunch of the defeated but y'all are welcome so dig in!' A fleeting sadness crossed her face when she turned to him. 'Robin never let me do this. He said it wasn't appropriate and people would think me odd.' She shrugged. 'I'm odd here anyway and always will be. I'll never be considered Cornish if I live here for fifty years, so there's no point pretending. I am what I am.'

Nathan swept her into a hug. 'Can this redcoat give the enemy a kiss?'

'I might let you.' She trailed her finger over his mouth. 'I'll be keeping you as a prisoner of war after everyone leaves.'

'Lock me up and throw away the key,' he jested.

'Oy, you pair, get your hands off each other. Some of us are starved. You going to feed us or not?' Vernon Bull grabbed a paper plate off the stack.

The man might be gruff and his manners left something to be desired, but he'd welcomed Chloe back with the closest thing to a smile anyone in Penworthal had ever seen. In an unheard of move he'd even allowed Chloe to take charge of the shop tonight while he was at the barbecue, although he'd promised to return by eight o'clock to lock up for the night.

After a whirlwind of activity getting everyone settled with their food and topping up drinks, Nathan made a grab for Melissa. 'Sit down and I'll get us a plate each.'

'Oh no you don't. You'll fix my burger all wrong.' She gave him an arch look. 'What d'you put on yours?'

He couldn't admit he'd rarely ever eaten one. 'Uh, ketchup, I suppose.'

Her eyes rolled. 'You're lame. Robin was no better. Even after living in New York he never got rid of his Britishness that way. Watch and learn.' She dragged him to the table. 'I'll do you a classic cheeseburger. That shouldn't stretch your culinary tastes too far.'

Nathan watched in amusement as she laid a slice of cheese on a burger and put it back on the grill long enough to melt. The meat was laid reverently on the bun, topped with a large slice of tomato, a thin slice of onion and a pile of shredded lettuce.

'It should really have sliced dill pickles too, but I've never managed to track down the right sort here. I'll have to grow small cucumbers and pickle my own. Do you want mustard as well?'

'Yes, let's go all in.'

'Right.' She squirted a swirl of each on his burger and slapped the top of the bun on, then added a scoop of homemade potato salad and a heaped ladle of baked beans to the sturdy paper plate. 'Don't go thinking they're the Heinz variety either because they most definitely aren't. It's my mom's recipe. Sweeter than you'll like, I expect, but you lost the war and you're on my turf so you can try them.' Soon she had her own burger similarly made. 'Don't you dare cut it in half or eat it with a knife and fork either. Put your hand on the top and squash it down a bit then pick it up with both hands. Don't set it down again either until you've taken a few bites and it's more manageable.'

'Yes, miss,' he grumbled, half-heartedly.

'Good. She's made herself scarce.' Melissa nodded towards the road where Josie's car was pulling out of the drive.

'How long are you going to keep this up?'

'Until she's got the guts to be honest with me.'

'And have you always been honest with her?' Heat crept up Melissa's throat that had nothing to do with the fire from the nearby grill.

'She swore that her brief marriage was history and continually trashed her ex-husband. Those were outright lies.'

'You didn't answer my question.' He knew there was more to the story presented to everyone about Melissa and Robin's supposedly perfect marriage. Robin had been his best friend, but that hadn't blinded him to the man's faults. Everyone had them. Robin had been a very black and white person. Obsessive over the things he loved, and those he hated. Middle ground didn't exist for Robin. He was easily bored too, so perhaps the old adage about marrying in haste and repenting at leisure had applied?

'No one is entirely, are they? But not like this.'

He allowed the subject to drop and asked instead whether she was enjoying the next month's book choice.

'Absolutely, and I plan to read the whole series. In September we're doing Rosamunde Pilcher's *The Shell Seekers*. I suppose you've read that too?'

'Nope, you got me there.' Nathan chuckled. 'My mum was a big fan of hers though, and some friends we knew had their house used for one of the German TV adaptations. For some reason she's immensely popular there.'

'That's fascinating. We'll have to do another of our literary treks around a few of the locations. If you're game, that is?'

'You know me,' he said with a grin.

'Sometimes I wonder.'

'What do you mean?'

Melissa picked up her burger. 'Can't let this go cold.' She took a large bite, making it impossible to speak.

Another subject for pillow talk?

* * *

Melissa was relieved when her phone buzzed, although she'd no doubt Nathan would pursue the topic they'd been discussing again later. Persistence was one of his good, or bad, traits. She stifled a groan when Josie's name flashed up on the screen. She'd fudged the truth by implying that Josie hadn't attempted to contact her — there'd been several rejected calls and deleted texts.

'Would it really hurt?' Nathan asked.

It wasn't in her nature to be mean and petty, but she possessed more than a smidgen of her mother's stubbornness.

'Fine.' Grudging, but the best she could manage. 'Hi, Josie. What's up?' The resentment she'd been holding onto flew out of the window as her friend's breathless words sank in. She glanced anxiously at Nathan. 'Yeah, he's here. Vernon is too. I'll tell them and we'll be right there.'

'What's wrong?'

Her heart thumped hard enough to make her ears ring. 'It's Chloe. There's been an incident in the shop.'

'Don't tell me she knocked over a stack of tinned peas and bruised her toes?'

'This is serious.' She struggled to keep her voice steady. 'Someone tried to rob the till but Chloe tried to fight him off. The boy had a knife.'

'She's been stabbed?' The blood drained from his face. 'Oh God, tell me she's not dead? How can I tell Cath that!'

'She's alive. Luckily for her, Josie came in right after it happened.' Melissa couldn't see through the tears welling up in her eyes. 'She did first aid and called the ambulance. We need to tell Vernon.'

'Why don't you do that while I drive to the shop?'

'You're in no fit state to get behind the wheel of a car.'

'I'm fine.' Nathan yanked his keys out of his pocket.

She snatched the Cornwall-shaped keyring away and held out his shaking fingers. 'See? You'll have an accident and that won't help anyone. We're wasting time. Come on.' They pushed through her guests, ignoring their puzzled looks, and found Vernon stretched out in a deckchair in front of her garden shed. Sometimes words weren't necessary for people to know something was wrong. The older man jumped to his feet before they reached him and Melissa raced through Josie's garbled message. 'I've only been drinking Coke so I'll drive us.'

The three-minute ride stretched into eternity and she jerked the car to a stop outside the shop. Her heart leapt into her throat at the sight of the small crowd gathered to see what was going on. She kept a tight rein on her emotions until the sight of Chloe, sprawled out on the tiled floor, almost brought her to her knees. Josie was crouched down beside her, pressing a blood-soaked towel to the young woman's stomach. Her friend turned around and her bright green eyes flashed the clear message that this wasn't good.

'I hoped you were the paramedics. She's drifting in and out of consciousness and I'm concerned about shock.'

Nathan knelt on Chloe's other side and touched her lifeless hand. 'I'm here, Chloe love.' Her eyes fluttered open but didn't appear to focus. 'Did they say how long they'd be, Josie? Why aren't the police here?'

'There's been a fatal multi-car accident on the A30 near Bodmin and the emergency services are tied up there.'

'Then we'll have to take her ourselves,' Melissa said firmly.

'How about I ring them again and ask for an update and their advice?' Nathan's reasonable suggestion frustrated her but she said nothing while he pulled out his mobile and made the call. After a brief conversation he hung up and grimaced. 'They say it'll be at least another half an hour but didn't give an outright no when I raised the possibility of driving Chloe ourselves.'

Deep frown lines creased Josie's brow. 'Thirty minutes is too long.'

'How about we use my van?' Vernon offered. 'We can make a bed in the back.' The poor man clearly blamed himself.

Melissa had never felt so useless as Josie issued instructions about what they needed to do, all the while continuing to monitor Chloe. It didn't take long to get the van set up and they carried Chloe out on an improvised stretcher.

'Do you want us to ride with you, Josie, or should we drive in front to clear the way?' Nathan asked.

'You go first. Flash your lights and blow your horn and if other drivers think you're an idiot, that's tough.'

He turned to Melissa. 'Would you give me your keys? I know the roads far better and I'm okay now.' Nathan held out his steady hands for inspection and gave her a questioning look. Reluctantly she passed them over.

In her car he adjusted the seat and mirrors before thrusting his phone at her. 'Do you think you could break the news to Catherine while I drive?'

'Of course.'

He pulled away from the curb and in the rear-view mirror she watched Vernon ease out behind them. After scrolling through for Catherine's number, she held her breath as it rang. No way could she leave this sort of message in a voicemail. But the woman answered on the second ring and Melissa prepared to ruin Catherine's day, and possibly the rest of her life.

CHAPTER NINETEEN

Nathan clasped his head in his hands and prayed, something he hadn't done in a very long time. The comfort of Melissa's hand wrapped around his was the only thing stopping him falling apart. The subtle drift of her perfume helped blot out the pervasive hospital smell of disinfectant mixed with worry that hung around them like a toxic cloud. Chloe was now in surgery. Catherine and Johnny were hot-footing it from Sussex. There was nothing useful he could do and the sense of helplessness was killing him.

'Anyone fancy a coffee?' Josie's mouth twisted in a wry smile. 'Calling it that should really be outlawed under the Trades Descriptions Act but there we are. I suppose if they described it as lukewarm brown sludge, they wouldn't get many takers.'

Despite his best effort he couldn't smile.

'I'm not making light of Chloe's situation, you know.'

Nathan nodded. 'I'll risk the coffee. Milk and sugar please. Melissa?' The two women hadn't spoken directly yet; instead they'd funnelled all their conversations through him. She let go of his hand and stood up.

'I'll come too. I need to stretch my legs. We won't be long.' She must've sensed his dismay at the break in physical contact because a soft kiss brushed over his cheek. Her lips lingered and she whispered in his ear. 'I need to talk to Josie.'

'I'll be fine. I mean it. Take as long as you need.' He dredged up a wan smile. 'You know I like my coffee lukewarm anyway.' That preference was a hangover from when he was a boy and used to beg to taste his mother's coffee. She refused to let him touch it until it was cool enough not to burn his mouth, and the habit of drinking it that way never left him. Nathan watched the two women walk away and crossed his fingers. If being forced into this awful situation together helped repair their broken friendship, some good would come out of the whole dreadful day. The image of Chloe, always so full of life and bubbling over with the next drama, sprawled on the floor of the shop with her hated blue nylon overall stained with blood would never leave him. They still knew very little about what happened because his niece was in no condition to tell Josie very much. Her sketchy description of the young man who attacked her and the fact Vernon Bull had never invested in a security camera left the police very little to go on. They could only hope that when she came around from surgery — he refused to allow the alternative to enter his brain — she'd remember enough to help catch her cowardly attacker.

His phone pinged with yet another text from Vernon. The poor man was distraught and mired in guilt. He'd been desperate to stay with them after their high-speed dash to A&E, but they'd persuaded him to go home on condition that they relayed regular updates. Nathan had nothing new to pass on yet because the doctor had warned them they wouldn't know the full extent of Chloe's injuries until they got her into the operating theatre. Nathan tapped in a quick response and returned to his default position, head in hands, shoulders slumped. The sound of voices took him by surprise and he glanced up to see Melissa and Josie walking towards him chattering animatedly.

'There you go, one order of brown sludge.' Melissa thrust a paper cup at him.

'You aren't taking a chance yourself?' He noticed the bottle of Coke in her other hand.

'No way!'

Josie brandished her own coffee cup. 'I'm immune after all these years.'

'At least I'm in the right place if it does a number on me,' he joked. The brief lapse into normal behaviour sent a wave of guilt sweeping over him.

'Don't beat yourself up.' Josie wagged a finger at him. 'How do you think people in the medical profession, the police and so forth handle the dreadful stuff we're forced to see and deal with? If we didn't resort to dubious humour we'd go crazy.'

'I suppose, but it still seems . . . wrong.'

She dropped down on the chair beside him. 'How much longer before Chloe's parents arrive?'

'A couple of hours. If I hadn't fixed her up with this job—'

'Stop that right now.'

'Yeah. Stop that,' Melissa chimed in. In the depths of his misery he couldn't help the glimmer of amusement that popped up. The two women were ganging up on him now after not speaking to each other in days.

'Life is messy. Unpredictable. Chloe's not a kid,' Josie said firmly. 'You can't wrap her in cotton wool.'

Knowing she was right and accepting it were totally different animals, but for the sake of keeping the peace, he agreed. Nathan caught Melissa's raised eyebrow. He hadn't fooled her. No surprise there.

'Josie Hancock?' A tall, burly man with salt and pepper hair strode towards them. 'DI Harry Bishop.'

'It's Senior Staff Nurse Hancock actually.'

'Excuse me, ma'am.' His deep-set blue eyes sparkled. 'I need a statement from you about the incident with Miss Chloe Waters. Is there somewhere quiet we can talk?'

The waiting room was a long way from peaceful, with two toddlers running rampant and a sour-faced man berating some unfortunate on his mobile phone.

'Of course. Follow me.' Josie sprang up and led the detective out of the room.

'They'd make an interesting pair,' Melissa mused.

'You're matchmaking? Now?'

'Sorry. That was crass.' Her face burned with embarrassment.

'No, I'm the one who should apologize.' Nathan shoved a hand through his hair and smiled when she reached out, smoothed it down and tucked a rogue curl away from his face. 'We're all on edge.' She snuggled next to him and rested her head on his shoulder. Together was all that would work right now.

* * *

Melissa held it together for Nathan's sake. Just. The weary surgeon looked relieved to be delivering mostly good news. The knife hadn't touched any vital organs, although they'd been forced to remove Chloe's damaged spleen. He hurried to assure them that apart from lowering the effectiveness of the immune system, making her more vulnerable to infections, Chloe could live a perfectly normal life without her spleen.

'I'm afraid because it was an emergency we didn't have time to do keyhole surgery so she'll have a larger scar,' the doctor explained. 'Chloe's in the recovery room now and you'll be able to see her as soon as she's awake enough for visitors.'

She glanced at Catherine and Johnny, and noticed their strained grey faces were a shade less taut now.

'I'm going home now I know she's out of danger.' Josie stood.

'How will you get there?'

Her friend's face turned pink. 'DI Bishop offered me a lift. He's going back to Penworthal to supervise the investigation at the shop. There's no point him hanging around here because it'll be a while before he'll be able to question Chloe.'

When they'd fetched their drinks together earlier, Josie had told her all about her ex-husband and admitted that she'd been a fool over him, out of loneliness. A little spirit-lifting in the form of a ruggedly handsome, divorced detective inspector might be exactly what the doctor ordered.

Nathan jumped up too now and reached for Josie. 'If it wasn't for you . . .' He choked up.

'It's my job.'

They all knew it was far more than that. Josie took her responsibilities seriously, leaving little time for anything else.

'I'll see you all later.'

'Hang on, please.' Johnny joined them. 'You haven't given us a chance to thank you properly yet either.'

'I appreciate it, but as I said, it's my job and I'm only relieved there was a good outcome.'

Catherine roused herself to join in her husband's thanks, but it sounded automatic. Ninety-nine per cent of her concentration was focused on her daughter. Until she saw Chloe with her own eyes, that's how it would be.

'I really must be going. I'm back on shift in six hours and I need to snatch some sleep.'

'Of course.' Johnny shook her hand vigorously. 'Thank you again.'

Through the door, Melissa spotted the detective hovering and the man broke into a shy smile when Josie walked out.

'Trust you to be right.' Nathan chuckled. 'I should've expected no less.'

'Glad to hear you're catching on.'

'Nathan.' Catherine snapped her fingers to get his attention. 'We plan on staying here tonight. I assume you'll stay with us, so why doesn't Melissa get a ride home with Josie?'

He tightened his grip on her hand. It wouldn't do to let him start an argument in a misguided attempt to stick up for her.

'Good idea.' She gently pulled away from Nathan. 'I'll catch up with them.' Before he could say anything else she ran out of the waiting room and sent a text asking Josie to wait for her as she speed-walked through the deserted corridors.

They were a quiet threesome in Harry's unmarked police car, all too tired and caught up in their own thoughts for conversation. Melissa's eyelids drooped, and she was surprised to open them again and find they were driving through Penworthal. The village was eerily silent and dark with no one in sight.

'If you give me directions, I'll drop you both home,' Harry said. 'I'll follow up with you later, Josie . . . about Chloe.' The shy glance he slid across wasn't totally professional, but Josie's flushed cheeks suggested the detective's hint of personal interest wasn't unwelcome.

On the pavement outside their homes they waved Harry off.

'How about a proper cup of tea?' Josie suggested.

She should turn down the offer so her friend could rest, but maybe they needed this more than sleep? 'Sure. You going to tell me what you've discovered about the dishy detective?'

'Maybe.'

Not everyone gets second chances in life. She'd been fortunate enough to get one with Nathan and now another was on offer with Josie. They were lucky women indeed.

CHAPTER TWENTY

Nathan watched Chloe from his kitchen window. She was stretched out on a sun lounger under the shade of a frilly pink and white striped umbrella. Her floaty white dress trailed on the grass and from this distance she looked pale and fragile. Next to her, Toby knelt on the grass reading aloud. The cynical side of him suspected the scene was staged to replicate the one in *Sense and Sensibility* when the doting Colonel Brandon recites poetry to the recovering Marianne. That reminded him of Melissa. Only a couple of nights ago she'd confessed to having fantasies about them doing the same thing and he'd promised to fulfil them one day.

'What're you smiling about?' Catherine bustled in and turned on the kettle. She followed his glance out of the window. 'No one would think she was deathly ill a week ago. Do you really think it's okay if we leave? Johnny says we should but I'm not sure.'

'She'll be fine. I promise I'll keep a close eye on her. The doctors say she's bounced back incredibly well from the operation and is almost off the painkillers.' His niece hadn't had any problems tolerating the low-dose antibiotics she'd been put on for the foreseeable future. Chloe hadn't objected to being mothered — or smothered — for a few days after the attack, but her tolerance soon waned and the normal niggles between mother and daughter restarted. 'I'm sure Johnny needs to get back to work and you must have a lot of commitments too.'

'Well, he does have an important meeting in Brussels next week and I'd hate to miss the Women's Institute annual general meeting on Tuesday. They rely on me to chair it.'

Of course they do. 'There you go then. It's settled.'

'I'm warning you now, I shall ring every day to check how she's doing until I'm certain she's fully recovered.'

'Of course.'

'Oh, there you are, Johnny.' Catherine switched her attention to her husband who had wandered in to join them.

'We'll leave tomorrow afternoon. I'll cook us a proper Sunday roast before I go so at least Nathan will have some leftovers in the fridge.'

He didn't point out that he'd managed to take care of himself all these years without fading away yet.

'I suppose you'd better invite Melissa to join us,' she said with a martyred air.

'What *is* your problem with her?' Nathan had had enough. 'She's never been anything other than friendly and gracious with you so what've you got against her?'

'I'm not sure you want to know.'

'Careful what you say, love.'

She brushed Johnny away when he touched her shoulder. 'If he's blind to what she's really like, then as his older sister I've a right to look out for him.'

'It's not our business.' Johnny's insistence grew more strident.

'What is it you think you know?' Nathan's stomach churned.

'From what I've heard, Melissa's having financial problems. She latched onto you fast enough, didn't she? Goodness, she must've thought it was Christmas when you fell head over heels for her. A single man with a beautiful mortgage-free house and a healthy bank balance.'

'Who told you that pack of lies?'

'Mr Bull at the shop.'

'Vernon Bull? Why would he know about it?'

Catherine held up her hands. 'Don't shoot the messenger. Mr Bull told me in confidence that until last week Mrs Martyn was months behind in paying her account at the shop. Her debit card was rejected a couple of times too, so now she always pays him in cash.'

'That's hardly proof of anything. Robin was a risk-taker in business, that's true, but successfully so as far as I'm aware. Melissa is a top-notch freelance editor and never short of work.' They'd never specifically discussed their finances but he hadn't got the impression she was struggling. He wouldn't call her an extravagant woman — she loved charity shops and frequently bought own-brand products at the supermarket — but surely thriftiness was a positive trait?

'Mr Bull also let on that the funeral director who took care of her husband's arrangements had to send his bill repeatedly before he started to get any money out of her, and then it was in instalments.'

'Even if that's true it's completely unethical of him to share that information with the village shopkeeper!'

His sister shrugged. 'They're on the parish council together. I suppose he thought it was right to warn other businesspeople in the area.'

'I still say it's rubbish.'

'You would,' she said darkly. 'Surely it wouldn't do any harm to raise the subject with her? If you warn her what people are saying, then she'll have a chance to put things straight.'

Why did he feel he'd been cleverly manoeuvred? 'I certainly will. I'm sure Melissa will have a perfectly reasonable explanation for everything.'

Catherine's bland smile didn't fool him, but he quashed the urge to question her any further. There was only one person whose explanation he cared to hear.

* * *

'Oh, hi, what a nice surprise. I wasn't expecting you.' Melissa wound the towel she'd been rubbing her wet hair with around her head. 'Come in.' Nathan's smile didn't reach his eyes and he didn't rush to kiss her either. 'What's wrong?'

'Why should there be anything wrong? Can't a man turn up on his girlfriend's doorstep without a written invitation?'

She plastered on a smile and assured him that he was always welcome, but the sharp edge to his voice worried her. 'Why don't you fix us a coffee while I finish drying my hair and throw some clothes on?' Normally she'd joke about being naked under her bathrobe and ask if he preferred that she stayed that way, but for some reason she held back. 'Is everything still good with Chloe?'

'Yeah, she's doing really well and Catherine and Johnny are leaving us in peace again tomorrow.' His smile inched back and she remonstrated with herself for panicking over nothing. Upstairs she tousled her hair dry and raked a comb through it before throwing on an ankle-length turquoise floral skirt and plain white T-shirt. Melissa padded downstairs barefoot and hesitated in the lounge door. Nathan's face was grim as he stared out of the window.

'Oh, I didn't hear you come down.' He swung back around. 'The coffee's on the table.'

Melissa plopped down on the sofa and struggled to hide her dismay when he didn't join her. She tucked her feet under her and took a sip of her drink.

'Would you like to come for lunch tomorrow? Catherine's cooking. A full Sunday roast, of course.' A sardonic smile lifted the corners of his mouth. 'She's determined to feed me up before leaving.'

'Yeah, that'd be great. And?'

'And?'

'Don't play games. Sit down, for heaven's sake, and tell me why you've been glowering ever since you arrived.' A dark flush inched up his neck and he couldn't meet her eyes when he perched on the opposite end of the sofa.

'I heard something today that . . . disturbed me. I don't believe for a moment it's true but—'

'Oh for God's sake spit it out.' Melissa's heart sank as he started to speak and a wave of nausea swept through her. If she admitted everything it would wreck his memories of Robin, but if she lied then this beautiful thing between them might crumble into dust. 'I'm not after your money, Nathan.'

'I never thought so.'

'So why ask these questions?'

'Because I need the complete truth.'

Melissa pressed her hands around her coffee mug to stop them shaking. 'Catherine's information is maybe seventy-five per cent correct but I'm working hard to straighten things out.' Doubt flickered on his face. 'I don't need your money. I only need . . . you.' Her voice broke. 'Do you believe me?'

* * *

He absolutely did believe her, but wasn't certain that he could live with only knowing part of the story. 'Yes. Yes, I do.'

'Do you mind if we leave it there for now?' She set down her mug and reached for his hands, sending her warm touch flooding through him. What they had was far too special to throw away. Nathan could accept there would always be parts of her marriage she kept to herself. One hundred per cent honesty was an unattainable pipe dream.

'Of course not.' He slid one hand through her silky, peach-scented hair to caress her neck. 'I nearly chickened out of asking anything except whether I could take you to bed when you opened the door in that robe. That was a below the belt move.'

'Only if it was deliberate, which it sure wasn't.' A smile played around her lips. 'Now this.' Melissa's fingers brushed the fly of his trousers. '*That's* a below the belt move.'

'Good,' he rasped.

'Are you sure we're okay again?' Her hesitation showed.

'Yeah, we really are.' Nathan buried his last sliver of remaining doubt. Later he'd decide whether to have a quiet word with Vernon Bull.

'So, are you in a hurry to be anywhere else, Professor Kellow?'

'Nowhere.'

'In that case I suggest we take this to the bedroom.' The grey-green depths of her mermaid eyes rested on him.

Nathan wasn't stupid enough to believe they'd heard the last of Catherine's story. Vernon had shared the news with his sister who he barely knew, so who else was under the misapprehension that Melissa was one step away from bankruptcy? He pushed that thought away and reached for the woman offering herself to him.

CHAPTER TWENTY-ONE

Melissa stopped in the middle of weeding and rested back on her heels, turning her face to the sun. She revelled in the heat tamed by the breezes sneaking in from the coast. The only fly in the ointment was her continuing indecision about whether to bring the insinuations about her out into the open or wait until they died a quiet death. For the last couple of weeks that was the only thing marring her otherwise perfect times with Nathan. For a man genetically inclined to keep the peace, he'd made it crystal clear he disagreed with her reluctance to challenge Vernon Bull. She pushed a lock of hair out of her face and was grateful she had an appointment for a trim this afternoon. Very late last night she'd sent off the final round of edits to her most challenging author ever, a man she never intended on working with again, so was looking forward to a free weekend, starting with tonight's pub quiz.

'What didn't you understand about the phrase I never want to see you again?' Josie's strident voice rang out.

'You can't live without me. Us. And you know it.' Christopher Deacon's cocky drawl made the hairs on the back of Melissa's neck prickle. 'When are you going to admit it?'

'Ouch! Get off me!'

Melissa sprang to her feet and raced across the grass. 'Are you all right?' The couple stood outside Josie's door and Deacon was gripping her friend's bare arm. The doctor threw her a venomous glare.

'This is none of your business,' he barked. 'We're having a private discussion. Aren't we, Josie?'

Her friend's pale, drawn face remained unreadable.

'Do you want me to call the police, Josie?'

'We don't need Mr Plod, thank you.' Deacon scoffed. 'He's history, isn't he, sweetheart? She won't be seeing him again.'

Melissa's blood ran cold. Physically challenging the man wasn't an option so she needed to be clever. 'I was about to stop and fix myself a coffee, would y'all like to join me?'

'Not for me. I need to get to work.' He flung Josie's arm away. 'I'll be back.' Deacon stormed off down the drive and jumped into his flashy sports car.

'His Terminator imitation is pretty lame.' Her friend's attempt to make light of the situation trailed away. 'I'd love a coffee but I'm running late and need to get ready for work myself.'

'You don't want to discuss what just happened?'

'Not really. I'm fine. Christopher tends to overreact.' The attempt at a careless smile was feebler than her ex's attempt to imitate Arnold Schwarzenegger. 'We're through. It's all good.'

'If you say so.' Despite their own recent reconciliation, they weren't quite back to their previous closeness. They passed the time of day when they were on the way in or out of their houses, but apart from that Melissa was either working or with Nathan. She hadn't exactly been spying on her neighbour but it would've been hard to miss a certain handsome grey-haired detective beating a path to Josie's door on several occasions. 'Will you be home from your shift in time for the quiz?'

'Hopefully. In your pillow talk with the opposition, has he revealed any secrets about their strategy?'

'We don't waste time in bed talking trivia!' The quiz had become a running joke between them, which was ironic considering neither of them had volunteered to join their teams in the first place. Contrary to what she'd just said, though, they *did* sometimes swap trivia facts. Their specialities were similar — literature, history and music — so the gaps in their knowledge mainly came down to the natural differences that came from being educated in different countries.

Josie's phone buzzed and she frowned down at it before shoving the mobile in her pocket.

'If that's your ex again you should report him for harassment. You could get a restraining order.'

'Don't be daft. You're blowing all this out of proportion. I'll see you later. Bye.' Her friend turned away and disappeared back into her house, slamming the door behind her.

Later on she'd ask Nathan's advice. If he didn't think she was too far out of line she'd get on the phone to DI Harry Bishop tomorrow and see what he had to say about the situation. She'd bet anything the detective wouldn't sit back and do nothing.

* * *

Nathan grimaced at his reflection in the mirror. Chloe had taken full advantage of his indulgence after her recent ordeal to talk him into buying a whole wardrobe of new clothes. After being dragged around every men's shop in Truro, he'd given in to every one of her suggestions, anything to put an end to the ordeal.

You're not bad-looking for a man of your age but you dress like an old geezer. You aren't fat so why buy everything a size too big? And talk about dull. You need a decent hair cut too that isn't out of the 1940s. I can't believe Melissa lets you walk around like this.

On his own he would never have paired slim-fitting stone-washed jeans, an untucked navy and white shirt and a soft grey-collared cardigan. Chloe swore it wasn't too young on him but he was far from convinced. By the time he emerged shell-shocked from a hairdresser's with his hair tapered at the sides, swept off his face and lightly gelled, he was even more dubious.

If his friends, and even worse Melissa, laughed their heads off he'd return to his familiar summer uniform of khakis and whatever T-shirt was clean.

'Ready, Uncle Nat?' Chloe flung open the bedroom door. 'I'm meeting Toby at the pub so we can walk over together.' Her wicked dark eyes gleamed. 'Don't want you chickening out, do we?'

'Don't we?'

'You look great.' Her gaze softened. 'It's not that dramatic, just more — you.' She made a grab for his arm. 'Come on. You can buy the first round to thank me. Toby and I won't be staying long so you'll have to let me know how the quiz goes later.' She giggled. 'Hopefully that'll be sometime tomorrow. There's a beach party in Newquay.'

'Are you sure you're—'

'Yeah, I'm good. The doctor cleared me for all activities.' She poked him in the ribs. 'And I do mean *all* so I'm looking forward to Toby taking full advantage of *that* little fact.'

'Good Lord, Chloe, I don't need all the details, thank you very much. What am I supposed to say when your mum rings?' Catherine was still burning up the phone lines every day, despite his assurance that it was unnecessary.

'Tell her I'm staying the night with a friend who lives in some remote place where there's no mobile phone coverage,' she said airily.

Downstairs they headed off and strolled down the road. A pang of sadness struck like a dart to the bull's-eye. If he had a daughter, would she fuss over him the same way? He'd never know now because that ship seemed to have sailed. They said you couldn't miss what you'd never had, but was that true?

'Hi, Melissa!' Chloe waved frantically.

Nathan's spirits lifted as the lady in question strolled towards him. Her face altered as the gap between them lessened. Puzzlement. Close scrutiny. A wave of panic swept through him.

'Well, aren't you a sight for sore eyes, handsome man.' Her glorious smile broke free and she flung her arms around his neck. Her kiss sizzled all the way to his toes. 'Someone's had a makeover.' She stroked his hair, tweaked the collar of his shirt and nodded. 'You've done good, Chloe.'

'How do you know this isn't all my own doing?' The women laughed at his feeble protest. 'Are we going to the pub or not?'

'We sure are. I'm going to show you off.'

If they hadn't both linked arms with him, Nathan would've backed out. Before he knew it, they were inside the Rusty Anchor and, apart from the usual friendly greetings, no one appeared to be paying him any undue attention.

'Come have a drink with your enemies first.' Melissa tugged him towards her gaggle of girlfriends chattering away at their favourite table by the unlit fire.

By chance, he caught a fleeting glance between Amy and Becky, intercepted by Evelyn with a stern headshake. It didn't strike him as the sort of joking reaction he'd expect about the two of them walking in together. Had they all heard the rumours going around the village too? Melissa was oblivious and beamed at him. Nathan did his best to laugh when she joked about not letting him off his leash because he looked so yummy.

'I ought to join the others. I'll see you later.' He pressed a kiss on her cheek and headed for the bar. His quiz team companions weren't renowned for their subtlety, so if they'd heard the rumours about Melissa he'd soon know about it.

* * *

She squashed a flare of disappointment. One minute Nathan was fine, the next not so much. Perhaps she'd gone a little too far with her joke about showing him off. He could be sensitive at times. For now, she'd enjoy her friends' company instead and sort things with him later.

'Does anyone want a drink while I'm getting one?' she asked. 'Then you can catch me up with all the gossip. I've been out of the loop a bit this week with one thing and another so . . . what's up?' Everyone was giving her strange looks and a gaping pit opened in her stomach. 'You've been listening to the dumb story about me that Vernon Bull's spouting, haven't you? Tell me no one believes it?' Amy and Tamara couldn't meet her gaze when she glanced around the table. 'Wow! Y'all do, don't you? It sure is good to know who my friends are.' She smacked the side of her head. 'Yeah, that's right. I don't have any.' The nagging sensation of being unfair lingered, but her righteous anger overrode it.

'That's not true, Melissa,' Evelyn spoke up. 'We'd love to hear your—'

'You can stuff your stupid quiz and book club. I've had enough.' Through a veil of tears, she threw off Becky's attempt to stop her. With her hand on the door she turned back and yelled across the pub. 'Nathan, I'd pay attention to your buddies if I were you and stay away from me before I get my hands on your bank account!' The sight of his shocked, white face made her freeze. It took every ounce of determination she could drag up to force her feet to move again. Back out in the street she set off running.

Halfway up the hill she gasped at the sting of a raw blister on her right heel and slowed down. The slim white sandals weren't designed for speed. Melissa glanced behind her, unsure if she was relieved or saddened that no one had chased after her. The lump in her throat grew. How did everything go wrong so fast? Because she hadn't been honest, that's why. The anger and sadness she'd experienced over Laura's betrayal and Josie's hidden secrets should've taught her a lesson, but clearly she hadn't learned it well enough.

She limped home and let herself into the empty house. Acting on autopilot she headed for her bedroom and dug out an overnight bag from the back of the wardrobe. She randomly threw in some clothes, then added her phone charger, passport and laptop. She was done.

Before she drove away she allowed herself one last glance in the rear-view mirror.

CHAPTER TWENTY-TWO

Nathan glared at Paul. 'I don't want to hear any more crap about Melissa. She's straight as an arrow and I trust her completely. I'm going after her so feel free to talk about us as much as you want.'

He'd barely sat down before it started, the concerned looks and offers of more drinks than he could possibly manage. Paul had clearly been nominated as spokesman because he launched into a barrage of questions.

The anger bubbling up inside Nathan had been on the verge of erupting when Melissa's thick drawl filled the pub. Instead of going straight to her and making his solidarity clear, he'd stared blankly and said nothing. Huge mistake. That was when her face turned to stone and she rushed out of the pub. Now his priority was to find her and apologize.

'We're worried about you, mate.'

'Mate? We're not mates.' He scoffed. 'Mates wouldn't take me for a fool. They'd trust I know what I'm doing and help stamp out these stupid rumours.' It made him uncomfortable to recall how Melissa had skirted around a full explanation of her financial difficulties, but he ploughed on. 'Good luck with the quiz. You'll need it.'

Everyone stared as he followed Melissa's example and stormed out of the pub. Nathan hesitated, unsure whether to go home for his car or run after her?

'Uncle Nat, are you okay?' Chloe grabbed his arm. She must've followed him out.

'They're idiots, the lot of them, Professor Kellow,' Toby said earnestly.

'Call me Nathan, please.' He managed a fleeting smile at his niece. 'Or Nat, if you must.'

'We'll give you a lift to Mrs Martyn's house.' Toby pointed to his battered old red Mini.

'I couldn't trouble you. It's—'

'Trouble us?' Chloe scoffed. 'You've rescued me big-time this summer. I owe you.'

'Owe me? I nearly got you killed!'

'Don't tell me you've been thinking that all this time?' Her voice turned shrill. 'That was bad luck.' She looked about to say more. 'We'll talk about this properly later. Right now, *we're* going to help *you* for a change.'

She'd be horrified if he pointed out how very much like her mother she sounded.

'Hurry up and get in.' Chloe folded the front passenger seat forward and clambered in the back.

At the top of the road they stopped outside Melissa's house. His gut told him she wasn't there as soon as he stepped out of the car. The blinds were closed and there were no lights on. To convince himself, he hurried up the path and rang the bell. No response. Nathan pulled out his keyring then shoved it away again. He couldn't use the spare key she'd given him. If she *was* in there and wasn't answering then she didn't want to speak to him.

'No luck, Uncle Nat?' Chloe yelled.

He shook his head and trudged back down to join them.

'Have you tried her phone?'

'Not yet.' It would be a fruitless exercise but he gave it a try anyway. 'It's turned off. Should I leave a message?'

'Nah, it'll be pointless. Let's put our heads together and think where she might've gone.'

'What about your party?'

'It won't get really underway for hours yet,' she said blithely. 'Get in.'

It was easier to obey than argue.

'Do you think she's likely to go back to America?'

'I doubt it.' She'd be too proud to flee back to her family and give them the opportunity to say they'd told her so. A flash of inspiration hit. 'Dorset maybe?'

'Why there?'

'We've just finished reading *The French Lieutenant's Woman* together.' Amused glances flashed between the two young people. Their idea of romance wouldn't be dissecting literary fiction. 'We talked about spending a weekend in Lyme Regis.' He smiled sadly. 'She wanted to follow in the footsteps of the tragic figure of Sarah Woodruff and walk out on the Cobb. The three possible endings offered in the story fascinated her. Of course there's the Jane Austen connection too, because the same spot features in *Persuasion* when Louisa Musgrove falls and cracks her head on the seawall.'

'Hopefully she doesn't take method acting too far and replicate that,' Chloe said wryly. 'How about we take a chance and steer our trusty vehicle in that direction?' She patted the dashboard.

'I don't know. I could be wrong and you've got better things to do than—'

'No, we don't,' she declared. 'It'll be an adventure. Beach parties happen all the time down here, but turning detective to track down a missing person is far more exciting.'

He held back from pointing out that Melissa had only been gone for about half an hour and was hardly a criminal fleeing justice, or even a wife being searched for by her desperate husband.

Chloe showed them her phone. 'I've got the route.' She fitted the mobile in a clamp fixed to the dash. 'Let's go.'

She was her mother's daughter all right.

* * *

Melissa rubbed her eyes, blinked hard and opened the window. Air conditioning was no substitute for a dose of bracing fresh air. She refused to dwell on the fact that this was the furthest she'd ever driven on the wrong side of the road. She whizzed by the exit for the next service station and kept going. The sat nav insisted this was only about a two-hour drive, a distance she wouldn't think twice about doing back home simply to go shopping. *Yeah, but then you weren't exhausted, frazzled and angry.*

When she left Penworthal she'd no more idea of where to go than the man in the moon. It occurred to her to hop on the first plane out of the country but the high cost — both financial and emotional — stopped her. Her bank account wouldn't accommodate a last-minute plane ticket without going further into the red. If she begged her parents for the money they'd willingly send it, but that touched on the "emotional" element. Having made the break and crafted a new life for herself, she refused to go home with her tail between her legs — at least not yet.

Her spirits lifted as she left the motorway for the quieter A35 road and the last part of the journey. The memory of Nathan's rumbling voice reading *The French Lieutenant's Woman* filled the car as if he were sitting next to her, describing the town of Lyme Regis and Sarah Woodruff's walk out onto the Cobb, the stone structure built as a breakwater to protect the harbour. What was he thinking now? She should've been more transparent with him, but at the time her veiled explanation had suited them both.

Melissa slowed the car as she entered the town and started to check for somewhere to stop for the night. Many of the small houses she passed had B&B signs stuck in their front gardens but she preferred the anonymity of a cheap hotel. Her heart sank when she couldn't spot anything like a Travelodge, and before she knew it Melissa found herself in the centre of Lyme Regis within sight of the beach. Too tired and fraught to search any further she turned reluctantly into the car park of the Royal Lion Hotel and crossed her fingers they'd have a room available. At this point she'd take anything and worry about the cost later.

Reality only sank in when she reached her single room. She collapsed on the narrow bed and worked to steady her erratic breathing. The loud rumble coming from her stomach reminded her she'd skipped dinner, but she was too tired and out of sorts to go downstairs to the hotel restaurant or head back out in search of anything else.

She dragged herself off the bed, fixed a cup of coffee from the beverage tray and wolfed down the meagre packet of digestive biscuits. In the hope of a distraction she turned on the television but the first programme that came on was *Antiques Road Trip*, a show she and Nathan loved watching. Melissa jabbed the remote to turn it off and a veil of tears clouded her vision.

Exhaling a weary sigh, she stripped off her clothes and wriggled into an old faded blue nightgown. Robin had converted her to sleeping in the nude, but since his death she'd reverted to the habits of her childhood — until she and Nathan got together. A sharp pang of longing for him struck like a knife to the heart. He had a weakness for sexy, slinky nightwear and relished peeling it off to reveal her bare skin, ready and aching for his touch.

Melissa foraged around for her toothbrush and headed into the minuscule bathroom. Normally she took her time removing her make-up, washed her face and applied a night cream, but she didn't have the energy to bother with the whole tedious process tonight. Back in the bedroom she slipped between cold white sheets that smelled of commercial cleaning instead of the air-dried freshness she'd become accustomed to. One of the many things she loved about living in England was that hanging washing out to dry was commonplace, instead of the refuge of those who either couldn't afford a tumble dryer or were assiduous environmentalists.

Against all the odds she must've dropped off to sleep at some point because out of nowhere she startled awake. The glowing red numbers on the bedside clock informed her with an offensive jauntiness that it was 3 a.m. Wonderful. In a couple of hours the sun would rise again, being no respecter of people who hadn't slept or were unsure how they would face the day ahead. Melissa took a fast shower and dragged yesterday's clothes back on over clean underwear. She'd fix a coffee and read while she waited for the time to pass. Unfortunately, she'd forgotten to pack her Kindle so the only book to hand was the well-worn paperback of *The French Lieutenant's Woman* she'd snatched off the hall table on her way out of the door.

Why did everything come back to Nathan? *Because he's in your heart, you silly girl. The two of you are meant to be.* Josie had trotted out the gentle admonition when Melissa tried to brush off their deepening relationship as nothing more than her first foray into single life after being widowed.

Sitting cross-legged on the bed she opened the book and lost herself in the world of Victorian England.

CHAPTER TWENTY-THREE

'I'm too old for this,' Nathan groaned. Spending the night in a pint-sized Mini had been a terrible idea for a six-foot-tall, forty-year-old man whose joints had protested loudly at being cramped in unnatural positions. When they'd arrived late the night before he'd suggested they book into a hotel but his young companions — led naturally by Chloe — persuaded him this would be more "fun". After parking on the seafront, Chloe offered to swap seats so he could at least stretch out a little in the back. Not that he'd slept because he was too worried about Melissa, along with the shaming possibility of being moved on by the police. Now he was in desperate need of a bathroom and coffee, in that order.

'Relax, Uncle Nat.' Chloe pointed across the road to a row of shops. 'There's a café that's open. They're bound to have a loo, then you can treat us to a fry-up.'

The thought of food turned his stomach but he'd wrecked the couple's weekend plans so the least he could do was feed them. Nathan glanced at his phone and saw a slew of missed calls from Catherine, Josie and Evelyn, but nothing from the one person he desperately wanted to hear from. Toby locked the car and the three of them trudged over to the Golden Cobb Café. He thrust a bunch of money at Chloe and told her to order whatever they wanted, then dived into the gents. After relieving his aching bladder Nathan scrubbed a hand over his grey, stubbly face and splashed cold water over it in a vain attempt to wake up. He didn't have a comb in his pocket so made do with using damp fingers to flatten down his hair.

'There you go. One weak, sugary coffee.' Chloe slopped a brimming mug down on the nearest table. 'I've ordered you toast and marmalade, okay?'

He managed a faint smile. 'How did you—'

'Guess you didn't want a full English?' she chirped. 'Your horrified look when I mentioned it maybe?'

Nathan slumped on the wobbly red plastic chair and sipped his coffee, letting the caffeine and sugar seep in and start to work its magic.

'I'm going to the loo,' Chloe said.

He stared out of the window at the flat blue water winding like a wide silk ribbon past the harbour to the sea. The dark stone of the Cobb stretched out to the left and a few people were strolling along there already. They were probably locals enjoying the relative solitude before the daily rush of visitors arrived.

The mug slid from his hand and somewhere in the fog of his brain he was aware of warm liquid landing on his trousers. A swathe of silver hair. The pop of a bright pink sweater. A woman's distinctive, purposeful stride.

'Uncle Nat! What have you done to yourself?'

'What do you mean?' He followed the direction of Chloe's puzzled gaze to his stained clothes. 'Oh, right. It's Melissa. Look.' Springing to his feet, Nathan pointed wildly towards the Cobb. 'You and Toby stay and eat your breakfast.'

'Are you sure it's her? You don't want to be arrested for accosting a strange woman who happens to—'

The last part of the warning drifted over his head. All he cared about was catching up with Melissa before she disappeared again.

'Watch where you're bleedin' going, mate.'

He'd sprinted into the road without checking for traffic, forcing an oncoming driver to slam on his brakes, and the battered Land Rover had screeched to a stop only inches from him. Nathan waved a hand in apology but kept running, almost knocking over a lady walking a miniature white poodle. From here he could see that Melissa clutched in her hand the old orange Penguin Classic book he'd given her. He yelled out her name and she stopped. Turned. Saw him. Every drop of blood drained from her face.

'How did you find me?' she said breathlessly.

'Are you pleased I did? I really hope you are, but if not I'll go away.'

'Don't go.'

He threw his arms wide open and waited with a thudding heart.

'Go on, love,' a ruddy-faced man encouraged, egged on by several other walkers who'd stopped to see what was happening.

Melissa smiled and threw herself into his embrace, burrowing her head in his chest.

'I smell awful,' he warned. 'I slept in a car last night and dumped coffee over myself when I spotted you.'

She glanced up and amusement danced in her beautiful mermaid eyes. 'I love you but you do stink a bit.'

'You worried me to death running off that way.' It suddenly sank in that Melissa had said she loved him. Nathan experienced a surge of joy that made it a struggle for him to continue with what he'd been trying to say. 'Please, don't ever do that again. I know you had good reason and those rumours were nasty, but—'

'Shush.' Her finger pressed to his lips. 'Let's get away from here.' She nodded towards the strangers standing and gawking at them. Several were taking pictures with their mobile phones. If they weren't careful they'd go viral on Instagram, TikTok or whatever the favoured social media platform of the week happened to be.

He gathered his thoughts enough to quickly run through how he got here, so she'd understand he couldn't run off and abandon Chloe and Toby.

'I'm surprised you didn't hire a bus and bring the whole village with you,' she said dryly.

'A lot of people felt bad after you left so I'm sure I would've had plenty of takers for seats.' She needed to hear he wasn't the only one who cared. 'Let's go. If the café lets me back in, I suggest we have breakfast.'

'Awesome. I'm starving. I couldn't face any food last night so I haven't eaten anything since yesterday lunchtime.' She patted her hips. 'I can't have these fading away again when I've managed to put on a few much-needed pounds.'

'I'll feed you as much as you want. Then we're going back home to sort out this whole sorry mess.'

* * *

Melissa hovered on the verge of tears. Nathan made it sound so simple. She swallowed hard and tried her best to smile.

'A couple of minutes ago when you said you loved me I got distracted by all those people fussing around us so I never said I loved you in return. This is me doing it now instead.' Nathan's shy smile touched her heart.

'And I love nothing better than hearing it. Now why don't you lead me to this greasy spoon. Isn't that what y'all call our equivalent of a diner?'

'That's right.' With a fake sigh he loosened his arms and reached for her hand instead. 'The show's over,' Nathan joked with their observers. Ragged cheers and suggestive comments rippled through the air, following them back down the Cobb. 'This isn't quite the highbrow literary experience I'd imagined when we talked about coming here.'

'Absolutely not! In the book I got the impression Sarah and Charles's thoughts were on a much higher plane.'

'We'll come back another day.'

He meant every word. That was one of the things she loved most about this man.

Chloe was signalling frantically from the other side of the road and waving her phone around.

'Oh God, what drama is it now?' Nathan joked, steering them towards his niece, and checking for oncoming traffic this time. 'I've found Melissa and we're des—'

'You might want to hurry up and leave because your friend Josie could be in trouble,' Chloe gabbled. 'Mrs Taylor? The old schoolteacher woman? She rang. I don't normally answer numbers I don't recognize but I was distracted.'

Melissa clung on to the last shreds of her patience as the young woman rattled on.

'She'd heard through the village gossip tree that we came after you and hoped we'd tracked you down by now so I told her—'

'Chloe, just tell us what's wrong. Now.' Nathan's firm tone put a stop to his niece's rambling story.

'Fine,' she huffed. 'Josie's ex has — well, taken her I guess you'd say.'

'Taken her where?' Melissa joined in.

'Don't know.' Chloe shrugged. 'That's the problem.'

'Have they called the police?'

The girl smirked. 'Yeah, and Romeo turned up. You know, the cute detective she's shagging who was on my case. He wasn't happy from what the old bat said.'

'What did you tell Evelyn?'

'That we'd be back as soon as we could. I guess that's right?'

'Of course.' She and Nathan spoke in unison. 'To heck with breakfast.'

'Don't worry, we've got that covered.' Toby held up a white paper bag and two takeaway cups. 'Bacon sarnies and coffee made to Chloe's specifications.'

'You're an angel. Let's get on the road . . . Oh, I almost forgot. My car is at the hotel and I've got a bag to pack.'

'We can all pile into my car for now and I'll drop you off,' Toby offered.

'That's kind, but there's really no need. I'm at the Royal Lion Hotel and you can almost see it from here. It's only a few minutes' walk.'

'I'm coming too.' Nathan slid his arm around her. 'I'm happy to drive us back to Cornwall, unless Melissa objects.'

'You won't hear any argument from me on that score.' She threw up her hands in mock surrender. 'I'm still not a big fan of your roads.'

The next few hours flew by and dragged at the same time, which made no sense. Melissa spent a chunk of the journey texting with Evelyn and the rest of the group. No one would've known there was a problem if Becky hadn't walked up to Josie's to return a cake pan and seen Christopher Deacon lingering outside the door. Luckily, she had the foresight to duck behind an overhanging rhododendron bush before the doctor spotted her, and she watched him lead Josie out to his car. By their body language and the man's grim expression it seemed clear this wasn't a planned date. Now, Becky was kicking herself for not intervening, despite everyone telling her she could've made things worse. Melissa felt a niggle of guilt. Because she'd stormed out of the pub last night, she'd never got around to asking Nathan's opinion about whether to tell Harry Bishop about Josie's ex. Maybe if she had . . .

'Any update?' Nathan asked.

'Not really.' Melissa frowned. 'DI Bishop is hampered by regulations because there's no concrete proof that Josie's in danger. In the police's eyes, Becky is putting two and two together and making at least five, possibly six.' She dug her nails into her palms. 'I'm damn sure Josie hasn't gone with Christopher voluntarily. The other day I heard her telling him very clearly that they were through and ordering him not to come back again.' She swallowed hard. 'Josie looked scared.'

'You think it's possible he's hurt her in the past and could do so again?'

She pressed her hand to her mouth to stop herself crying.

'Josie's smart. She's used to dealing with unstable patients in her job so she'll know what to say and how to act.' Nathan's attempt at reassurance only worked so far.

'I sure hope you're right.'

They said very little for the rest of the drive and eventually the village came into sight.

'Go straight to the Rusty Anchor. Everyone's there.'

Nathan parked as close as he could and they ran hand in hand to the pub. It was still only nine o'clock in the morning but her friends must've prevailed on Pixie to open early.

'There you are.' Evelyn looked relieved. She hurried across the room to greet them and uncharacteristically threw her arms around Melissa. 'I'm so sorry about that ridiculous—'

'It's okay. Don't worry about that now.' The lump in her throat grew to mammoth proportions as she looked around at them all. 'I should've been more honest with y'all in the first place. We'll sort it out later. Right now, let's focus on Josie.'

'Harry Bishop's on the way. He's off-duty so the powers that be can't tell him off as long as he doesn't incite us to commit unlawful acts or something along those lines. He's a good man.' Evelyn wasn't one to throw around compliments lightly, so that was high praise. 'And so are you, Nathan. We're relieved you've brought Melissa back where she belongs.'

Where she belongs. Oh God, she'd lose it any second now.

'It was partly for selfish reasons.' Nathan turned bright red.

'Doesn't matter.'

'Is this the right place for the council of war?' Harry Bishop strode into the pub. Worry was etched into every inch of his face.

'It sure is.' Melissa's voice cracked.

'Don't worry. We'll find her.'

He must trot out the same routine platitude at work every day, but the depth of sincerity in his rumbling Cornish voice took her breath away.

'Is there any coffee going?' Harry asked. 'If I don't mainline a hefty dose of caffeine soon I'll fall asleep.'

'Course there is, my lover.' Pixie beamed at him. 'I'll bring some out.'

Once the drinks were sorted everyone's eyes fell on the detective and he seemed momentarily disconcerted at being put on the spot.

'Right, well, let's start with what we know for certain.' Harry pulled out a fountain pen and battered blue exercise book, the kind Melissa remembered using in school as a child. Those low-tech methods warmed her to him even more. Not that she didn't love the fancy bells and whistles on her computer and phone, and revelled in the wonder of e-readers, but it didn't alter her habit of printing off her authors' manuscripts on paper. The slower, more tactile way of reading enabled her to order her thoughts more clearly. Nathan was the same. Another reason they clicked.

She exchanged a fleeting smile with her lover. Melissa enjoyed that slightly risqué word for their relationship. Boyfriend was too teenage and partner too businesslike. A surge of hope ran through her, knowing that Harry wouldn't rest until he brought Josie back safe.

CHAPTER TWENTY-FOUR

Nathan glanced at the GPS again. 'Are you sure this is the right place?' The dilapidated farmhouse at the end of a bumpy one-lane track appeared abandoned.

'It is according to the land registry information.'

'I hope Harry doesn't get in trouble over all this.'

Melissa had half-jokingly called him too straight-laced for his own good in the pub earlier. Harry had made it clear he couldn't pass on any information to them, but had dropped heavy hints about how best to track down information about people online. As the most computer-literate of the group, Melissa was designated to follow up on his ideas. Now they knew plenty about Dr Christopher Deacon, including his home address and phone number, and the couple of other properties that he owned, including this isolated building. She'd discovered more disturbing facts about him in the process. After his brief marriage to Josie he'd remarried on two other occasions, and one of those ex-wives had accused him of mental cruelty in their divorce case.

'There's no reason why he should. All this information is in the public domain. How we discovered it is no one else's business. We're simply internet savvy.'

'Right.' Nathan sighed. 'How close do you want me to drive?'

'Park over there.' She pointed to a tangle of blackberry bushes almost as tall as she was. 'They'll be heavy with fruit by the end of August so that's only another month. We'll have to come back then and pick some. I've an awesome blackberry cobbler recipe to try out on you.'

'Doesn't all this cloak-and-dagger stuff bother you?' Nathan couldn't help wishing they'd been assigned to one of the tamer tasks, but wouldn't say so out loud for fear she'd laugh at him. Becky and Amy were watching Deacon's classy flat in Mylor overlooking the Fal Estuary. Evelyn was detailed to phone Deacon's parents and pose as a retired doctor trying to get in touch with one of her former medical students.

'He's hardly going to shoot us, is he? This is Cornwall, not Tennessee.' Melissa's eyes sparkled. 'I'm pretty sure you can handle yourself, Professor Kellow, and I'm no pushover.'

One night in bed she'd dropped in a warning about her black belt in karate. As a young woman she'd enjoyed the sport and, although she hadn't done any in years, felt sure she could take anyone down if necessary. Nathan didn't doubt that for one moment.

'Don't slam the car door when you get out.' Melissa warned. 'We don't want him to know we're here until we're ready to show ourselves. The element of surprise is crucial.'

'He's hardly Ronnie Kray.'

'Ronnie who?'

'A London gangster who had an identical twin brother, Reginald. The two of them were infamous back in the late fifties and sixties. They were thugs of the worst sort who acquired celebrity status by somehow mixing with all sorts of well-known people.'

Melissa scrambled out of the car. She crouched down and crept along the gravel path, dodging behind the overgrown grass and bushes whenever she could. Nathan followed along because it was easier than arguing. There were no signs of life and it seemed to him far more likely that Deacon had taken Josie to a decent hotel to talk her round, rather than this hole-in-the-wall.

'Why would he buy this dump in the first place?' Nathan mused. 'From what I've heard about Deacon he doesn't strike me as the type to enjoy hands-on renovations in his spare time.'

'I suppose it's an investment. Don't you know Cornwall is *the* place to live these days?' Melissa scrambled further along and peeked around the far corner of the house. She wore a triumphant smile when she scurried back. 'His fancy sports car's there.' Her gaze fixed back on the building. 'OMG, look. That's got to be Josie.'

Through the smashed windows Nathan caught a flash of something red in the room to the left of the front door.

Melissa whipped out her phone. 'I'm calling Harry.'

'Now? But we don't know it's—'

'I'd recognize her hair anywhere. She dyes it herself and the brighter the better is Josie's motto.'

'If you are right, at least he hasn't buried her in the back garden yet.'

'You're not taking this seriously, are you?' Melissa glared. 'If one of my exes kidnapped me are you going to sit by the fire with your feet up reading a book and not worry about me?'

'Of course not!' he protested. 'I'm concerned we might've overreacted, that's all. We don't know she's been—'

'Do you seriously think she'd come to this dump of her own free will?'

He'd learned to be cautious from his father. Think first. Think again. Then make a considered decision about whether to act. Harold Kellow had courted his future wife for nine years before he proposed, and they were engaged for five long years before finally walking down the aisle.

Nathan back-tracked. 'Sorry, I'm on edge. Ignore me.' He wilted under her searching look. 'Please.'

'Fine.' Melissa texted as she spoke. 'I've sent the signal.'

Privately, he suspected that by the time Harry tracked this place down, whatever was going to happen would've taken place, but he kept his mouth firmly shut.

* * *

Behind her casual banter, Melissa's stomach was in turmoil. If this turned out to be a fool's errand, Josie might be furious with them. But wasn't it better to make idiots of themselves over nothing than her friend ending up hurt, or worse? Nathan hadn't seen the barely suppressed fury in Christopher Deacon's face when she'd interrupted his "talk" with Josie the other day.

'What's the plan? We can hardly knock on the door and claim to be passing by.'

A perfectly valid question and she wished she had a smart answer. 'We'll be completely honest.' Nathan's eyebrows shot up into his hairline. 'Follow my lead.'

'Willingly.'

She debated whether to shout out Josie's name before knocking on the door, to see if anyone would answer. The decision was taken out of her hands when it suddenly opened.

'Well, well, we have visitors. How interesting.' Christopher Deacon's smirk widened. 'I wondered when you would show yourselves. A little word of advice — if you're going into the private detective business I suggest you take a course in spying on people first. At the moment your attempts are laughable.'

'I want to see Josie.'

'Josie? What on earth makes you think she's here? I'm here to check on my property, that's all.'

'We spotted her through the window,' Nathan joined in.

'Really?' The doctor's grating upper-class drawl set Melissa's teeth on edge. 'Ah, you mean you saw a woman with red hair and *assumed* it was Josie.' The corners of his thin mouth twisted. 'Crystal, darling, come and meet some friends of mine.' Deacon's emphasis on the word friends made Melissa want to vomit.

A woman strolled in from a room at the back to join them. The slender, elegant stranger's resemblance to Josie began and ended with her vivid red hair. Her form-fitting, ice-blue linen sheath and designer heels were a million miles from her friend's nursing scrubs or chain-store jeans. Nathan introduced them as if they were invited guests.

'Crystal is an interior designer and I've been showing her my architect's plans for this place and picking her brains. Now you've seen my little retreat is there anything else I can do for you, only we are in rather a hurry? We managed to get dinner reservations at Nathan Outlaw's Michelin-starred New Road restaurant in Port Isaac and I would hate to be late.'

'So where's Josie?' Melissa was tired of pussy-footing around.

'How should I know?' He plucked an invisible thread from the cuff of his immaculate dark navy suit.

Nathan shifted to stand in front of her, making Deacon uncomfortable enough that the doctor took a step back. 'You were seen outside her house yesterday, and walking her to your car in such a way that the witness was concerned for her safety.'

'So why didn't this person call the police?'

There was silence.

'For God's sake, man, don't tell me you've got them involved?' He grabbed Nathan's arm. 'I gave her a lift. That's all. Her car was in for its MOT.'

'But why were you there in the first place?' Melissa jumped back in. 'I heard her telling you never to come near her again.' Suddenly their adversary didn't look quite as confident.

'I stopped by for a quick word. Nothing sinister, I can assure you.'

'So where did she ask you to take her? And don't bother saying to work either because we know she wasn't in uniform.'

'I said I was on my way to the hospital to check on a patient and she asked for a lift to the train station.'

'I'm sure the Truro station's got CCTV so it'll be easy to prove one way or the other,' Nathan interjected.

'She asked me to drop her a little way down the road from the station. What she did then I've no idea.' Deacon shrugged. 'Good luck proving otherwise.'

'So you don't have any objection if we check around outside?'

'Feel free,' he scoffed. 'You won't find her lifeless body stuffed down an old mine shaft or buried in a shallow grave in the woods.' Deacon reached for his companion's hand. 'Let's leave Sherlock and Dr Watson to their investigations.'

They were shooed back outside, but before they could start their search a familiar dark grey saloon swept up the gravel road and screeched to a halt. Harry Bishop leapt out and planted himself in front of the startled doctor.

'If you've harmed Josie, I'll—'

'Good Lord, what is wrong with you people?' Deacon pushed the detective away. 'I'll have you know I play golf with the Chief Constable and he'll be hearing about this outrage.' He gave Melissa and Nathan a dismissive sneer. 'I suppose I can make some sort of excuse for them, but you should know better, Detective Inspector. If you stop this ridiculous nonsense right now I'll consider letting it slide, but if I get one more question or hear another suggestion that I've hurt Josie Hancock in any way you'll be hearing from my solicitor and your career will be toast.'

Nathan gave Harry a quick rundown of what they'd found out, while Deacon glared at his watch.

'I'm extremely sorry to have inconvenienced you, sir,' Harry said through clenched teeth. 'I'm sure you understand that I had to check things out.' He nodded at Melissa and Nathan. 'Please accept my apology if these two got carried away, but it was done out of concern for their friend.'

Deacon managed a condescending nod. 'Of course. I'd hate to think of Josie in any trouble and I do hope you find her soon. Now, you'll have to excuse us.' He steered Crystal away and a short time later they drove off.

The three of them stared at each other and Melissa waited for Harry's inevitable reprimand.

'I'll have to put in an official report about all this, with the conclusion that there's no proof Josie is in any danger. She's a grown woman and presumably had her reasons for wanting to leave.' Harry sounded grim.

'Aren't you at least going to check around the property?' Nathan suggested.

'Do you honestly think there's any point?'

'I suppose not. I'm sorry if we've made things worse. I hope you won't get in trouble because of us?'

'I shouldn't think so. I'm something of a maverick anyway and it's been made perfectly clear I won't rise any higher in the ranks now.' A sardonic smile lifted the corners of Harry's stern mouth. 'I'd hate being chained to a desk anyway. That's one reason Josie and I hit it off. She told me she's turned down promotions several times because she prefers to be hands-on with patients rather than pushing paper.'

'I guess we'd better go on home.'

They climbed into their respective vehicles and Nathan started the car, turned around and drove off without a word.

'Sorry,' she apologized.

'You've nothing to be sorry for.' His hands gripped the steering wheel. 'We both know she would never have gone with that creep voluntarily or let us all worry this way.'

'So what're we going to do?' she asked.

'I don't know yet. But if Harry lets this go, he's not the man I think he is. It's getting late, so why don't we convene another council of war tomorrow morning?'

She berated herself for having allowed the disloyal thought that Nathan was ready to give up to creep in. 'I'm definitely in.'

'I knew you would be.' A smile played around his lips.

CHAPTER TWENTY-FIVE

Crouching under a blackberry bush for the second day in a row wasn't top of the list for how Nathan would choose to spend his Sunday.

'There's no sign of Deacon's car. Let's go.'

He couldn't help thinking that Harry's superiors would be seriously unimpressed at the way the DI was spending his day off. It couldn't be legal to poke around private property without a warrant or the owner's permission. Nathan's question on those same lines had been shot down by Melissa and her gang of would-be detectives in the pub this morning. No one else had discovered anything useful yesterday. It'd struck him as reckless when Tamara suggested they return to the house when Deacon wasn't around, but he'd decided the risk to his own reputation was less than the damage that refusing to go along with the mad plan could do.

They hurried across the scrubby grass towards the house.

'Put these on before we go in.' Harry yanked out three pairs of latex gloves from his pocket and passed them round. 'We'll check the building first then spread out around the grounds.'

Inside, Nathan checked out the kitchen while Melissa did the same in the living areas, and the policeman took the risk of climbing the rickety stairs for a look in the bedrooms. This would've been a worker's cottage once, a simple two-up and two-down structure built from Cornish granite. All Nathan found in the kitchen was a cracked porcelain sink with the remains of a wooden draining board, two free-standing cupboards and a pine table that listed to one side on a broken leg. The footprints in the dusty flagstone floor probably belonged to Deacon and his companion from yesterday.

'Nothing here,' he yelled, and wandered back out to join Melissa. She was scrutinizing every inch of the empty living room as if it might give up more secrets if she persisted.

Harry cautiously made his way back down the stairs and shook his head. 'Outside?'

'Of course.' Melissa's enthusiasm was unwavering, but the detective's face had sunk in deeper lines. Now there were few signs of his earlier optimism.

They split up again, under instructions to check for any obvious disturbance in the grass or earth, or anywhere a person might be hidden. To Nathan this all felt a bit *Midsomer Murders* and unreal. Half an hour later they met back by Harry's car.

'What now?' Melissa's sweaty hair was sticking out in all directions and her clothes were limp and crumpled.

'I don't know.' Harry sounded despondent.

'How about we assume for a moment that Deacon's telling the truth.' They both stared at Nathan as if he'd lost his marbles. 'We've confirmed that he's a slimy creep, but that's not illegal. Perhaps something made Josie desperate enough to beg a lift from her ex to get to Truro in a hurry.'

'You mean she perhaps got some kind of important news? If her car was off the road, why didn't she call me for help?' The detective's frustration bubbled over.

'Because she didn't want you to intervene in a professional capacity?' That earned Nathan a grimace from Harry.

'Maybe it's something to do with Laura?' Melissa suggested tentatively. 'We could head for Newlyn where we spotted her the other day? Either that or track down Barry and see if knows anything.'

'Who are Laura and Barry?' Harry frowned.

'Hasn't Josie mentioned them?'

'Obviously not, or I'd know who they were, wouldn't I?'

'You explain, Melissa.'

By the time she'd finished talking Harry's expression had lightened a few shades.

'Josie's daft sometimes. I wouldn't have tried to interfere officially about all that.' Now he sounded indulgent rather than furious. 'Penworthal is closer so let's go back there and see if this Barry chap is around first.' He jerked his thumb and nodded to the car. 'Hop in.'

Melissa snuggled into Nathan's shoulder. 'Pining for your old boring life, are we?'

'Not a bit.' One day he'd tell her how much he absolutely meant that.

* * *

'So how're we going to handle this?'

Melissa's question made Harry shake his head. '*We* aren't doing anything. I'll be upfront with this Barry Day and tell him I need to get in touch with Josie to follow up on Chloe's stabbing case but can't find her. I might bend the truth slightly and claim that I heard a rumour she might be visiting Laura so could he give me his wife's address.' He fixed his steely gaze on her. 'We've no proof all this mess has anything to do with Josie's disappearance. It's pure speculation on your part.'

Knowing he was right didn't sit easily with her. People frequently mistook her quiet manner for timidity, but underneath the polite veneer Melissa was still her mother's daughter. Sybil Rutherford wasn't a woman to sit back and watch the action taking place in front of her. Nathan squeezed her hand and, when she turned to him, the twinkle of mischief lurking in his bright blue eyes lightened her resentment a fraction. He could read her moods like one of his well-loved, well-thumbed books and had recognized her frustration.

'I'd like you to show me where he lives then make yourselves scarce.'

They were standing outside the pub, so Nathan pointed across to a narrow road running next to the hairdresser's shop.

'That's Wesley Lane and the Days' house is number sixteen. There's a good chance you'll see Barry's white van parked out front, with it being a Sunday.' Nathan shrugged. 'Of course, he's probably at the pub by now. Melissa and I could wander in for a drink and take a look around, if you like?'

Harry looked dubious.

'We wouldn't say anything beyond a normal hello, would we, Melissa?' His tone made it clear she'd better play along or they wouldn't be allowed to do anything.

'Absolutely not. If he's there we'll text you and leave him well alone.'

'Why doesn't that ease my mind?' A resigned sigh slipped out of Harry. 'Fine. Go ahead.'

Before he could burden them with any more restrictions she tugged on Nathan's hand and dragged him towards the pub.

'Remember what he said.'

'Yes, dear. Of course.'

Nathan groaned. 'Oh God, when you turn all sweet and compliant I get worried. I remember Robin . . .' He couldn't meet her eyes. 'Forget that. Let's go.'

'No. Finish what you were going to say first. We've got to stop putting my marriage in a box marked "Do Not Open".' Her heart thudded. For the last couple of months she'd yearned for this confrontation, or at least thought she had. Now they hovered on the verge of it, the certainty drained away.

'It wasn't much, honestly . . .'

Silence. That was the way to make him talk more. She'd discovered that early in their relationship and used it to her advantage several times.

'Fine,' Nathan muttered. 'Robin said you were like a Matryoshka, you know, the Russian nesting dolls?'

'Yeah.'

'He hinted he'd never know the real you because you buried it under all those other versions of Melissa.' His eyes glistened. 'Did you keep them there for a reason with him? I need to know because I don't feel that way about you. Perhaps I'm deluded but I don't find you the least bit hard to understand.' Nathan's mouth curled in amusement. 'Apart from when another weird pithy Southern saying pops out of your mouth which needs translating into the Queen's English.' He chuckled. 'Although I suppose I should call it the King's English now.'

'Let's go to your place. The pub isn't the place for this sort of talk.' She hesitated. 'Or is Chloe at yours? Not that I don't love the girl to death but—'

'You don't want her throwing her two-penn'orth in.'

'Her what?'

'Two pennies worth. It means—'

'We'd say your two cents worth instead.' Melissa grinned. 'And yeah, you're right on that score.'

'She and Toby went to the beach for the day.' He rolled his eyes. 'They told me not to worry if they're not back tonight.'

'But you will anyway.'

Nathan shrugged. 'It's hard not to after what happened. Anyway, forget about Chloe and her love life for now. What about Barry?'

'Damn. I forgot.' Her face burned. 'What sort of friend am I?'

Nathan wrapped his arms around her. 'A loving one, but flawed like the rest of the human race.'

'We'd better poke our heads in first to see if he's there.'

'It's okay. We've waited this long for that talk so a few more minutes . . . or hours . . . won't hurt.'

Won't they? The shallowness Robin had referred to typified their marriage. Whirlwind romances weren't always a success. When she and Nathan did get around to this much-needed conversation, would it damage the memories of his old friend? Change how he felt about her? About them?

'Don't look so worried.' Nathan's gentle smile stirred her as it always did. 'The truth won't alter anything. Let's go and see if Barry is propping up the bar.' He loosened his embrace and reached for her hand. 'If you're a good girl I'll treat you to a sweet sherry.'

Melissa wrinkled her nose. He'd about died laughing once when she'd insisted the old-fashioned drink was nothing more than repackaged cough medicine. 'You sure know how to spoil a lady.'

'I hope so.' A new intensity burned in his eyes. 'Maybe she'll let me prove it?'

'I think she might.'

'That'll suit me for now.'

It would her too.

* * *

Barry's bleary eyes and swaying figure told Nathan he'd been in the Rusty Anchor since opening time. They'd come face to face with Pixie marching him out of the pub. The young landlady swore she was an inch over five feet tall but he suspected that was wishful thinking. It was doubtful she weighed much over seven stone soaking wet either, but despite her petite stature, she had no problem dealing with difficult customers.

'Go back to yours and sleep it off, Barry love,' Pixie said kindly. 'Don't come back 'til tomorrow.'

'Would you like us to walk him home?' Melissa's offer surprised Nathan until he registered the gleam in her eye. She was back in Sherlock mode again. He was definitely the Dr Watson in this relationship. 'We don't mind, do we?' She angled a smile his way.

'Of course not. We'll take care of him, Pixie.' Nathan hitched his arm under Barry's to haul him more upright. This would be a wasted attempt in his view because they'd surely get nothing coherent out of the poor bloke today.

'Cheers. Come back for a drink on the house later.'

'Sure thing.' Melissa waved Pixie away. 'Go see to your customers. We're good.' She grabbed Barry's other arm and they set off across the street, stumbling like kids at a three-legged race on school sports' day.

Outside the house they propped Barry against the wall and Melissa held on to make sure he didn't topple over.

'Where is Harry anyway?' Nathan pulled out his phone to call the detective and saw he'd missed an incoming text. 'Ah, that explains it. He's been called back to the station. Harry wants an update from us but he says not to go to Newlyn or anywhere else searching for Josie today.'

'Spoilsport,' she murmured.

Sensible man, Nathan thought. Luckily Barry was the sort of old-style villager who never locked his door, so they didn't have to search his pockets for a key. They heaved him in over the couple of steps and half-carried, half-walked him into the living room. The detritus strewn around the place was indicative of a man used to having someone pick up after him. Discarded pizza boxes. Greasy fast food wrappers. He avoided looking too closely at the various stains marring the plain beige carpet.

'Laura would have a fit to see this mess.' Melissa shook her head.

'Left me, didn't she,' Barry moaned.

'Have you seen her recently?'

'Nah.' He shook his head then issued a loud moan, slapped his hand over his mouth and was violently sick all over himself and the floor.

'We'll have to clean him up and leave him to sleep it off,' Nathan said.

'Can you get him upstairs?' She glanced around in disgust. 'I wouldn't let a pig sleep here.'

'I should be able to manage it.'

'Oh well, at least this means we've no excuse for not having "that talk".' Melissa's air-quotes made him smile.

He basically dragged Barry up the steep stairs and into the shower, then found a relatively clean pair of sweats and a T-shirt and wrangled him into the bed. Melissa would've insisted on stripping the sheets but he figured they'd been slept in long enough that Barry must be immune to any ill-effects by now. Loud banging noises from downstairs and the low hum of a hoover told him she was making progress in restoring the house to a marginally less germ-ridden state.

Nathan left Barry snoring under the duvet and found Melissa in the kitchen. She was in the middle of washing up what must be a month's worth of dirty dishes. Next thing a tea towel was tossed his way.

'Dry these and then we're out of here.' She levelled a shrewd look at him. 'And don't purposely take your time either.'

Earlier she'd been disconcerted by him understanding her so well, and here she was doing the same. A good or a bad thing? He wasn't sure.

CHAPTER TWENTY-SIX

Nathan wrapped a soft plaid blanket around Melissa's shoulders and eased her back against his chest. It remained to be seen whether Chloe's new sun lounger would bear the weight of them both without collapsing.

The church clock finished chiming midnight.

'So, we've put off talking about your marriage for *another* day.' His voice rumbled in the still night air. The heat of the day dissipated early here, leaving behind a freshness that wouldn't be found in Tennessee until at least October.

'We absolutely needed to eat.' Melissa craned her neck around. 'That spaghetti carbonara you whipped up sure hit the spot.'

'It did indeed.' His fingers stroked her hair. 'I love smelling my shampoo on you.'

She hoped the velvety darkness hid her blush, but that was doubtful because he'd turned on the fairy lights around the patio and they vied with the sprinkling of stars dotting the inky sky. The shower and hair wash were necessities after their leisurely late lunch morphed into a long afternoon nap. Nap? Who was she kidding? Not much sleep occurred, if any. Somehow the evening slipped away from them too, in that lazy Sunday sort of way. They'd polished off an extremely good bottle of chilled Sauvignon Blanc along with another box of her favourite cheese straws while watching *Antiques Roadshow*.

'There are things I want to tell you too,' Nathan said. 'But—'

'You need me to share a few things first.' The effort to inject positivity into her voice took everything she had. 'Marriage first or finances? Actually the two are intertwined, so if you don't object I'll do them together.'

'Sweetheart, it's not so much that *I* need to hear them but *you* need to get them out.' He hesitated. 'At least I think you do. Correct me if I'm wrong and we'll leave it alone.'

She couldn't lie. 'When I met Robin it dazzled me that this handsome, clever, witty man with his to-die-for British accent found me fascinating. I'd spent several years climbing the publishing ladder in New York but outside of work I was lonely. So lonely. I'd even considered chucking in my job and finding something in Nashville nearer my family. When I took Robin home to meet my folks Mom tried to make me see sense and not rush into anything. She didn't *dislike* Robin but . . . she wasn't convinced he was right for me. Daddy was a hell of a lot more forthright and said he'd need to know him a whole lot better before he'd trust him.'

'I must admit I wasn't the only one who was surprised when we heard the renters had left *Gwartha an Dre* and the two of you were moving back in.' Nathan hesitated. 'Don't take this the wrong way, but no one thought Cornwall was exciting enough for Robin any longer. On the few occasions he came back to visit his parents he never stayed long and always seemed relieved when the time came to leave.'

'I'm pretty sure he liked the idea of sweeping back in with his American bride and making his old friends envious.' Melissa nibbled her lower lip. 'The money side of things came into it too.'

'I'd always had the impression he was doing well financially.'

'That's what he wanted everyone to believe. Including me.' The wobble in her voice wouldn't go away. 'But like a house built on sand, when the first rains came it all washed away. Call me naive—'

'I'd never do that.'

'You'd be right though.' Everything flooded back and she fought against crying. She'd already shed far too many tears over how stupid she'd been. 'Early on in our relationship I tried to talk about money but Robin brushed it off. He filled my head with exaggerated stories about his wealth, including the sprawling estate he owned in Cornwall.'

'Sprawling estate?'

'Yeah, but at least he told me the truth about that before we arrived. I suppose he hadn't much choice.' She tried for a smile. 'When he first suggested we come here to live I wasn't totally on board. I wasn't sure about going freelance or how I'd fit in. Our discussions got pretty . . . heated because he repeatedly steamrollered over my concerns. That's when he admitted his credit cards were maxed out and he owed money all over the place.' She swallowed hard. 'He basically said if we didn't take advantage of a free house, he'd be forced to declare bankruptcy.' Conflicting emotions crowded out her lover's smile. 'You don't believe me.'

'Of course I do.' The protest sounded hollow.

'I don't blame you for doubting me. You and Robin grew up together, and let's call a spade a spade — you didn't even like me until a few months ago.'

'That's not true.' Heat flushed his face. 'The bit about not liking you, I mean. The other part you're both right and wrong about. I'm not making much sense, am I?'

'From a literate, articulate man I might've expected something better.' Her feeble attempt at injecting a light note into the difficult conversation fizzled like a damp firework.

'Don't get me wrong, I'm not blind to Robin's faults,' Nathan said. 'He'd always been reckless, but I secretly admired that because I'm inherently so much more cautious.' He shrugged. 'In a way we balanced each other out. You know the way he could light up a room.' Nathan's head drooped.

'God, this is coming out terribly. Can you explain a little more about how he got into so much trouble?'

Melissa didn't blame his reluctance to believe her, but it still stung. 'By living a hugely more extravagant lifestyle than he had the money to support basically.' Cautiously, she touched his arm. 'Are you starting to understand?'

* * *

Nathan was realistic. There were lots of things he wasn't great at, but he'd been on the receiving end of enough dubious explanations from his students about late assignments and the like to recognize a half-truth when he heard one. He suspected that Melissa was muddying the waters out of fear. Fear that he'd put his long-standing loyalty to Robin first, leaving his feelings for her to trail a distant second. 'Yes. So tell me, are you still in financial difficulties now?'

'Would you care to see my bank statements?'

'Don't be like that.' He reached for her hand but she pulled away. He said, gently, 'You initiated this conversation remember?'

'Yeah, I did, didn't I? I'm getting there now. There was no life insurance because Robin stopped paying the premiums, so I've been slowly paying off his debts as and when I can.'

'And the things Vernon Bull told my sister?'

'I'm ashamed to say they were basically true. My card was declined because the minimum payment I made didn't reach them on time.' She shrugged. 'As for the funeral director, I've just paid the final instalment.' Melissa's wry smile wrenched him in two. 'I didn't expect him to broadcast my business around the village, or at least to Mr Bull, which proved to be almost the same thing. I've trimmed my budget right back and am now seeing the light at the end of the tunnel. By the new year I should be totally back on track. You sure find out who your friends are in a case like this, though. When Evelyn and the others fell over themselves to apologize when we came back, I said I was fine with it but—'

'You're not really and I don't blame you.' He grimaced. 'We've all let you down. Robin was my oldest friend but that doesn't blind me to the fact he let you down too.' Nathan's breath caught in his throat. 'Can you forgive me? Any of us?'

'Yeah, because I love y'all and I know I'm at fault too. If I'd been honest in the first place none of this would've happened.' She splayed her trembling hands over her knees. 'There's more. I'm pretty sure you have your suspicions but I've never confirmed them. Our marriage *was* on shaky ground by the time he got sick, and I'm pretty sure it wouldn't have lasted much longer. But once he became ill, nothing else mattered, and afterwards . . . getting through each day was all I could manage.' Tears glistened in her eyes.

'I'm not surprised. I can't begin to imagine how dreadful it was.' Heat zoomed up his neck. 'And I was one of the people who made things worse . . . If it will help, I'll gladly lend you any amount of money you need and you can pay it back when you're able.'

She looked sad. 'I'm not taking your money, Nathan. I can't. Your sister has already marked me down as a gold digger and I doubt she's the only one. Handsome, single, solvent. You've got it all.'

'I do now, but that's only because I love a certain beautiful American lady and she loves me back. Before that it was all nothing. Empty.' He turned thoughtful. 'Funny how life turns out, isn't it? In the space of a few months I've acquired a lover and a lodger. I'm not sure I'll get rid of Chloe anytime soon either. She's considering enrolling in Truro College to see how it goes but wants to hold onto her job in the shop too. My dramatic niece loves having something to complain about and gets a kick out of stirring things up with the customers. Surprisingly, she's even talked Vernon into making a few changes that are apparently bringing in more business.'

Melissa laughed. 'I couldn't wrap my head around the miserly Mr Bull offering a free piece of fruit to any children in the shop with an adult. And there's a wider selection of toiletries, including make-up. I bet those are Chloe's doing.'

'They are indeed. Vernon's falling over himself to keep Chloe around because his wife's told him she's done with working all hours and if he doesn't get permanent help she's off to live with her sister in Wales.'

'That obviously put the frighteners on him. I do like Chloe.'

'Me too.' Nathan stroked her silky hair. 'Time for bed?'

'You sound like a tired father doing his best to persuade a fractious toddler to stop playing.' She stifled a yawn. 'Okay, you win.'

He expected conditions to come along with her swift concession, and remained suspicious long after they were tucked up in his bed under the faded rose-pink bedspread.

CHAPTER TWENTY-SEVEN

'Still nothing from Harry.' Melissa glared at her phone as if that would stir it into action. 'Or Josie.'

Nathan peered over the rim of his tortoiseshell-framed glasses. He'd been self-conscious of wearing them ever since Melissa had pointed out how unbearably sexy they made him in her eyes, completing the whole rumpled professor look. 'Are you glued to work today?'

She'd distracted herself for the last couple of days by starting the first-round edits for a debut author she'd taken on, a laborious process but extremely satisfying. Last night she'd stayed up late trying to sort out a particularly knotty problem with the manuscript. She'd been so in the zone that she only stopped when her head drooped over the computer. 'I ought to be but my brain's kinda fried. Why?'

'How about another research day out? You've got *The Shell Seekers* at book club next month in September, right?'

'Yeah, but I haven't finished reading it yet. Work's been a bit manic plus I couldn't resist racing through the rest of the Janie Bolitho books. My excuse is that I looked on those as background for next week's discussion of August's book, *Snapped in Cornwall*.'

'It won't matter.' He leaned back in the chair and took off his glasses, dangling them from one finger. 'When they adapted the Rosamunde Pilcher book for television, they filmed a lot around Cornwall. A couple of the locations are in the far west of the county.'

Melissa guessed she was supposed to read something into that but was too tired for subtlety. 'And your point is?'

'St Michael's Mount and Lamorna are only a few miles from Newlyn.'

The penny dropped. 'You devious man, Dr Kellow!'

'DCI Harry Bishop can't stop us from doing a little sightseeing, can he?' His face was suffused with mischief.

'In your pretty car?' It was a running joke with them that she fancied his car almost as much as she did its owner.

'Your wish is my command.'

'I'll jump in the shower first and then you can have a turn.' The disappointed expression he fixed on her made her laugh. 'Yeah, I know I'm a spoilsport, but we'll never make it out of the house on our mission if you join me.' She turned away before he picked up on the emotions flooding through her. It saddened her that only Robin's untimely death had given them this gift.

'You're not the only one struggling with guilt.' Nathan's raspy voice stopped her at the bottom of the stairs. 'It doesn't always sit easy with me, being here in my best friend's house, going to his bed with his wife, and on my worst days feeling . . . relieved he's not around.'

Melissa knew he needed to hear that she felt the same way, but couldn't make herself say the words. In the deafening silence she watched disappointment flit across his face. With a sharp nod she ran off upstairs and only allowed the tears to flow once she was in the sanctuary of the pulsing shower.

* * *

While he drove, Nathan kept up a running commentary about where they were going and what he knew about *The*

Shell Seekers, all to the background of their favourite Classic FM radio station. It was either that or tackle the elephant in the room, which she was clearly avoiding. If she had commiserated with him earlier and admitted to having the same guilty feelings about their relationship, it would've lessened his own unease.

'I know you've been to St Michael's Mount before so I suggest we just drive through Penzance to look over at it on our way to Lamorna. I did check online and there's a day tour you can take around several of the locations connected with Rosamunde Pilcher, but I promise I'll be cheaper.'

'If the price is a damn sight more honesty from me, I'm not sure it will be.' Irony laced her words. 'I can't believe this gorgeous weather. Y'all are so lucky and don't realize it half the time.'

Nathan rested his elbow on the open window and inhaled deep breaths of the soft salty air while the welcome breeze cooled his face. 'I do. I've travelled enough to appreciate it.'

'Oh, wow, there it is!' She pointed to an island of jagged rock not far off the shore with a small castle perched on top. 'I still remember the first time I saw it on a grey day, rising up out of the mist.'

'Never gets old, does it?' A trickle of envy that he hadn't been the one to take her on that initial visit dimmed the moment. 'The road to Lamorna goes through Newlyn so we could stop there for lunch if you like?'

'Yeah, that'd be good. Do you really think—'

'I don't know but it's worth a try.' Anticipating each other's sentences came naturally these days.

Fifteen minutes later they were fortunate enough to snag a parking space close to the harbour. It was the first of August today so the first full week of the school holidays, which meant there were a lot more people milling around than on their last visit. That could be seen as a plus or a minus, because the two of them wouldn't stand out as much but neither would their quarries. Over succulent crab sandwiches, made with the morning's fresh catch, and glasses of crisp pear cider in a shady pub garden they debated the best way to track down Laura, and possibly Josie too.

'I reckon Laura must be working somewhere because she must need the money. Barry's hardly going to be shelling out, is he? Newlyn isn't exactly New York, so we can easily cover it on foot and ask after her in all the shops and eating places.'

'I suppose.'

'Try not to be too enthusiastic.' She shook her head. 'Let's hurry up and go back out. If we split up we'll get through quicker.'

Nathan thought she sounded like a Sergeant Major ordering recruits on the parade ground and considered saluting. He trudged off in his allotted direction and tried to push away memories of their recent fruitless search around Christopher Deacon's derelict property. For a moment he thought he spotted Josie's vibrant red hair across the road, but thankfully realized he'd made a mistake before accosting a stranger. His optimism was waning when he decided to take a break and join a queue in one of the ice-cream shops.

'I should've known you pair wouldn't listen to sense.'

He stopped studying a chalkboard with the flavour choices on offer and turned around to meet Harry Bishop's sharp blue eyes.

'Don't bother spinning me a yarn about being out sightseeing either. This one's already tried it.' The detective pulled Melissa forward and her red face matched Nathan's own. 'She trotted out the whole innocent "we're tracking down book locations and only stopped here for lunch" rigmarole.'

There was little point in arguing.

'We might as well join forces,' Melissa suggested. 'Forces. Get it?' She laughed at her own joke but Harry's stern features didn't crack. 'I've asked all over the place but with no luck so far.' She sighed. 'An ice cream might help make the little grey cells work harder.'

'Melissa? Nathan?' Laura gaped over at them from behind the counter. A clean white overall with the shop name embroidered on the front was stretched over her baby bump and she wore her blonde hair scraped back in a tight ponytail. 'I've done nothing wrong!' she yelled at Harry. 'Did Barry send you after me?' The colour left her round freckled face. 'I thought the police didn't—'

'They don't. I'm not here officially.' Harry shifted from one foot to the other. 'Are you able to take a break and come talk to us?'

'I suppose.' Laura sounded less than thrilled but turned to mutter something to the only other employee, an older grey-haired lady. 'I'll meet you outside.' She patted her stomach. 'Loo first. One of the penalties.'

They left without buying any ice creams and made their way across the road to lean against the harbour wall. Nathan wasn't sure what size can of worms they'd opened but there was no closing it back up now.

* * *

'So what're you all doing here if you're not trying to drag me back to Barry?' Laura joined them, her arms folded protectively over her stomach.

Everyone's gaze landed on Melissa. Somehow, she'd become the unelected spokesperson. She explained as well as she could but her friend said nothing, turning away to stare out to sea. Around them the usual noisy seagulls swooped, intent on snatching food from unsuspecting tourists.

'Have you seen Josie?' Harry asked. 'All we want to know is that she's safe.' His voice turned gruff. 'I'm worried about her. I care . . . a lot.'

'I haven't *seen* her.' The emphasis on the word "seen" made the back of Melissa's neck prickle.

'But she has been in touch sometime since Saturday?'

Laura avoided eye contact.

'Our main problem is we don't know whether Josie's ex was lying about dropping her off in Truro. We really need your help.'

'She swore me to secrecy. I don't know how she did it but Josie tracked me down here and—'

'I'm sorry, that was our fault,' Melissa admitted. 'Nathan and I spotted you when we were here a few weeks ago.' She whipped out her phone and found the covert picture she'd taken. 'I showed the other girls too.'

Laura's hand flew to her mouth. 'Oh God, please tell me Barry hasn't seen this? He'll kill me. And with Jake. It's not what it looks like. Not exactly.' Her head drooped. 'I suppose you all hate me?'

'Hate you? Don't be an idiot. I suppose we were more . . . disappointed. We would've understood if you'd shared what was going on.' She didn't know what her friend meant by the picture not being what it seemed because there didn't seem much room for confusion. It was a struggle but she tried to give Laura the benefit of the doubt.

'Would you really? I doubt that.' That sad sense of resignation tugged at Melissa's conscience. After all, she'd hidden her own financial struggles and the truth about her crumbling marriage from the same friends. 'Barry's a good man, but I can't see a way for us to ever be together again. Not now.' She twiddled with the ends of her ponytail.

'But that's what you'd want if it was possible?'

'I fell in love with Barry when I was sixteen and he'll always be the only one for me.' Tears trickled down her blotchy cheeks.

'Then you need to tell him that,' Nathan urged.

'It's not that simple.'

Melissa hugged her friend. 'I know.' She slid a "back-off" look Nathan's way. Coming down hard on Laura wouldn't help. 'What time do you finish work?' She'd noticed her friend sneaking anxious glances at her watch.

'Not until six.'

'How about if we come back then and treat you to a meal? That way we can have a proper catch-up?'

'Well, okay.'

'Great idea,' Nathan chimed in. 'We're off to do some more sightseeing so we'll leave you to get back to work.' He clapped Harry's shoulder. 'Come on, mate, you can join us for a paddle at Lamorna Cove.' The morose detective looked less than thrilled.

Laura eased herself away from the wall, one hand sliding down to rub the small of her back, then lumbered across the road.

'Yeah, I know we could've pressed and maybe got something out of her but it wouldn't be fair. There's a Southern expression about catching more flies with honey than vinegar.'

'I hope you're right.' Harry shrugged. 'We'll go to the beach, if that's what you had planned. Good thing I wore shorts.' His resting expression was naturally severe but a smile broke, taking years off him. 'My car is—'

'If you don't object we'll go in mine.' Nathan smirked at Melissa. 'It's part of the package deal today to please a certain American.'

Blushing was juvenile at her age but there was no stopping it and Harry's curiosity made it worse. His expected questions didn't come, however, but somewhere in the recesses of her mind she knew she was about to fall for a clever trick. The police wrangled out a lot of their confessions because criminals, like a large proportion of the human race, couldn't tolerate a vacuum. 'Yeah, Nathan's car is the attraction, all right. I mean, what else could there be to keep me interested?' From the corner of her eye she caught Harry's satisfied smile. 'Let's get a move on so I can follow in Penelope Keeling's footsteps.' Harry looked puzzled again. 'She's the main protagonist in *The Shell Seekers*, our book club choice for September. She's in her sixties and looking back over her life, but also talks about the present time and her relationships with her adult children. Penelope's father was an artist in this part of Cornwall around the time of the Second World War. Lamorna, and Newlyn itself, became famous for the school of painters who lived and worked there around the turn of the twentieth century.' Melissa heard Nathan smothering a laugh. 'Sorry, the professorial habit must be catching.'

'You're a breath of fresh air after a lousy week. I see now why you and Josie hit it off. She lifts my spirits too, the same way.' His face sank in deep lines. 'If any of the blame for her disappearance lands on me I'll never forgive myself.'

'I can't see any reason why it should. Do you?' Melissa was afraid of the answer.

CHAPTER TWENTY-EIGHT

Nathan popped a hot chip in his mouth. Over-salted and over-vinegared, according to Melissa's taste buds. He'd argued there was no such thing. The impromptu picnic was Laura's idea because she'd been stuck inside all day. To keep her sweet they bought fish and chips, piled into the car and drove a little way out of the village to park on a craggy headland overlooking the silvery blue sea.

Nathan was still mulling over Harry's revelation that Josie had got a little "freaked out" — his exact words — when he sprang it on her that he'd booked a weekend trip to the Scilly Isles for them.

'Josie told me several times she's heard people say how beautiful they are, especially the gardens, and would really enjoy going one day. I assumed she'd love that I'd paid attention and planned it for us.'

Nathan had sympathized with the poor man, while Melissa saw it from a different point of view. She'd explained to them that Josie's ex-husband had a habit of doing similar things, using them as a way of controlling her and their life together.

'So was Lamorna Cove crowded?' Laura started to pull the crispy batter off her fish. 'It gives me heartburn,' she explained.

'Oh, right. No, it was quiet.'

'I did discover you've got to be pretty determined to find it.' Melissa chuckled. The only way to reach the tiny unspoiled harbour was by a narrow road that meandered through some shaded woods. Apart from a small car park and a café there was nothing else to attract visitors apart from the view. 'But it was sure worth it though. Most places around here are. The cove is stunning and so peaceful. Well, it was until these two had a stone-skimming competition like a pair of little kids.' She rolled her eyes at Nathan and Harry.

Laura gave a weak smile. 'I've been thinking all afternoon about how much I should or shouldn't say about Josie.' She'd eaten very little and wrapped up the remains of her meal. 'I'm not adding anything to the little I told you earlier.'

Nathan saw his own disappointment mirrored in the others' faces.

'All you need to know is that she's okay. Josie's a grown woman and when she's ready to get back in touch she will.'

'Is she going to make us wait months like you've done to Barry?' Melissa's bluntness made Nathan wince. 'Do you know what I reckon? You *want* him to find you, and my guess is that Josie feels the same about Harry.'

'How would I know what she wants?' A deep flush stained Laura's cheeks. 'We're mates, yeah, but not that close.'

'And you?'

'I dunno. Josie offered to go back to Penworthal with me to pick up a few things. I s'ppose she thought if Barry saw me, he might . . .' Her shoulders drooped. 'It's more likely he'd throw me out on my ear and that'd be that.'

'If I were in Barry's situation I'd want to hear what you had to say and talk it through.' Harry tossed a chip at the seagull who'd been lurking near them on the grass since they arrived. 'If you love someone you don't stop just like that.' He clicked his fingers. 'I'm pretty sure Josie will contact you again to see if you want her help. When she does, could you make sure to point out to her that I'm not Dr Christopher Deacon. I'd *never* make her do anything she didn't want.' A faint smile lifted one corner of his mouth. 'Tell her I'll be on the ferry from Penzance to St Mary's next Friday — Ninth of August — and I'll have a spare ticket if she's interested in joining me.' He screwed up the remains of his food and levered back up onto his feet to wander over and toss the greasy package in the bin. 'I'm ready to go pick up my car, if that's all right?'

'Of course.' Nathan followed Harry's example and ditched the rest of his food. 'We can give you a lift to where you're living, Laura, if you'd like?'

'No thanks, down by the harbour again is fine.'

Melissa shrugged behind her friend's back. They obviously weren't trusted not to go running back to Barry and tell him where to find his errant wife. Since his own personal life had become more complicated, Nathan was more in tune with other people's. Until Chloe and Melissa both pointed it out, he'd been unaware of his long-time habit of keeping an emotional distance between himself and other people. The barriers were down now. It would be only too easy for the three of them — including a detective inspector, for God's sake — to discover Laura's address, but going against her wishes would be wrong.

They piled back into the car and when they reached the harbour Laura couldn't wait to clamber out, say a brief goodbye and disappear in the direction of the ice-cream shop.

'Well, that's been a dead loss all around.' Melissa's lips pinched together.

'I wouldn't say so.' Harry's satisfied tone surprised Nathan. 'I'm relieved to hear that Josie's okay. She'll be back. As for Laura, I'm pretty sure the other man isn't in the picture any longer — if he ever really was.'

'What're you getting at? We saw them all loved-up, didn't we, Nathan?'

'I guess we'll have to have a little faith in Laura's explanation.' His cautious response made Melissa roll her eyes.

'I'll let you know if Josie gets in touch,' Harry promised. 'You can stop playing amateur detectives now.'

Melissa glowered at Nathan when he fervently agreed with Harry. It was clear she wanted the search for Josie to continue. Once they were alone he'd need to say something, but her tight expression told him it'd better be the right words this time.

* * *

Anger trumped guilt in Melissa's head right now so the apology she should rightfully make remained stuck in her throat.

'I'm sorry, love, but you can choose to stay mad or not, it's up to you. We can't force Laura to bare her soul to us, and Harry has accepted he needs to back off tracking down Josie.' He mitigated it with a tentative smile. 'Do you want to head back to Penworthal and report to the rest of the girls?'

She managed to nod, torn between disagreeing for the sake of stubbornness and desperate to discover what her friends made of the day's curious happenings. Nathan's lips twitched with amusement but she did her best to ignore him. Silently reaching for her seatbelt, she was relieved when he took the hint and followed her lead.

On the drive home she sensed them both fighting not to laugh. They were hopeless at being mad with each other. Robin had been an expert at holding grudges and she didn't miss that one bit.

'If you grip the door handle any tighter you'll wrench it off.'

Melissa loosened her left hand and shook out her fingers. Every time she thought about Robin and the way they'd been together it made her tense.

'Your place or mine?' He turned off at the signpost for the village. 'Or do you want to convene a meeting at the pub?'

'Pub,' she said decisively. After tapping in a group message, she hit send.

'We've done our best.'

'Yeah, I know.' Her phone pinged with replies, making her smile. 'We're on.'

'Do you want me to drop you off and disappear?'

She was torn.

'I won't be offended.' Nathan's even temper and calm disposition were yet more things to love about him. 'Do you want to come over to my place when you're through?'

'Sure. That's a date.'

'Chloe's off with Toby. Another beach party.' He rolled his eyes. 'I wish I had half her energy.'

Melissa ran her fingers along his leg and stroked the hair-roughened skin exposed by his shorts. 'Save yours for better endeavours.'

'Willingly.'

'In fact, if we go to my place instead, I've got something you might like to see. Did I mention I found a brand-new set of gorgeous lingerie in one of the charity shops in Bodmin last week? I'm guessing it was an unwanted present.'

'You know you didn't.' The mock-complaint made her laugh.

'Wanna take a guess?'

'Red lace? White silk?' he growled.

'Turquoise satin. Very little of it though, considering what it must've cost originally.'

'Worth every penny, I'm sure.' Nathan cleared his throat. 'I'll pull in outside the pub and let you out. But I'm not going to be a gentleman tonight and offer to walk you to the door. I'd embarrass us both.' His gaze dropped to the visible evidence of their teasing conversation.

'Good plan.'

'You're a cruel woman sometimes. Out you get. Go make fun of me to your girlfriends.'

'I'd never do that.'

'I know. Don't look so serious.' He rubbed a warm thumb down her cheek. 'I was joking.'

'I knew that, but still . . .'

'Oh Melissa, what am I going to do with you?' Nathan leaned across to kiss her and the fleeting taste of him left her craving so much more. 'That'll have to do for now. Off you go.'

'Giving me something to think about, were you?'

'Always.' He shooed her away. 'Go, before I lose the self-control to be Mr Nice Guy.'

With a wicked laugh, she threw open the car door and leapt out. She spotted Evelyn and Amy strolling towards her and ran off to join them.

Half an hour later she glanced around their silent gathering and sighed. Even the generous inroads they'd made into Pixie's two-for-one cocktail specials hadn't dented the collective air of gloom.

'I used to think we shared everything important.' Becky sounded wistful. 'How wrong was that?'

Evelyn picked up her glass of vibrant Tequila Sunrise and took a large gulp. Once she'd heard the first sketchy details of Melissa's day their de-facto leader had abandoned her usual modest half of shandy and declared her need for something stronger.

'I've no right to criticize either of them though, do I?' Melissa took the plunge. 'I've lied through my teeth to y'all over and over. I didn't do it on purpose but I did it all the same.'

'Why?' Amy's blunt question made her sit up straighter. 'No one's marriage is perfect. We wouldn't have thought any less of you.'

'I suppose like lots of folk I hoped it'd get better and we'd be okay. Then when Robin got sick it would've seemed disloyal.' She bit back a sob. 'And trashing him — us — after he died was worse.'

'What about your money problems? What's the excuse there? The same, I suppose?'

A trickle of irritation ran through her. 'I was all set to tell you everything tonight but I'm not so sure now.'

'Girls, let's be careful what we're saying.' Evelyn set her drink back down. 'Tempers are running high and words can hurt. They're not easily forgotten.'

Melissa had had a myriad of discussions with Nathan along the same lines, often involving literature, but many other times about regular everyday life. Words had tripped them up on more than one occasion. 'I didn't share my financial difficulties for the same reason most of us keep secrets — I was embarrassed. Embarrassed, and convinced that I could sort it all out on my own without anyone else needing to know.' She hung her head. 'Even my best friends.'

'Perhaps we can all learn a lesson from this.'

Melissa grinned. 'You'll always be a teacher, won't you, Evelyn?'

'I can't help it. Sorry.' Her friend didn't sound the least apologetic.

'In case you're still worried, I'm almost out of the woods with Robin's debts. I'll still need to be super-careful how much I spend for a while longer, but that's no bad thing.' She angled a sharp look in Amy's direction. 'I've never taken a penny from Nathan either.'

'No one thought that, dear girl.' Evelyn threw a quelling look around the group as if daring them to argue.

'Yeah, they did.' Melissa was done with waffling. 'That disappointed me but I guess at the end of the day y'all don't know me like you know each other.' She let that hang. Hopefully it would sink in that Josie and Laura had belonged to the group from day one and see how that'd worked out. Amy turned pale but kept her arms folded and chin tilted in the air.

'Time isn't always a critical factor in these things, is it though?' Evelyn probed. 'Love is the same. It can take years to develop or spring up overnight.'

'I still think it sucks,' Tamara declared, 'And if Laura and Josie were here now they'd get a piece of my mind.'

'Why don't you go right ahead and spit it out then?' Josie's scathing voice rang out. The whole pub fell silent.

Melissa choked on her martini. Tamara turned the same bright pink as her Cosmopolitan cocktail. Amy, Evelyn and Becky, who'd had their backs to the door, swivelled around in unison.

They'd spent the last hour pulling Josie and Laura apart, because everyone was hurt by how they'd both deceived their close-knit group. Now those same two friends stood there, arm in arm.

CHAPTER TWENTY-NINE

The toast was snatched out of Nathan's hand before he could take a bite.

'I'm starved, Uncle Nat. Don't suppose there's any bacon?' Chloe pleaded. 'Oh, hi, Melissa. Sorry to interrupt.' She nudged his arm. 'At least you're both dressed. I suppose I should've knocked. You might've been—'

'But we weren't.' The stern professor tone failed on his niece who blithely carried on chattering about a sick party she'd been to. Luckily, he was up to date enough to realize that was a good thing instead of assuming everyone was unwell, although no doubt a few suffered ill-effects from whatever they'd ingested. 'We're in the middle of having breakfast like normal people on a Friday morning when they don't have to hurry off to work. Talking about work—'

'I've plenty of time for a quick shower before I slip back into my elegant overall and turn up for my shift at the coal face.' She wrinkled her nose. 'Needs must if I'm going to stay solvent. Mummy's cut off my allowance.'

He couldn't hide his shock. Everyone knew Catherine was less than pleased with her daughter's decision not to go back to Oxford, but he hadn't expected her to go this far.

'Don't worry, Daddy sneaks me some behind her back and I've discovered the joy of trawling the charity shops for cool clothes.' Chloe peered at Melissa. 'You look wrecked.'

'Thanks. I'm a bit tired, that's all.'

'What's wrong?' She tossed Nathan a stern look. 'Has Uncle Nat done something to upset you?'

'No! He's been wonderful . . .' Melissa's face crumpled and tears inched down her face. She'd been like this since last night, leaving Nathan as drained as her. By now he'd heard every excruciating detail about Josie and Laura's unexpected appearance and the ensuing argument.

'Is it . . . you know, like . . . the menopause?' Chloe pulled out a chair and sat down.

A strangled laugh burst out of Melissa. 'I realize at almost forty I'm ancient compared to you, and some women do experience an early change of life, but I'm not one of them. Me and my girlfriends had a bit of a frank exchange of words last night and it's kinda upset me.'

An understatement, if ever Nathan heard one. She'd been a blubbering mess when she'd returned from the pub, and between brief snatches of sleep it'd continued all night. Typically, Melissa heaped most of the blame on herself. He'd attempted to point out that she was one of seven people involved, but that was swept aside as if he hadn't spoken.

'Wow! I thought you lot were tight.'

'Yeah, we did too. Guess we were wrong.'

'I've had run-ins with my besties before. It either blows over or the relationship's run its course. That's life.'

Nathan didn't expect Chloe's philosophy to go down well but Melissa simply went quiet instead of disputing his niece's blithe assertion. She plucked another tissue from the box and blew her nose.

'Tell me everything,' Chloe urged. 'If you want to.'

Nathan suspected his niece would regret asking. He leaned back and listened patiently to another recitation of the whole sorry mess. Apparently, after they left Newlyn yesterday, Josie had contacted Laura again and talked her into joining her so they could both confront their demons. Instead of the support they'd taken for granted from their old friends, they'd been shocked to walk into an unexpected ambush. Everyone had turned defensive and the end result wasn't pretty. Unless a miracle happened, the August book club meeting in a few days would be short a couple of members and a dismal gathering.

'So what's the skinny on Laura's baby?' Chloe leaned closer. 'Did she tell you more about the guy in the picture?'

'Nope.'

'She can't expect much in the way of sisterly solidarity then, can she?'

'Maybe not.'

Chloe looked wary. 'And Josie? Has she still got a bee in her bonnet over that yummy cop being all nice and whatever?'

Phrased that way it sounded irrational, but his niece wasn't mature enough to see past the obvious.

'I get you're trying to help, and I appreciate it, but there's not much you can do,' Melissa said. 'You'd better hurry up and go to work because — to paraphrase Chaucer — baked beans and jam tarts wait for no man.' Chloe looked baffled. 'You've heard the old saying — time and tide wait for no man?' Nathan joined in laughing when Melissa burst into giggles but Chloe stared at them both as if they were lunatics. Not everyone appreciated their literary jokes. One day she'd admitted that Robin had ordered her to stop doing it around him because other people would label them as pretentious. Nathan hadn't said so but he suspected his old friend was too proud to admit he didn't understand half of his wife's bookish references.

'Fine.' Chloe dragged back up on her feet. 'I know when I'm not wanted.'

Neither of them rushed to contradict her and, once she'd gone, Nathan reached for the teapot and topped up their cups.

'So, what's on the agenda today? I'm almost afraid to ask.'

* * *

Melissa knew she should crack a joke about seeing what other absent friends needed tracking down, but she couldn't force one through her tear-swollen throat. She'd had more than her fair share of miserable times over the last few years, but last night had sneaked a place in the top ten. What hit her hardest was seeing Josie hook her arm through Laura's and the two walking off together.

'I've got work to do so I should go home.' Nathan's eyes didn't hide disappointment well, but she steeled herself against giving in. 'I could cook tonight, if you like?'

'I'm pretty ragged.' She dredged up a weak smile. 'If even Chloe says I'm looking old and haggard, that's a big clue written in bright lights. I could probably do with a night alone to catch up on my sleep. We both know I won't get a lot of that if I'm with you. Don't take that as a complaint either, but you know I'm right.'

'Fair enough.'

Sometimes his reasonableness irked her. What would it take to stir Nathan enough to make him blow his top? Now she *was* being ridiculous. How many times had she longed for Robin to be more even-tempered?

'Are you going to tell Harry about Josie and Laura turning up?'

'Yeah, I think so. The whole thing happened in a public place — very public — so I'm not breaking any confidences.'

'You don't have to do this alone, love.'

'Yeah, I know, but—'

'But nothing. I totally appreciate you need to work but don't push me away. I could still help with the other stuff.'

'I'm not!' A rush of heat raced up her neck. 'Well, maybe I am, but I don't mean to.' The mellow notes of Elgar's "Enigma Variations" started to play and she stared around, looking in vain for her phone.

'Is this what you're looking for?' Nathan swiped the mobile from behind the jar of marmalade and passed it across the table.

'Thanks.' She grimaced at the screen. 'Oh heck, it's Harry. I bet he's heard already.' She took a steadying breath before answering. 'Hiya, I was just going to—'

'I need you both at the Days' house. Now.'

'Why?' Melissa listened with a sinking heart. 'We'll be right there.' The call ended and she stared at Nathan, too choked up to speak.

'What's wrong?'

'It seems Josie engineered a meeting between Laura and Barry but it's gone pear-shaped and he won't let them out of the house.' The lump grew in her throat. 'Josie managed to call Harry, but when the police turned up Barry came to the door and waved a carving knife around.' Tears blurred her eyes. 'Josie always has to damn well try to fix things. She couldn't leave it alone.'

'I'll go and get some shoes on.'

After he left the kitchen, Melissa allowed the peacefulness of his house to work its usual magic. Chloe frequently derided Nathan's house as old-fashioned and complained that it needed major renovation because she was too young to appreciate its Victorian charm. True, the bathroom was out of the ark and the kitchen appliances needed upgrading, but with those things fixed and the whole place given a fresh lick of paint it would be close to perfect in her eyes. The problem was that *Gwartha an Dre* was equally lovely. A sliver of amusement snaked into her stressed-out brain. Their houses only became an issue if their relationship gained a level of permanence, and it was too early to think along those lines. Evelyn's words flew back.

'Time isn't always a critical factor in these things, is it though? Love is the same. It can take years to develop or spring up overnight.'

It shamed her to admit, even if only to herself, that the first kernel of her love for Nathan took root during her marriage. Was this their right time now? How could she trust her decision-making skills after she'd rushed into a whirlwind romance with Robin that had foundered at the first obstacles?

'Right.' Nathan reappeared in the doorway and fixed his worried gaze on her. 'I'd ask if you're okay but that'd be daft. You look—'

'Worse than I did before? Don't fret, it's a conversation for another day.' Melissa stood up. 'Come on. I promise it's okay. Trust me.'

'I do.'

Those two simple words — spoken quietly and with such sincerity — stopped her halfway across the room. Only the touch of Nathan's warm hand on her arm brought her back to earth and gave her the impetus to keep walking.

'I've told Chloe what's going on and she'll lock up when she leaves for work.'

She managed to nod and they hurried outside in time to see a police car with lights flashing and siren blaring rush past. 'Oh, Nathan.'

'Josie's wily. She'll know how to handle Barry.'

'I hope you're right.'

'It's your turn to trust me now.'

'I do,' she whispered. The significance of the moment resonated with them both and she reached for Nathan's comforting warm hand.

CHAPTER THIRTY

The fake optimism he put on for Melissa's sake sprang from wanting to make her feel better. Sad to say, the last time he saw Barry Day was in the pub a few days ago, when Laura's husband had been a sorry sight — grey-faced and rumpled, propping up the bar and moaning about his dismal life. A man who'd lost everything he cared about. Not a good omen.

Melissa ground to a halt as they turned the corner into Wesley Lane.

'I don't believe it. The media is here.' She jabbed a finger at a silver van with the logo of one of the local TV stations emblazoned on the side. Nathan recognized the smartly dressed blonde brandishing a microphone from the midday report.

'Slow news day.' His laconic response made her glare. 'Sorry. I don't mean to be heartless.'

'You'd never deliberately be that. I get it. You're worried too but falling back on the old stiff-upper-lip Brit thing out of habit.'

He didn't contradict her.

They stood at the back of a growing crowd being held at bay by a police cordon. Over people's heads Nathan spotted Harry's thatch of salt and pepper hair.

'I can't see anything.' Melissa raised up on tiptoe but couldn't hold the position for long and flopped down with a puff of annoyance.

He whipped out his phone and sent a quick text. 'I've let Harry know we're here.'

'What's happening now?' Chloe wriggled in next to them. 'Mr Bull's sent me to get an update. He's rubbing his hands with glee at the extra customers coming in.'

'He would.' Melissa rolled her eyes. 'If he'd lived in Paris during the French Revolution, he'd have been one of the ghouls sitting around the guillotine for the best view.'

'We don't know any more than you, we've only just arrived.' Nathan kept one eye on his phone but it remained frustratingly quiet.

'They say he's got a knife.' Chloe paled under her golden tan. This must bring back harrowing memories of her own ordeal. She'd laughed it off when the doctors and the police suggested counselling, but on several occasions when his niece thought no one was looking he caught her frowning and rubbing at her stomach. It couldn't help her recovery to know that the police had made very little progress so far in catching the culprit.

'Yeah, but I expect Barry's trying to be a bit macho and look threatening,' Melissa said.

Nathan didn't necessarily agree with her blithe statement but she caught his eye and nodded, giving him a clear hint to play this down.

'She's absolutely right, Chloe. This is Barry we're talking about. He's a quiet, gentle man who loves his wife and would never harm her or anyone else.'

'I hope you're right.'

Clearly he hadn't convinced her, so maybe he'd better not take up acting again anytime soon. The thought horrified him. His one and only stage appearance had been as a street sweeper in a school production of *My Fair Lady*. He'd tripped over the lead actor who fell into a line of chorus dancers, making them topple like dominoes. Nathan was only there in the first place because Robin had talked him into joining the drama group so they could hang around the young, blonde, big-breasted drama teacher — Hayley Porter, a name that had inspired many an erotic teenage dream. Years later he and Robin had smiled over their pints when they read a newspaper announcement of Hayley's marriage to another female teacher.

'Uh, Professor Kellow, sir?' A red-faced young police officer touched Nathan's arm. 'DI Greene wants you to come with me.'

'Me?'

Melissa shrugged her own confusion back at him.

'The suspect is asking for you.'

If he repeated his question the officer would think he was a penny short of a shilling. His father used that old-fashioned phrase donkey's years ago. He doubted this officer had even heard of the pre-decimal currency.

'Well, go on,' Melissa urged.

Both women stared at him as if to say, why are you still here? He could hardly admit he was scared. He plastered on an upbeat expression and trailed after the officer, studiously ignoring the curious stares they got. The crowd had dwindled when people discovered things weren't as riveting as they appeared on the telly, drifting off back to their homes. What he couldn't fathom was why Barry had asked for him. They were mates only in the loosest sense of the word, but the man must have far closer friends.

'There you are. Good man.' Harry seized on him like manna from heaven. Thank goodness he couldn't see Nathan's insides churning like the sea on a rough day. 'And no, I don't know why Barry wants you in particular but he's insistent.'

That answered his unspoken question. Nathan glanced across at the Days' house and was surprised to see it looking eerily normal.

'He's got Laura and Josie in the kitchen at the back. We've spoken to him on the phone and so far the only demand he's made is to see you.' The glimmer of a smile flickered in Harry's troubled eyes. 'I'm guessing Josie might've suggested that because you know everyone involved and you've got a calm, quiet way about you.' He frowned. 'My bosses aren't pleased. We don't normally let civilians get involved and I can't force you to do this if you're at all uneasy.'

Uneasy? That didn't even begin to cover it. 'I'm surprised you're here. You know, with Josie and whatever.' Wasn't there a conflict of interest, or whatever was the police equivalent?

'They decided my knowledge of the situation outweighed the disadvantages but I'm not in charge.' Harry's jaw tightened as he gestured to a short woman with cropped ginger hair giving orders to some uniformed officers.

'So what do I do?' He could hardly stroll up to the door and ring the bell.

'We'll ring Barry and tell him you're here. See how he wants to play this. While we're waiting for a response, why don't you get over to the police van for a stab vest.'

The blood in his veins turned to water. Horrific images of Chloe on the floor of Vernon Bull's shop ran through his head on a continuous loop.

Harry gripped his arm. 'You sure you're okay with this?'

Before he could lose whatever nerve he had left, Nathan nodded and strode off. All he wanted was to get through this without making a fool of himself. Or ending up in hospital. Or the morgue.

* * *

Melissa gnawed her lip. She itched to beg the bored people chattering around her to stop complaining about mundane topics like Asda having Halloween chocolate on sale already or the scandalous cost of their child's new school uniform.

Nathan had updated her by text that Barry was refusing to talk to anyone but him. A few minutes later her heart leapt in her throat as she watched Nathan walk slowly up to the Days' front door and disappear inside.

'Uncle Nat will be fine.' Chloe squeezed her arm. 'He'd better be, or Mum and Dad will turn up again and I can't handle that.' An embarrassed flush lit up her neck and face. 'Sorry. This isn't about me, I get that.'

'Don't worry. I'm sure you're right and he'll be back out before we know it.'

'Isn't that your phone? I'd recognize your ringtone anywhere.' By her screwed up face, Elgar clearly didn't rate highly.

She stared at Harry's name flashing on the screen and felt her knees buckle. Chloe snatched the phone and answered in her usual carefree way, listening for a few moments before ending the call with a cheery goodbye.

'Harry says you can come join him if you promise not to interfere. I didn't say that was asking for the moon.'

'I'm perfectly capable of keeping my mouth shut when necessary.' The attempt to sound offended failed when she couldn't help smiling. 'You stay here.' She refused to be responsible for Chloe getting in any more trouble. Her poor parents had been through enough recently.

'Don't worry. I'm not going anywhere near another crazy person if I can help it.' Her voice trembled. After this, Melissa was determined to join the chorus of people begging the young woman to talk to a counsellor. Traumatic events didn't melt away like snow in the sunshine, and burying them was asking for trouble later.

The same police officer who'd escorted Nathan away a short while ago reappeared and led her through the thinning crowd.

'Oh, Harry.' The sight of the grim-faced detective made her eyes sting. She noticed a sharp-faced redhead with an impressive number of pips on her uniform giving them a piercing stare.

'That's my guvnor, Superintendent Margaret North, known behind her back as Mighty Maggie. If she asks, you're a long-time friend of Laura's who has insight into her present mental and physical state.' One corner of his mouth twitched. 'That's not stretching the truth too much.'

'Was Nathan okay when he went in?' Stupid question. Of course he wasn't. She'd seen the wariness under his tight smile.

'He seemed to be. I caught a glimpse of Josie too when she opened the door. That's all I can tell you.'

'The police aren't going to do anything rash, are they?'

'We're not rushing in with guns blazing, if that's what you're concerned about. At the moment it's a wait and see situation unless anything happens to make us decide differently. I mean, if *they* decide differently. It's not up to me.'

'Pity.'

'Maybe. Maybe not.' His shoulders lifted in a shrug. 'I'd hardly be objective now, would I?'

In the distance the church clock struck one and right on cue Melissa's stomach rumbled. It seemed obscene to feel hungry but she'd only played around with a slice of toast at breakfast and been too overwrought to eat dinner last night. Harry threw a sad smile her way but they didn't speak. What was there to say?

* * *

The surrealness of this whole situation wasn't lost on Nathan. When he stepped inside the house, Josie greeted him as if he'd been invited for afternoon tea. The only thing she had a chance to whisper as she led him back through the house was to treat Barry as normal. It'd been unnecessary to point out that as far as he knew, none of his other friends had ever threatened people with a carving knife. In the cramped kitchen he discovered Laura and Barry sitting on opposite sides of a square grey formica-topped table, as they must've done on so many other days, tea mugs at hand. They were chatting quite amiably about how the garden was looking and whether the shed needed repainting.

'Another bloody hot day, isn't it?' He knew his comment was lame, but innocuous seemed safest for a minute.

'It certainly is. Tea?' Josie said brightly.

'Yeah, that'd be great. All right if I sit down?'

'Of course.' Laura's eyes turned suspiciously bright. 'We're grateful you've come, aren't we, Barry?' Her husband managed a weak nod. 'We need your help to get out of this . . . situation we're in.'

'I'm happy to do whatever I can.' What on earth did they think he could possibly achieve? 'Why don't you tell me what it is you want so I can pass that on to the police?'

As Barry leaned across the table the movement sent a whiff of rank body odour Nathan's way. Combined with the stifling air and the additional heat created by four bodies crammed into the room, it made his head throb.

'What I *really* want the police can't help with. They can't make my wife fall back in love with me or force her to come back here to live. And they sure as fuck can't make that baby mine. Can they, Mr Professor?' Barry's voice shook.

'No.' There was no point lying. He gestured to the knife loosely clutched in his friend's left hand. 'That won't do any of those things either, will it? You and Laura having a heart-to-heart talk to see if you can work your way through this together. That's the only solution.' He hesitated. 'Deep down you know that, don't you?' Nathan heard Josie's sharp intake of breath and wondered if he'd spoken out of turn.

'I never fell out of love with you!' Laura gasped and turned white. Josie rushed to crouch down by her and rested her hand on Laura's stomach.

'Why didn't you tell me you were having contractions?'

'I thought it was the false ones again. I've been having those for weeks.' She bit back tears. 'I didn't know, did I? I've never got this far before.' A blending of pain and wonder suffused her face and she cried out, grasping Barry's hand. 'I'm sorry for everything, love. Please let Nathan go and fetch help. I know he can talk them into letting you be with me.' Her fierce confidence left no room for the doubts filling Nathan's own mind.

'Is that okay with you, mate?' he asked.

'Anything Laura wants.' Barry heaved a sigh, weary and defeated. 'Beg them, Nathan. Afterwards they can throw the book at me. I don't care.'

'Fair enough.' Nathan sprinted from the kitchen as a howling cry ripped out of Laura. He flung open the front door and blinked as a battery of cameras flashed in his face. A stern-faced police officer rushed towards him but his attention zeroed in on Melissa. She stood by Harry Bishop's side, staring at him as if she'd seen a ghost.

CHAPTER THIRTY-ONE

Melissa watched anxiously as Harry and his boss continued what looked like a heated discussion. Her heart had leapt in her throat when Nathan emerged from the house a few minutes ago. All she'd been able to do was rake him with her eyes as the police rushed to speak with him, relieved to see that apart from his pallor and tight jawline he looked unscathed. It tore her apart when he turned around and went back inside.

She jerked her head as an ambulance appeared from around the corner. It stopped to allow two paramedics to jump out and they disappeared inside carrying their equipment. Everything happened quickly after that and next thing Laura was carried out on a stretcher with Barry holding one of her hands and Josie the other. The police surrounded them and hustled Laura and Barry into the waiting ambulance, which drove off with its lights flashing and sirens blaring. A wave of joy surged through Melissa as Nathan reappeared and this time weaved out around the remaining police and ran to her, wrapping his arms around her in a tight hug. He buried his face in her hair and the familiar warmth and scent of him brought her to tears.

'Please don't cry, please. I'm fine and it's all going to be okay.'

Maybe it was and maybe it wasn't. In that moment the only emotion flooding her body was gratitude that Nathan was safe. She could never have forgiven herself otherwise. Harry joined them, clutching Josie by the hand. Her friend looked pale and was unnaturally quiet.

'I'm taking this one to hospital,' he said. 'I guess you're coming too?'

'Yeah, of course we are.' Melissa flashed a tentative smile at Josie and received an equally wary one in return. 'When is Laura's baby actually due?'

'Not for another month.' Josie sounded concerned.

'Is that—'

'I can't say. The stress of all this probably brought it on.' She grimaced towards the house. 'If anything goes wrong, part of the blame lies with me. I talked her into coming back and trying to sort things with Barry. The idea was that if that failed she'd pack the rest of her stuff and move out.' A tear trickled down her cheek. 'Stupid. Stupid.'

Arguing the point now would be a waste of breath. Words weren't always the best solution.

* * *

Nathan's gaze drifted around the labour and delivery waiting room. He wondered if the walls had absorbed all its various occupants' joys and sadnesses over the years. At three in the morning there was little else to occupy his brain.

Josie hadn't been allowed to stay with Laura so she'd stretched out on a couple of the uncomfortable grey plastic chairs and crashed. They'd probably served as an impromptu bed on many other long nights. He shifted his right knee an inch in an attempt to bring some feeling back to his leg but stilled it again when Melissa stirred in his arms. She'd curled up with her head in his lap and followed Josie's example hours ago, leaving him the only one awake. Miraculously, when they'd arrived, Laura's vital signs were good and the contractions had slowed enough for her to get some rest.

There'd been no recent update from Harry. He wasn't an official part of the police presence at the hospital but had been allowed to wait outside Laura's room. Nathan had been forced to stop himself checking his phone obsessively and rationed himself to once every half hour. There were five minutes to go until his next fix. A loud buzz startled him and his heart raced as a new text popped in from Harry.

Things are moving here again now. They're taking Laura to the delivery room.

'Anything?' Melissa yawned and stretched back up to sitting.

'Yes, are you psychic or something?'

'Just desperate for the loo.' She seized his phone, scanned it and grinned. 'Right. After I pee I'll update the others.'

It had heartened him when she'd initiated a flurry of texts and calls between the group, who weren't holding onto any ridiculous resentments now one of them needed support. A wave of sadness engulfed him over the way he'd treated this amazing woman after Robin died. If she told him a million times that she forgave him, he'd still never totally forgive himself. Knowing he'd been attracted to her all along only made his behaviour worse. If he was still alive his father would look down his nose and reprimand his only son, telling him that wasn't the action of a gentleman. Harold Kellow would've perfectly suited the role of one of Jane Austen's severe clergymen or domineering fathers.

'Don't look so grim. I'm sure it's gonna be fine.'

'What is?' Josie's eyes flew open. As soon as they shared the news she jumped to her feet. 'I'm going snooping.' Nathan was amazed to see her so wide awake, as if she'd enjoyed eight hours in her own comfortable, warm bed. She laughed at his surprise. 'You haven't worked shifts for almost twenty years. My body's used to this.'

'Say hello to Harry from us,' Melissa said. 'You scared the poor guy, you know.'

'I was an idiot.' She couldn't quite look at them. 'I should've apologized the other day but I was in stubborn mode and—'

'We all were.'

'Let's talk later.' Josie's colour deepened. 'After I've straightened things with Harry. I know he seemed fine earlier but that could've been down to relief that I wasn't in a body bag. I shouldn't assume he'll forgive me but—'

'That guy will forgive you anything,' Melissa chirped. 'He loves you.'

'People throw that word around far too easily.'

'For heaven's sake, go find out something — anything — before we all go crazy. I need a bathroom before I wet myself.' Melissa frowned. 'Should I go ahead and call the girls or wait?'

'Call them. When I examined Laura at the house there were no real concerns, but with her history . . . Anyway, even in the most normal pregnancy no one can ever be a hundred per cent certain.'

They left him alone and Nathan wandered over to the window, flexing his legs to get the blood flowing again. He peered out over the deserted car park and the only person he spotted was a solitary nurse walking towards the entrance, his steps slow and deliberate, as if he wasn't quite awake. There were still another couple of hours before sunrise and if the situation was different Barry would be the typical expectant father now — nervous and excited. How must he be feeling? Nathan couldn't begin to imagine how difficult a time he faced helping his wife through the ordeal of labour in their unique circumstances.

All he could do now was hope.

* * *

Melissa never wanted to come down from this high. The sight of Laura holding her tiny dark-haired miracle baby, wrapped in a soft pink swaddle, would linger with her forever. No matter what her friend had gone through or done to get to this point, her blissful expression now was reminiscent of classic Renaissance paintings of the Madonna and child. Barry's face was wreathed in smiles too as he beamed at his wife and the child in her arms. Was there a chance they could become the family they'd always wanted, or was that an impossible dream? Had too much been said or unsaid?

'Celebrate life, Melissa. Nothing else is important right now.' Evelyn's calm, measured voice penetrated her wistful mood.

'I know you're right but—'

'But nothing, dear.' The teacherly edge sneaked back in.

One by one their friends had turned up. They'd filled the room with chatter, drinking from thermoses of tea and coffee and sharing a generous selection of snacks while they waited for news. It'd seemed forever before Josie raced in to tell them that their group had a new honorary member — a healthy little girl weighing in at a small but sturdy six pounds three ounces. They'd been allowed to take it in turns to pop in to say hello, but Laura needed to rest so the girls had disappeared in dribs and drabs back to their homes.

A wave of affection swept through her at Nathan sitting patiently in the corner with his head in a book.

'You ought to take that man home to bed.'

Melissa stared at Evelyn as though she'd grown two heads, because the older woman often tended to be somewhat straightlaced.

'I wasn't always a crotchety old widow, you know.' Evelyn's face flushed. 'You might not think so but we've got a lot in common.'

Her mental attempt to draw up a list began and ended with their obsession with books.

'Apart from our passion for literature, we were both widowed far too young and neither of us have children.' Evelyn's pale eyes misted over. 'You've cultivated the mask that most people see extremely well, and mine's been in place so long I hardly remember what's underneath.'

How could she have been so wrong? She should've learned her lesson that no one was quite what they seemed. They all had one face they showed to the world and another reserved for a few special people, or sometimes, if they were unlucky, no one. Her family would be horrified to discover that until she and Nathan became close, that was the case with her.

'When I lost my husband everyone encouraged me to open my heart to meeting someone else, but I lied and insisted I could never do that because Sam was the only one for me. My soulmate. But the truth is I was simply too scared. When we met I'd been a shy, newly qualified teacher and pathetically grateful because this handsome, dashing man wanted to marry me. After a while I realized I'd been a deliberate choice on his part because it meant he'd always be — as you Americans say — the top dog in our marriage.'

Melissa couldn't wrap her head around the picture of Evelyn being anything other than a strong, confident woman.

'It's too late for me now, but don't you dare miss out on this wonderful chance at happiness you've been offered.' The penetrating look returned. 'You've already hinted that *your* first time around wasn't everything it appeared on the surface either.'

'You're right. You're so right.' Admitting the truth was empowering. From the corner of her eye she noticed Nathan stop reading to tune into their conversation. She tossed him a brilliant smile. 'I am amazingly lucky and I'm going to do exactly what you recommended.' Nathan's tired face lit up. Melissa threw her arms around Evelyn and sensed the older woman stiffen. 'We'll have to see about whether it's too late for you or not. I bet Nathan knows some suitable—'

'No. No. No. A thousand times no. I've no interest in a dusty old academic who's looking for a housekeeper and nursemaid.' The steely head teacher persona returned. 'Promise me you won't even consider something so patently ridiculous.'

'I promise.' Normally that level of meek agreement would stir her friend's suspicions, but she clearly wasn't on her A game this morning. Melissa hadn't promised anything about finding a *non*-dusty man, had she?

CHAPTER THIRTY-TWO

'Who the heck are you, and where's my sister?'

Nathan dried his right hand with the towel he'd been rubbing over his hair and stuck it out. The hulking, dark-haired man ignored his friendly gesture and continued glowering. 'Nathan Kellow. You must be either Pat or Bryan. Melissa's . . . upstairs.' She'd been naked when he threw on some clothes and came to answer the door. Her last words were for him to hurry up so they could jump back into bed. Not something her brother needed to hear. 'Come in. I'm sure she'll be thrilled to see you.'

'Yeah, well, our folks were worried about her so I drew the short straw and they packed me off to check on her.' The tone suggested he wasn't best pleased. Cornwall must not have been top of his must-see travel list. 'I'm Pat. The oldest. Melissa mentioned some guy she'd been seeing but we didn't know it was serious.' He left unspoken that any man in his sister's house at 7.30 in the morning fresh out of the shower wasn't there to read the electric meter. 'If you've taken advantage of her while she's down and vulnerable after losing her husband, you'll have—'

'Patrick Henry Rutherford, where on God's green earth did you spring from?' Melissa flew down the stairs and launched herself at her brother. Pat lifted her off the ground in a giant bear hug. 'Why didn't you tell me you were coming?'

'Mom and Dad wanted it to be a surprise.'

'Was the idea to catch me out or something?'

Pat dropped his arms away and glared at Nathan again. 'Yeah, and I succeeded by the look of it. Is this guy the one you told our folks about?'

Melissa linked hands with Nathan. 'Yeah. I'm not working through all the single men in the village, you know. This is Professor Nathan Kellow and we were about to have breakfast. Are you hungry?'

'Sure am. There's a hole where my stomach used to be. All they served on the sleeper this morning was crappy coffee and weird soggy bacon in a bread roll.'

'The sleeper? Oh wow, that's something I've wanted to try in forever. Robin refused to travel down that way because he said it was cramped and tedious.'

'It's not bad for regular people but it is kinda cramped if you're my size.' Pat's craggy face softened. 'The damn beds are several inches too short for a guy like me.'

At a shade over six feet, Nathan didn't consider himself short, but the American beat him by at least six inches.

'I bet you're dying for a hot shower?' Melissa beamed at her brother. 'Don't fret. I wouldn't condemn you to one of the regular Brit-sized ones more suited to one of Snow White's dwarfs. I'll show you where it is so you can freshen up while we fix you some decent food.' She wrinkled her nose. 'I'm not a fan of regular British bacon either — believe it or not, they import a whole lot of it from Denmark. I buy what they call streaky bacon because it's the closest thing to ours. I hope you're staying a while?'

'A week or so maybe? I haven't booked my return flight yet.'

Nathan kept his own agreeable expression in place. The idea of being scrutinized by Melissa's older brother for an extended period, and possibly found wanting, wasn't a cheering one.

'Awesome! The guest bedroom is ready to go and there's a king-size bed.' Her eyes sparkled. 'It's especially for oversized visitors.'

Nathan started to feel like a third wheel. 'How about I leave the two of you to have a good catch-up and I'll see you later? I've got some jobs to do around the house and my grass needs cutting.'

'Don't run off on my account.' Pat clapped an arm around Melissa's shoulder. 'The kid and I don't mind you hanging around, do we?'

'Take your bag upstairs and I'll be with you in a minute.' She wriggled out of her brother's grasp and steered Nathan towards the door. 'I'm sorry about this. I'd no idea—'

'I know, love.' A sigh slipped out. 'Is book club still on tonight?'

'Shoot. Yes it is, and I don't want to miss out. I've promised to clear the air about a few things, and it's important to be with the other girls anyway, you know what I mean?'

'Absolutely.'

'I don't suppose—'

'Would it help if I took Pat to the pub?'

'You're a star.' She flung her arms around his neck, tangled her fingers through his damp hair and seized his mouth in a teasing kiss. The heat seeping through her sheer pale pink dressing gown raised his temperature and the air around them filled with the scent of the floral soap and shampoo they'd both used. 'I'll make up for it later, I promise.'

'Not for at least a week you won't.' He tried to make a joke of it. There'd be no sleepovers while Pat Rutherford was on guard duty.

'He's not my keeper.'

'No, he's your older brother, and that's far worse if my dear sister is anything to go by.'

'You're probably right.'

'Hey, kiddo, where do I find a towel?' Pat's thick drawl boomed out.

'I'd better go.' Reluctantly, they moved apart. 'I'm coming,' she yelled up the stairs.

Nathan watched her retreating back wistfully.

* * *

If she wasn't so stressed out by the whole day, Melissa would've found Josie's bug-eyed stare amusing.

'You're her brother? From America?'

Pat looked amused rather than pissed off, so that was hopeful. With her oldest brother she could never be sure which way the wind would blow. They'd had one set-to already when she tore him off a strip for his rudeness to Nathan. He'd had no right to basically tell him he was surplus to requirements.

'Yes, ma'am.' If he'd been wearing the cowboy hat that didn't usually leave his head, he would've doffed it like a true Southern gentleman. 'The kid tells me I've got the pleasure of escorting you lovely ladies down to the little ole village for your book thingy.'

She almost pointed out that she was neither four years old nor a goat, but dredged up a smile for Josie's sake. 'Pat's going to have a drink with Nathan at the pub while we're at Tamara's. Shall we go?'

While they walked, she happily let Josie fill any gaps in the conversation with a no-breath-needed recitation of life in Penworthal. It left her mind free to run through the things she needed to confess at book club.

'There you are. The Rusty Anchor in all its glory.' Josie flung out her arm in a generous flourish. It'd be interesting to hear her brother's reaction later. Pat wasn't a great traveller — he'd gone to Mexico once on a stag weekend for their younger brother, and across the other border into Canada when an ex-girlfriend dragged him to a concert in Toronto. Being forced to listen to Justin Bieber and endure the company of myriads of screaming fans had put him off for life. He appeared to have little interest in seeing the rest of the world — Pat was far happier staying on the North American side of the Atlantic Ocean.

'Do you want us to come in with you?'

'I'm not a five-year-old starting kindergarten.' Pat scoffed. 'I'm big enough and ugly enough to take care of myself if your boyfriend is late.' His scathing dismissal of Nathan made her cringe. 'See ya later, ladies. Have fun.' It bewildered him why anyone would choose to spend an evening discussing books, and Melissa hadn't mentioned it was one of her and Nathan's favourite things. Pat would die laughing if she told him about their literary sightseeing trips. He'd rather watch a good football game or go fishing, preferably with a cold beer in one hand. The lukewarm temperature of British beer would doubtless join his litany of complaints.

After they left Pat to his own devices, Josie slowed her pace and gave Melissa a wary look.

'Are we going to clear up this nonsense between us before we get there?'

'That's fine by me.' That sounded grudging, which wasn't what she'd intended. 'Sorry, it's been a weird day and I need to clear the air with you guys about some stuff that's filling my head.'

'You mean about your money problems and that you and Robin weren't love's young dream?'

Her dismay must've been obvious because Josie exhaled a groan.

'Oh God, now I'm the one who's sorry. Harry says I'm so used to being bossy and in charge at work, it carries over to my private life. I've asked him to help me be less . . . abrasive.' The corners of her mouth twitched. 'It's a work in progress.'

'So you and Harry are good again?'

'Yes.' Josie blushed. 'We're off to the Scilly Isles on Friday.'

'I'm so relieved he managed to convince you he wasn't a controlling prick like your ex-husband.'

'You certainly saw Christopher's true colours the other day. I was an idiot for far too long over him. I even convinced myself I was partly to blame for his behaviour. Too many doctors have a God complex and he's one of the worst offenders.' She puffed out a breath. 'I was stupid to think I could wave a magic wand over Laura and Barry and put everything right, too. They love each other so much. I had the mad idea the baby would bring them together, as if it didn't matter who her biological father was. I put Nathan at risk in the process because I suggested him as a possible intermediary. If anything had happened—'

'But it didn't.' She grabbed Josie's arm. 'Let's get going.' Her friend still looked awkward. 'We're not going to be this idiotic ever again, are we?'

'I sure hope not because it's getting exhausting.'

They laughed, linked arms and marched off down the road.

* * *

'Nathan, I'm sorry to interrupt but are you free for a minute?' Barry hovered by the table.

'Could it wait? I'm here with Melissa's brother and—'

'Don't mind me. I'll get another beer and prop up the bar,' Pat said affably, and made himself scarce.

So far they'd got on okay, but it wasn't easy to find compatible subjects to talk about. Sports were the other man's passion, but Nathan's knowledge of American football, basketball and baseball would fit on the head of a pin. The only sport he followed to any great extent was cricket and that was double Dutch to the American.

'Sit down. What's up?'

'Laura's told me about him. Little 'un's father, like.' Anguish was etched on his tired face.

Nathan didn't feel equipped to deal with this. At work he followed college policy to the letter and steered students with personal troubles to the appropriate counsellor. 'Are he and Laura . . . ?'

'No. Turns out he *was* an anonymous sperm donor.' He turned bright pink and rubbed his hands on his thighs. 'The guy you saw her with is her cousin, Jake.'

If Melissa cozied up to one of her cousins that way he'd be distinctly unhappy, but he held his tongue. 'Oh, right.' He picked his next words with great care. 'So that's good, right? I mean, I know she kept it all a secret and went behind your back, but you've got a beautiful baby girl out of it.'

'So you'd be okay if Melissa lied through her teeth, took money the two of you were saving up and left you high and dry? I was worried sick because she nearly bloody died the last time she lost one of our babies.'

'No, I wouldn't be okay, but I'd ask for an explanation and try to listen objectively to her answer.' Remembering how unsympathetic he'd been at first when Melissa attempted to explain Robin's decision to discontinue treatment made him sick to his stomach. 'I'm not saying it'll be easy but what's the alternative? Lose the woman you love and the baby who'll make you the family you've always wanted.'

'You weren't so bloody noble when Melissa had that trouble the other day, were you? Took you a while to step up and be a man about things from what I heard.'

Over his shoulder Nathan watched Pat's expression turn to granite so he raised his own voice, the better to be overheard. 'You're right and I'm ashamed of myself. Be a better person than me.' That took his companion aback.

'I s'ppose I can give it a try.' Barry lumbered to his feet. 'Thanks, mate.'

'Anytime.'

'Let me get you a pint.'

'Nah, it's okay. Another time. You go off home.'

'Yeah, I'll do that.' Barry dipped his head.

As soon as he ambled off, Pat slid back in to take his place.

'You going to tell me what my kid sister's been up to or do I have to prise it out of her?'

Nathan's heart sank.

CHAPTER THIRTY-THREE

Several sets of astonished eyes stared back at Melissa. Josie and Evelyn didn't appear as dumbfounded because they knew most of her story already.

'You're a bloody good actress is all I can say.' Becky shook her head. 'You certainly had me fooled with your loving wife and devastated widow performance. And Robin flashing money around here all the time when he was up to his neck in debt? Unbelievable.'

'That's enough,' Evelyn chided. 'I'm sure you have your secrets too. No one's marriage is an open book.' A wan smile lifted her dour expression. 'Mine wasn't made in heaven either but I come from a generation that didn't believe in throwing our problems out in public for everyone to pick over.' She held a warning finger up to Melissa. 'Please don't take that as a criticism. I wish I'd had the courage to be as upfront. This is what good friends are for and I didn't give them the chance to help me.'

Now Becky wasn't the only one looking awkward. The knot of guilt tying up Melissa's stomach remained tight as a drum. Perhaps she should've learned from all the celebrities who splash every aspect of their private lives across social media and live to regret it.

'Poor Melissa's been through an awful ordeal and needs us to rally around her now. She deserves our support.' Evelyn levelled her best head teacher stare on Becky, then swept her gaze around the room. 'None of you had a problem being there for Laura at the weekend when she had the baby, and this is no different.'

'Well said.' Josie clapped. Two blobs of red flared in her cheeks. 'I know a good friend when I find one and she's the best. I wasn't smart enough to recognize it straight away but I got there in the end. She had my back even when I sure as hell didn't deserve it.'

Melissa blinked away a rush of tears.

'She was firmly on my side too when Nathan's stroppy sister threw a wobbly and tried to blame her daughter's escapades on my son,' Tamara declared. 'Anyway, I vote we remember what we're here for. We've talked about *Snapped in Cornwall* and sorted out Melissa's . . . niggling little issue, so now it's time for the serious business of the night — cake.'

Should she be relieved or slighted to have her troubles dismissed as a "niggling little issue"?

'I've made a lemon drizzle with a new recipe. There's Italian limoncello in it so there's a proper kick to it. There's plenty of wine on offer too, because we all know Rose Trevelyan liked a drop, didn't she?'

All the way through the light-hearted discussion they'd joked about the main character's tendency to open a wine bottle at the drop of a hat, especially when Detective Inspector Jack Pierce came on the scene. Josie was forced to endure a slew of nudge-nudge-wink-wink comments about her own handsome DI, including how often he frisked her and whether he brought his handcuffs on dates.

Everyone drifted out to the kitchen and suddenly the doorbell jangled.

'Who's that now?' Evelyn complained. 'It better not be anyone's husband or partner come to drag them home. They should know by now that book club night is sacred.' She bustled out to the hall and returned with a bright smile. 'Well, look who I found!'

The light purple smudges under Laura's eyes hinted at a lack of sleep but despite that her face glowed.

'Let's go back in the lounge, ladies,' Evelyn ordered. 'I'm sure our new mother needs a comfy chair.'

They gathered up their drinks and food and were soon settled in their original seats.

'I promised my mum I wouldn't be long. She's staying with me for a while to help out with the baby. Barry's kipping at a mate's house for now.' Anxiety pulled down the corners of Laura's smile. 'There's something I need to get off my chest.' She sighed down at the post-baby breasts straining the confines of a blue T-shirt. 'I'm afraid trying to squeeze into this was over-optimistic.'

'Are you having a glass of wine, lovey, or aren't you indulging?' Tamara asked.

'A small one should be fine. I fed Josephine before I came out.'

'Josephine?' Josie turned bright red. 'That's what you're calling her?'

'You don't mind, do you?'

'Mind? Far from it. But I can't believe after all—'

'If it hadn't been for you I wouldn't have a second chance with my Barry.' She nodded at Melissa. 'We're going to ask Nathan if he objects to us using Natalie for her middle name.'

'I'm sure he'll be honoured,' she stammered.

Laura flopped down on an empty chair. 'Barry knows the truth now, but I want you to hear it too.' Her agitated fingers pulled at her shirt hem. 'I couldn't tell you I was trying again for a baby because you'd have tried to talk me out of it. So would Barry. And logically you'd all have been right.'

'There's no logic when it comes to the heart, dear.' Evelyn's whispered words pulled at Melissa's heart. Nathan should have been the very last name on the list of suitable men for her to fall in love with.

'Josephine's biological father is an anonymous sperm donor. I was wrong to take money out of our savings behind Barry's back to pay for it. He'd planned to spend it on a conservatory and a Mediterranean cruise because the poor man thought that would make up for not having kids.'

Melissa bit her lip. Were some of Robin's extravagances intended as a substitute for the baby he refused to consider having?

'I did fudge one thing a bit with Barry, and I don't know now if I've done right or wrong . . .' She took a gulp of wine. 'Let's forget it. My hormones are all over the place. I don't know what I'm saying half the time. It'll keep for another day.' She pushed the glass aside and levered out of the chair. 'Thanks for everything, girls. There's nothing like old friends.' An apologetic smile came Melissa's way. 'And newer ones. We need to treasure each other more.'

Amen to that, she thought.

Nobody spoke right away, but then the speculation started and they all took guesses at what Laura had been on the verge of confessing. It was pretty much unanimous that there was more to Laura's clinch with her cousin than a simple comforting hug.

'If we're right, I think she should tell Barry,' Amy said firmly. 'If she doesn't she'll always be looking over her shoulder and worrying whether this Jake is going to stir things up.'

'Normally I'd agree with you. Honesty usually *is* the best policy.' Evelyn looked thoughtful. 'But I'm not sure that's true in this case. Barry's recent behaviour hasn't been exactly stable, has it? I fear it wouldn't take much to unsettle him again.'

'Yeah, we don't want a repeat of the other day,' Melissa said with a shudder.

Evelyn's tone softened. 'Laura and Barry will never make a go of things with little Josephine if they can't put all this behind them. I vote we say no more about this, unless Laura brings up the subject again of course.' Her piercing gaze swept around the group.

One by one they all nodded.

* * *

'So, are you gonna tell me here or should we go to your place?' Pat glowered, his default expression most of the time around Nathan. 'We knew something was up — the kid reckons she's so damn smart but we knew she was pulling the wool over our eyes.'

'It's not really my—'

'Don't give me that crap.' The American's booming drawl drew the attention of all the other customers. They'd become tonight's entertainment.

'Let's walk over to my house. There's a decent bottle of single malt I'm happy to share.' As he stood up, Pixie caught his eye from behind the bar and Nathan sensed her relief. The landlady couldn't be happy with the number of recent confrontations in her pub, mostly centred around him.

Outside he stopped still for a moment. 'Melissa says Carter's Run is smaller than this. You still live there, right?'

'Yeah. It's mighty pretty, but if you're looking for excitement you're out of luck. Suits me fine that way.' The first hint of a smile softened Pat's granite features. 'It's not exactly the bustling city here either so I'm taking a guess you must be the same? My sister says you've lived here most of your life.'

'I did go away to university and worked in London for a couple of years. Cornwall was always stuck in my head though, so I leapt at the chance when a job opportunity came up in Truro.' Nathan started walking and Pat fell into step beside him.

'You and Robin were best buddies.'

'Yes.' He needed to be cautious. He'd no idea how much Melissa had or hadn't told her brother about Robin and the deteriorating state of their marriage by the time he died. It stuck in his throat to malign his old friend, but if he fudged the truth too much he'd come out of it badly. He didn't doubt that Pat would report everything he heard straight back to the rest of the Rutherford family, and that could set them against Nathan before they'd even met. Not that the possibility of that happening had been discussed yet, but neither had anything else about where their relationship might be headed.

'We never really took to the guy.' Pat scrutinized him. 'You don't seem like you'd have much in common.'

Nathan played for time and pulled out his house keys. 'The teacher sat us next to each other the first day of primary school and that was it. We never questioned *why* we were friends, it just was always there.' He lifted his shoulders in a shrug. 'There was some rivalry when it came to exams — the two of us came in first and second in most of the classes we were in together. Then we went to Oxford at the same college.'

'You think he'd approve of you making a move on his widow?'

Nathan disliked the way that made his and Melissa's relationship sound sordid, and didn't answer. 'Here's my house.'

Pat let out a low whistle. 'Wow, that's some place.'

'It's early Victorian, built in 1842. Come on in.' He struggled to remember if Chloe was working tonight and hoped she didn't float down to greet them wearing nothing but a smile. Nathan could imagine her about to step in the bath when she realized she'd forgotten a match to light the scented candles she liked to stink up the bathroom with, and running downstairs without a thought as to who might be around.

'My God, all the antique nuts out where I live would pay a bomb for this kind of stuff.' Pat wandered over to take a closer look at the grandfather clock.

'It's not for sale.'

'Hey, keep your hair on, pal. I'm only making conversation.' Eyes the same curious shade as Melissa's studied him. 'Where's this drink you promised? Then you can tell me what that guy in the pub was ranting about.'

'Go on in and sit down while I fetch a couple of glasses.' After he pointed Pat in the direction of the living room, he retreated to the kitchen and sent Melissa a message letting her know *where* they were, and *why* they were there. With any luck she'd come to rescue him before he put his foot in it with her brother. 'Right, here's a treat for us.' He walked back in to join Pat, taking the bottle of Laphroaig he kept for special occasions off the sideboard. 'Water? Ice?' He'd got used to Melissa putting ice in almost everything. She'd explained it was a major reason why she bought the massive refrigerator in her kitchen, complete with ice and water dispenser on the door.

'I might not be the brightest bulb in the light socket but even I know you don't ruin good whisky with ice.' Pat guffawed. 'You got any brothers or sisters?' The change of topic threw him for a second.

'Uh, yes. One sister. Catherine. She's ten years older.'

'Bit of a tartar, is she?'

'You could say that. Doesn't matter how old I get I'll always be the annoying kid brother who needs watching out for.' Nathan took a couple of steadying breaths, then launched into the story Pat had asked for.

'You mean Robin left her high and dry for money and she's been paying off his debtors right, left and centre?'

'That about sums it up.' He stayed well away from the subject of Melissa and Robin's marriage; *that* certainly wasn't his story to tell.

'We would've helped her out. All she had to do was ask.'

'She had her pride.'

'You just wait 'til I see her and—'

'You might think twice about that.' His interruption made Pat frown. 'It might be best to wait and let her tell you in her own time.'

'But she's family. Looking out for each other is what we do.'

She'd told him that escaping her smothering family was one reason she'd returned to Cornwall. She had made Nathan smile when she'd explained what it would've been like if she'd stayed in Carter's Run.

'Everyone would use hushed sympathetic tones around me and say "Bless her heart, that's the poor Rutherford girl whose husband up and died on her".'

'I'm sure she knows that, but I'm not telling you something you don't already know when I say your sister's a very independent woman.'

'Is she okay for cash now?'

'Yes. She's not flush but she's getting by.' He held up the whisky bottle and Pat's grin widened.

'I'm liking you better than that other stuffed shirt already.'

He topped up their glasses and forced out a smile. No matter what, he still missed his old friend.

You think he'd approve of you making a move on his widow?

The unsettling question had wriggled into his brain and no doubt would keep him awake tonight.

CHAPTER THIRTY-FOUR

'Have a wonderful time.' Melissa hugged Josie and lowered her voice. 'Harry's a keeper. Don't you dare let that jerk of an ex back in your head again.'

'I won't. He's history.'

Melissa had brought her first coffee of the day out to the garden to snatch some much-needed time alone. There was no danger of Pat joining her because her brother never surfaced until at least nine. Ever since Nathan spilled the beans about her recent financial woes earlier in the week, her brother had been bending her ear non-stop. There was one constant theme — what were family there for if not to help when one of them was in trouble? He couldn't accept her determination to be independent and sort out her own problems.

'I hate to break up the party but if we don't get a move on we'll miss the boat — literally.' Harry broke into a broad smile. He'd wandered out from the house to join them.

'What time does *The Scillonian* leave?' Melissa asked.

'Quarter past nine from Penzance,' he replied with a slight shrug. 'Traffic shouldn't be too bad this early but it'll still take us a good hour to get there and park the car.'

'Take her, she's all yours.' Melissa playfully pushed her friend away.

'What am I — the parcel in the old children's party game?'

'Yep, and I'm the winner so I get to unwrap the last layer and discover my prize.' Harry waggled his dark eyebrows.

'You're both terrible!' Josie turned bright pink. 'I might change my mind if you're not careful.' She wagged a finger at her boyfriend.

There was no danger of that happening. Only the other day her friend had confided that she'd never felt such a sense of contentment with any man before. The short amount of time they'd known each other was immaterial. It'd been a struggle to hide her envy. Not that she and Nathan weren't the same way, but in their case the complications appeared more . . . complicated. Nathan had been in an odd mood since his conversation with Pat and strangely reticent to open up about what exactly they'd shared. Under the guise of giving her more time with her brother he'd largely stayed away and his absence was gnawing at her.

Josie thrust her soft tan leather weekend bag at Harry. Strictly speaking it belonged to Melissa, who'd offered it after cringing at the garish blue plastic backpack her friend initially packed. She'd told Josie in no uncertain terms that it was tactless to go off for the weekend with Harry using a bag emblazoned with the logo of a medical company specializing in erectile dysfunction drugs. She'd ignored Josie's protest that there were a pile of them free in the nurses' lounge one day, and that Harry was confident enough for it not to bother him.

'Carry that, if you're in charge.' There was no real annoyance in Josie's words as she smiled at Harry.

'Off you go.' Melissa watched wistfully as they left arm in arm.

'So where's lover boy these days, kiddo?'

'Pat? What on earth are you doing out of bed?'

Her brother ambled down the path taking large gulps from a steaming mug of coffee. 'Mom reckons I've pissed you off and should apologize. According to her, it's their fault I'm a caveman.' His cheeks turned ruddy.

Good on you, Mom. Sybil Rutherford's outspokenness didn't usually extend to her precious husband and sons.

'You're forgiven.' How could she stay mad at a brother who'd travelled four thousand miles from his comfort zone to check on her welfare?

Pat's gaze dropped to his large bare feet. As a kid he'd fought a long-standing battle with their parents over his dislike of wearing any sort of footwear and even now only put on shoes when he had no other choice. 'I might've poked my nose in with your guy too.'

Alarm bells jangled. 'In what way?'

'I said something I prob'ly shouldn't have,' he mumbled.

'What was it?' Melissa grabbed his arm so he had to look at her.

'I asked if he thought Robin would approve of his best friend making a move on his widow?'

'You said that? Seriously? Hell's bells, Pat, how could you?'

'I dunno, it just sorta came out.'

No wonder Nathan had stayed away. Those insensitive words would've sliced right through him. She thought they'd made peace with that particular elephant in the room, but had they both simply been saying what they thought the other needed to hear? As far as she could tell there were two choices. Allow this to fester and eat away at their feelings for each other or tackle it head on. Her lack of courage in forcing difficult conversations with Robin had tangled her up in a mess of mammoth proportions that she was only now unravelling.

'I sure am sorry.' Pat held his hands out as if to hold her off.

'Have I tried to hit you since I was five years old and you buried my Barbie doll in the compost heap? Remember how that ended?'

'Yeah, with your arm in a cast.' His mouth twitched. 'I didn't know you were going to fall on it wrong when I shoved you over.'

'You'd still have done it,' Melissa retorted. 'Now you're almost a foot taller than me and probably twice my weight. I doubt I'd come out of it too well this time either.'

His expression turned serious. 'I know my own strength these days. I've grown up, you know.'

'Yeah, well, I have too.' Hurt bloomed in his eyes, their unusual greyish-green a mirror-image of her own. 'I know y'all love me and would do anything for me, so I can admit I've maybe been a bit too stubborn.'

'Ya don't think!'

'I need to see Nathan.'

'You want me to come along too and grovel to the guy?'

'No thanks. I'll get dressed and wander down. It's a lovely morning for a walk.' She needed time to decide how to approach this. A simple challenge would only result in denial. Nathan would insist there wasn't a problem and wonder why she was on at him for being thoughtful enough to give her the space to make the most of her brother's brief visit. This needed a touch of guile.

'Best of luck, kiddo.' Pat bent down and kissed her cheek. He wasn't the most demonstrative of men, but there were tears glistening in his eyes.

* * *

'Uncle Nat, look who I found on the doorstep.' Chloe burst into the kitchen, dragging a red-faced Melissa by the hand. 'Don't worry, I'm off to have a shower.' She playfully sniffed her underarms. 'This health kick Toby's on will be the death of me. Don't tell Mum and Dad I'm voluntarily getting up at six in the morning to go running. They'll think I've lost my mind.'

'Or grown up, and that'd be terrible, wouldn't it?' That dry response earned a burst of laughter from Melissa and a fake glare from his niece. 'Do they know you've registered for Truro College?'

'Not yet.'

'Wow, that's great news, Chloe.' Melissa's smile did funny things to Nathan's insides.

God, he'd missed her more than anything these last few days. In a simple linen shift dress the same shade as her mermaid eyes, and with her bare tanned legs and cream tennis shoes, she could pass for little older than Chloe if it wasn't for her striking silver hair. He could even pick up her elusive scent from where he sat.

'Are you planning to study the same subjects?'

'Definitely not! I'm doing the HNC Business course. That lasts a year and if it goes well I'll probably go on to Plymouth Uni for another two to get my degree. Or I might decide to skip the degree to get a job or do some sort of traineeship. We'll see.'

'What made you take a U-turn in that direction?'

Flashes of heat lit up his niece's cheeks. 'Working in the shop. I know that's crazy but I've discovered I'm pretty good at sales and I've already come up with a few ideas to improve the business that Mr Bull's taken on board. The weekly sales display right inside the door. The made-to-order sandwiches. I talked him into buying a new pizza oven and they're selling like — hot pizzas!' Her eyes sparkled. 'I've got more satisfaction out of all that than I ever did writing essays on Plato or discussing the merits of the two-party political system. It'd be awesome to have my own business and be my own boss one day.'

'That's a terrific idea and I'm sure you'll ace the course,' Melissa said. 'I can picture you as the next successful entrepreneur on *Dragon's Den*, mentoring other young people.'

Nathan had never been a materialistic person so a tiny part of him was disappointed that Chloe had abandoned her academic career at Oxford. That was his problem though, not hers, and if this venture made her happy — something she clearly hadn't been before — he'd support her all the way. Melissa treated him to a sympathetic smile. She understood.

'We'll see.' Chloe's warm laughter filled the room. 'Right now I need to shower then drag on my fashionable blue overall. Sadly I haven't succeeded in talking Mr Bull into anything smarter yet. The good villagers of Penworthal depend on me to keep the shelves stacked.' She bounced out of the room, her footsteps echoing on the stairs as she raced up them two at a time.

'Oh for a fraction of her energy.' Melissa dragged out a chair and sat opposite him. 'Is there any coffee on the go or do I have to fetch it myself?'

Nathan sprang up. 'I'll get it.' He fussed around making her coffee the way she liked it — the opposite of his — scalding hot, black and sugarless. 'Don't get me wrong, I'm thrilled to see you but beautiful women don't usually bang on my door at half seven in the morning.'

'I hope I'm the only one.'

'You're all I need.'

'That's the right answer. I'm here because after I've had my coffee we're gonna take a walk.'

'Okay.' Nathan set a steaming mug down in front of her and dropped back in his seat. 'Where to? More research for next month's book?' He'd assumed their trip to Newlyn and Lamorna Cove had covered it for *The Shell Seekers*, but if she wanted to dig deeper that was fine with him.

'No.' She angled a searching look at him. 'Throw some clothes on and we'll go. We won't need the car. It's close by.'

From experience he knew that was all he'd get out of her until she was ready to share anything more. 'I assume Pat's still languishing in bed?'

'Believe it or not, he was up early today.' Something about the answer made him study her closer. There was an air of mystery about Melissa this morning that he couldn't quite put his finger on. 'Are you going to get dressed or not?'

This wasn't the time to crack jokes about preferring her to beg him to do the opposite and whip them off instead. He left her and headed off to get dressed. Impatience radiated off her when he came back down to the hall, stirring his curiosity even further. Nathan followed her outside and stopped at the gate. 'Are you going to tell me where we're going?'

Melissa linked her arm through his. 'We're off to see Robin.'

Whatever he might've expected her to say, it certainly wasn't that. 'Okay.' He wracked his brains. 'Is there a significance to today's date that I've forgotten?'

'Not in the way you think. Come on.'

They strolled along in silence and a wave of unease swept through him as they turned into the cemetery. He hadn't had the guts to return to his old friend's grave since his inauspicious meeting with Melissa several months ago. When she sat down on the warm grass he followed suit.

'Robin, we need to sort a few things out with you. My dumb brother put his foot in it and asked Nathan if he thought you'd approve of him making a move on your widow, and it's been bothering him no end. He needs to know you're fine with it.'

The breath left his body and he couldn't have spoken if someone had paid him a million pounds.

She took hold of his hand and rested her other one on the dark marble stone, linking the three of them together. 'I know we'd fallen out of love with each other before you got sick, but that happens to people all the time. If you hadn't gone and died I'd have wanted you to find happiness with someone else, and I'm sure you'd have done the same for me.' Sadness flickered over her face. 'I'm on track in sorting out the financial mess you left me in so I've been able to let go of my anger at you. I can remember you fondly now and the good times we had.' She lifted her hand from the stone to brush away a tear. 'Nathan feels guilty for falling in love with me and I don't want him being that way any longer.' Melissa turned to him. 'Do you want to say something?'

He froze.

'Pretend I'm not here and chat to him like you used to.'

Nathan knew he needed to be honest with his old friend now or it would haunt him later. 'I know you screwed up some things and I wish you could've asked for help, but you didn't so there's nothing I can do about that now. I'm pretty sure you guessed I was attracted to Melissa the first time you brought her into the pub.' He heard her quick intake of breath. 'But I hope you also knew me well enough to be sure I'd never have done anything about it. That's why I stayed away from you both as much as I could. Now things are different, but I still can't shake off the wrongness about us being together.' He puffed out a sigh. 'I'm not sure what I think is going to happen, mate. It sounds mad to ask you to send a sign.'

'Let's sit quietly a few minutes.' A flush brightened her cheeks. 'I find it helps. I came here the day after we slept together the first time because I needed to put it right with Robin.' Melissa grabbed hold of both his hands now and pressed them over her heart. 'I felt it here. A sense of peace.'

No better idea came to mind so he draped an arm around her shoulders and her head nestled against his chest. The rise and fall of her breathing soothed him. Whether that was what did the trick, or it was down to something indefinable he couldn't put a name to, the discomfort he'd been carrying around eased.

'Are we good now?' she whispered.

'Yeah.'

'Great.' Melissa stood up, brushed off her dress and patted Robin's headstone. 'See ya soon, and thanks.'

The whole scenario no longer struck Nathan as weird or uncomfortable so he followed her example and said goodbye to his old friend.

'Let's go home.'

CHAPTER THIRTY-FIVE

Melissa and Josie arrived at the pub in time to grab their favourite table and have a catch up before the rest of the group turned up for the quiz. Their lives had been so busy they'd hardly seen each other for the last three weeks. It was hard to believe in a couple of days it would be September already. After Josie and Harry came back from the Scilly Isles, he'd moved in with her. They'd decided that with their unpredictable work schedules it wasted too much precious time to always be travelling back and forth between their two homes. Pat had returned to Tennessee, leaving Melissa free to slip back into routine with Nathan again.

'So what's the latest with Laura?' Josie leaned forward. 'I spotted her and Barry out walking the baby together last week.'

'From what I've heard they're back together and he won't hear anything more said about little Josephine's parentage — as far as Barry's concerned, he's her father.'

'I tried to winkle out of Harry whether the police are going to charge him but I was firmly told to mind my own business. He said that I quite rightly don't discuss my patients so I shouldn't ask him for any details about his work either.'

Melissa suppressed a smile. It took a strong man to stand up to Josie, but the canny detective seemed up for the challenge. 'Things are going well with you two?'

'It's strange living with a man again — anyone, really — after being on my own so long.'

'Good strange or bad strange?'

Josie blushed. 'Almost all good.' She sipped her white wine spritzer. 'What about you and Nate? Will we hear wedding bells anytime soon?'

'I could ask you the same thing.' Deftly avoiding the question, she gulped her wine down so fast she almost choked.

'Harry and I have both been burned before so I don't see it somehow.'

'But would you say yes if he asked?' Her own feelings on the subject see-sawed from day to day. Not that Nathan had ever dropped any hints in that direction.

'I honestly don't know. Anyway, you don't get away that easy, what about—'

'Well done, ladies.' Evelyn set her handbag on the chair next to Melissa and smoothed a hand over her immaculate white hair, swept back in its usual elegant French pleat. She waved across at Becky and Amy who'd just walked through the door followed by Tamara.

Melissa felt she'd had a narrow escape. Although part of her wanted to be honest with Josie, she wouldn't know *how* to answer that particular question.

'Wonderful, Laura's here too,' Evelyn said. 'We've got a full complement now.'

There was the normal bustle while everyone found their preferred spots and got their drinks.

Little Josephine, who was already called Jo for short, was fast asleep, plastered to her mother's chest in what Laura had informed them was a baby wrap carrier. Supposedly they were very popular with all the new mums. Melissa avoided pointing out that it bore a strong resemblance to the wide strips of cloth used by generations of women to strap their babies on so they could continue working in the fields. It was touching to see Barry trail in with them, hefting a bag on his shoulder big enough to contain everything a tiny baby might need over the span of a couple of hours — or the next month, judging by the size of it.

'Have you all done your assignments?' Evelyn probed. Now they were an established fixture on quiz nights, they weren't allowed to turn up simply for a gossip and breeze their way through the questions. They'd each been allotted certain subjects and given a sheet of frequently used questions with hints about how best to study for them. When Tamara half-joked that it was like being back at school, Evelyn quelled her by asking if they wanted to make fools of themselves. When Tamara dutifully said no, they all obediently followed suit. Melissa was allotted flags of the world, not a favourite of hers but someone had to do it, along with brushing up on all things American.

'So, do *Proper Choughed* have all their brains here tonight?' Amy glanced across to where Nathan and his team were hunkered over the table with their heads close together. 'Looks like it. They're either strategizing over how to beat us or talking about last weekend's footie scores.' She chuckled.

Melissa smiled to herself. Nathan had no interest in football, so plotting the *Back of Beyond Brain's* downfall was a far more likely scenario. There was nothing like a little healthy competition to spice things up, although they didn't need any help in that direction. She hadn't shared details of their chat with Robin with anyone, because she suspected other people would find it strange, to say the least. But it'd worked for them. There was a new closeness between them and an ease she hadn't realized they were missing. 'Come on, girls, we're not going down without a fight.'

Pixie rang the bell, shouted her usual instructions and read out the first category. Literature. Over the crowd Melissa caught Nathan's eye. Bring it on.

* * *

'That bloody woman of yours is a pain in the ass,' Micky Broad complained.

Evelyn, surrounded by her acolytes, stood in front of the bar, brandishing the small silver cup that'd been fought over for more than a decade. The dent on one side attested to a particularly hard-won fight, resulting in the second-place loser throwing it at the winner but missing, sending the trophy crashing to the floor.

'She's smart.'

'Yeah, and a flamin' Yank. Bloody unfair. She was bound to know some obscure baseball player from back in the Dark Ages.'

He didn't contradict his teammate. It wouldn't do to point out that Melissa had been glued to an American sports trivia website for the last couple of nights so she wouldn't let her team down. Micky's view was that anyone who studied for the quiz was a loser, although Nathan had noticed him scrolling through Olympic medal statistics on his phone before they were forced to switch them off.

Behind the bar, Pixie lined up a row of bright cocktails for the quiz winners.

'Uncle Nat, it's him,' Chloe hissed in his ear.

'Oh, hi, I didn't know you were in tonight. Is Toby here too? Did you see the ladies—'

'Did you hear what I said?' She threw a frightened look over her shoulder.

'Who are you talking about?'

'The boy who stabbed me.' The tremble in her voice magnified and her eyes widened with panic. 'I'm sure it's him.'

'Sit down and don't draw attention to yourself.' He yanked out the chair Micky had vacated. 'I thought you told the police you wouldn't recognize him again.'

'Not exactly. I gave them a rough description but the details were too hazy to help them much. I did tell Harry there was something that struck me about the guy when it happened, but I couldn't remember what it was.'

'Until tonight?'

She nodded. 'I was getting a round of drinks in when I saw a man reach out his right hand to Pixie for his change.

There was a faint green snake tattooed around his finger. I remembered it was the last thing I saw before he stabbed me.'

While he listened, Nathan pulled out his phone and sent Melissa a text asking her to find out where Harry was.

He's at Josie's place. What's wrong?

Tell her to get him here now. Chloe's seen the man who attacked her and he's here right now. I need you to come over to join us. Please.

'Hiya, Chloe, long time no see.' Melissa appeared at their table and rested a reassuring hand on his niece's shoulder. 'How's the wonderful world of baked beans?'

'Fine.'

'I'm off.' Barry gave a sheepish grin. 'Laura and the little one are ready to go home.'

Tears pricked at Nathan's eyes. He wasn't an overly emotional man but if anyone deserved a happy-ever-after it was those two.

'You can have my seat, Melissa.' He switched his attention back to Nathan. 'Everything all right, mate?'

'It will be. You go on.' Barry didn't need any further interaction with the police, especially as he'd cheerfully told them all earlier that they'd let him off with a caution.

'So, you going to tell me a bit more about what's going on?' Melissa kept her voice low and a smile fixed in place, as if they were having a regular conversation.

He ran through the details of Chloe's revelation and, as he finished, she glanced down at her phone. 'Harry will be here in a couple of minutes.'

'Oh God, he's moving away from the bar. What if he leaves?' Chloe groaned.

Nathan pushed his chair back. 'I'll wander over and say hello, shall I? I might accidentally bump into him and spill his beer.'

'You need some back-up?' Paul playfully flexed one of his muscular arms.

He wondered how much his friend had pieced together from what he'd overheard.

'You don't need to bother telling me the ins and outs now. Who're we after anyway?'

'The young, thin guy near the bar in a faded red T-shirt and jeans. Straggly blond hair. Thin face. Wispy beard.'

Paul took a good look. 'Never seen him before. I think he could do with meeting a few of the regulars.'

'Yep, good idea. We can pretend we're going to get another round in.'

'No need to act.' Paul's rumbling laughter loosened Nathan's nerves a few degrees. 'Stay put, ladies.'

Melissa frowned, as if to ask if he was sure about this. He'd never been involved in a pub brawl before, but if that's what it took . . . Catherine and Johnny would never forgive him if he let Chloe down now, but more importantly he wouldn't forgive himself. He raised his voice. 'Must be my round.'

'About bloody time.' Paul spoke loudly enough for anyone around them to hear.

Their quarry had stopped to talk to one of the local teenagers, so Nathan ducked to the left and Paul automatically shifted right, ready to move in on him from both directions. Nathan was the closest so he pretended to stumble and plastered on a silly grin when the young man jerked around.

'Sorry about my mate.' Paul clapped a beefy hand on the boy's shoulder. 'We've just lost the quiz to a bunch of women and he's been drowning his sorrows. Let me get you another drink. You on pints or what?'

'No need, pal. I'm leaving. Forget it.'

They might not manage to delay him much longer without showing their hand. Sweat trickled down Nathan's back.

'Nah, can't do that, it wouldn't be right. What's your name? Haven't seen you here before. I'm Paul and this is Nathan.' The boy's pale eyes flitted between them.

'I'm, uh . . . Tommy.'

'Well, Tommy, you come with us.' Paul steered him back towards the bar and Nathan did his part by planting himself behind the two of them to cut off any possible escape route. Tommy sounded resigned as he asked for a half of Tribute and didn't say another word when Paul rambled on about the weekend's upcoming football matches and speculated on England's chances against Portugal.

'How'd the quiz go tonight?'

The sound of Harry's rumbling voice made Nathan sag with relief. He'd never been this happy to see a policeman. 'Second place again. Three guesses who beat us.'

'Do I need to ask?'

'Not really.'

Harry zeroed in on their new acquaintance. 'Are you a quizzer too?'

The young man's eyes widened. 'A what?'

'This is Tommy,' Paul said. 'We're buying him a drink because someone knocked into him. Can't hold your drink, can you, mate?' He punched Nathan on the arm.

'Well, Tommy — it's like this. I'd like a word with you down at the police station.' The abrupt change in Harry's attitude startled the young man, who turned white when the detective pulled out his warrant card. 'Just a few questions, that's all. At this stage.' Tommy's startled gaze shifted between the three of them. He peered over their shoulders as if sizing up whether to make a run for it. 'Don't even think about it,' Harry warned. 'I'll have the cuffs on you faster than you can blink.'

'Dunno what you think I've done but you can ask whatever you want. I've nothing to hide.' The bravado in his voice didn't match his slumped shoulders and hangdog expression.

If he was Chloe's attacker, why on earth did he come into the pub which was less than fifty yards from the shop? Anyone would think he *wanted* to be caught.

'Outside.' Harry gripped the boy's arm. Other people had started to notice that something was going on and Pixie looked worried. 'Nathan. Paul. Come with us for a minute, please, if you would.'

They walked past their table and he noticed Chloe burying her face in Melissa's shoulder. Outside the door a police car was parked by the curb and two uniformed officers jumped out. Harry passed Tommy over to them, issued some instructions, then turned back around again.

'You might warn Chloe that I'll need her down at the station in the morning.' He gave a tight smile. 'Thanks for your help. He would've got away if you hadn't acted fast. Chloe deserves justice.'

'She certainly does.'

Once the police left, they stood on the pavement looking at each other.

'That's a first for me.' Paul rubbed a hand over his thinning fair hair. 'Amy and her gang might've won the quiz but we've got the best story to tell.'

What had Melissa said the other day? Something about whether he missed his old quieter life? He didn't miss it one bit. Guilt sneaked in again. There'd been nothing exciting or gossip-worthy about what had happened to Chloe.

'Don't beat yourself up, mate. We've done our bit and it's up to the Old Bill now.' Paul shook his head. 'At least you're done being guilty over Melissa, aren't you?'

'How do you—'

'Small village, Professor. Jimmy Trevail was weeding the churchyard and spotted you and Melissa having a good old chinwag with Robin like he were going to answer you back.' A fleeting smile brightened his sombre expression. 'Were you asking his blessing?' Nathan didn't answer so his friend carried on. 'You planning to make an honest woman of her?'

He held off saying Melissa was as honest as the day was long and didn't need a ring to prove it. She'd been over the moon when Josie and Harry moved in together and he'd considered suggesting the same thing for them, but in the end something held him back. He couldn't work out if she wanted that, something more or neither.

'You've avoided the marriage noose longer than most of us, but there're worse things, you know.'

'I suppose. Let's go get that drink.' The sad headshake he received told Nathan what his friend thought of that lame response. Would Melissa think him equally sad if she found out?

CHAPTER THIRTY-SIX

'Yeah, Mum, I promise I'll think about coming for Thanksgiving. I appreciate Dad offering to buy my ticket but I need to do this on my own. You see that, don't you?' They were on delicate ground. Ever since Pat reported back to the family there'd been a new wariness in her parents' interactions, as if they were afraid of overstepping boundaries they hadn't been aware even existed. 'I doubt Nathan would be able to get away from work then, so perhaps we might do Christmas instead? The university shuts down for a couple of weeks over the holidays.' It was a subject they'd never touched on so she was making a lot of assumptions. She ran a hand through her hair and a blush worked its way up her neck, remembering the sensuous way Nathan slid his fingers through it in bed last night.

'Melissa, have you listened to a word I just said?' Sybil sounded irate. Mildly irritated was usually the most negative her perennially upbeat mother allowed herself to appear, so this must be serious. She could hardly admit to daydreaming about her lover. 'I said, if y'all can't get away for whatever reason, we'll come to you.'

Panic zipped through her faster than a Japanese bullet train. At almost forty she shouldn't be nervous about introducing them all, but the thought made her twitch. Would it be better done here or back on home turf? 'It's only early September so there's still tons of time to decide. Leave it for now, okay? Look, I'm sorry but it's my book club meeting tonight and I still need to get ready.' Thank goodness this wasn't a video chat or her mother would spot the soft lilac trousers and silk tunic she'd dressed in half an hour ago.

'All right, I'll let you go.' Her mother's martyred air didn't fool Melissa for a moment. Sybil would start a campaign to get the whole family on board so she'd be bombarded with similar pleas for a visit. A pang of homesickness struck out of nowhere. The leaves would change soon, and football season would start, then it'd be Thanksgiving — the time for pumpkin pie, hot apple cider and heavenly sweet potato casserole dotted with marshmallows, burned to a crisp the Rutherford way. Before she could make a fool of herself, Melissa said her goodbyes and tossed the phone on the bed. She wiped away a few tears before swearing out loud. Along with getting changed, she'd already put on her make-up. A quick peek in the mirror revealed the damage she'd done. It took several careful swipes of a tissue to fix the unsightly smears of mascara under her eyes.

She hadn't stretched the truth too much because now she genuinely was running late. Thankfully the meeting was next door at Josie's, but she'd promised to be there early for a quick drink and gossip. That wasn't happening now. Melissa slipped her feet into a pair of comfortable purple ballet pumps and hurried out of the door. As she scurried up the path, peals of Tamara's distinctive throaty laughter drifted out through the open front door. The minute she stepped inside her friend poked her head out from the living room.

'There you are! You're the last to arrive. What happened?'

'My mom rang as I was about to leave. Please tell me all the wine isn't gone?'

'We might've saved you a glass. Come on.' Josie steered Melissa towards the empty kitchen. 'What's wrong? You've been crying.'

'I haven't!' The protest died on her tongue. 'Not really.'
'You either have or you haven't.'

She explained about the phone call. 'It's not like me but—'

'You love your family and Tennessee's still home, right? That doesn't mean you're not happy living here.' Josie cocked her head to one side. 'Is Nathan still being all tight-lipped? You could ask him, you know.' Mischief sparked in her bright emerald eyes.

'Ask him what?'

'To move in with you or the other way around — after all, you love his house. You could even ask him to marry you if that's what you want.'

'I'm not doing either one! It's way too soon to think of anything long-term and I'm pretty sure he's commitment-shy anyway.'

'You daft woman.' Josie shook her head. 'I'd bet the only reason he stayed single was because he hadn't met the right one — or at least by the time he did Robin had already whisked you down the aisle. He's also looking for the sort of equal partnership his parents never enjoyed. Old Mr Kellow ruled the roost, and his sister strikes me that way too.'

Melissa couldn't dispute any of those things without lying through her teeth.

'Is he coming up this way later?'

'No, I'm going to him. Chloe and Toby are in Falmouth at a party.'

'How's she coping?'

'Now that the guy confessed? Relieved. I'm sure Harry didn't tell *you*, but he *did* share with Chloe some stuff about this Tommy Hunkin's background. She's soft-hearted enough to feel sorry for him now. Apparently his childhood was a revolving door of foster homes and as a teenager he got mixed up with a couple of boys who'd already been in trouble with the police. It was minor stuff until they talked Tommy into robbing the shop.' She half-smiled. 'They saw it as a soft target and convinced him all he had to do was show the knife and it'd frighten whoever was serving into handing the money over. None of them bargained on stroppy Ms Chloe. I think Tommy was so relieved when Harry turned on the thumbscrews that he confessed right away.'

'Harry did everything by the book and—'

'I'm teasing! I love that you're such a fiery tiger mom about him, it's so sweet.' Her friend pretended to gag. 'C'mon, let's get that drink you promised.'

'We'll have to ask the girls what they think.'

'About what?'

'Your dilemma.'

'Josie Hancock, you are absolutely not going to put my love life to a vote of the Back of Beyond Book Club.'

'Why not? You'll get heaps of advice and can take it or leave it.'

'Wonderful.' Her sarcasm went unnoticed.

* * *

Nathan paced around his study, or at least he tried to. The cramped room didn't allow for any serious pacing. Four of his generous strides took him right up to the fireplace before he needed to turn around and repeat the procedure towards the window.

He flung himself in his father's old chair and fretted. Was he more like Harold Kellow than he cared to believe? Too cautious for his own good? After all, he loved Melissa, so what was the problem? Their relationship was so comfortable and they were already quasi-living together, swapping from one house to the other as and when they wanted. Naturally, they'd both had adjustments to make. At first she rolled her eyes when he left things out of the fridge that he wasn't used to being in there — who on earth bothered to refrigerate marmalade? The heavy-handed way he slathered it on his morning toast meant a jar was finished long before it could go mouldy. He found her habit of flinging enough talcum powder around the bathroom to ensure it was under a permanent layer of magnolia-scented dust mildly annoying. But compared to the myriad of pluses arising from them being together, everything else was minor.

The sound of footsteps in the hall startled him.

'Hiya, why are you hiding out here in the dark?' Melissa rested one hand on her hip and the other against the door frame. The combination of her hair draped coyly over one eye, the sensuous silky outfit and bright crimson lips recalled an old-time movie star. A drift of her perfume came his way and Nathan automatically stood up.

'I didn't expect you yet.'

'Yeah, I know.' A teasing smile lifted her mouth. 'I left early. Before cake.'

'Before cake?'

'Josie even bought Chelsea buns from our favourite bakery in St Austell, to mimic the ones Noel serves in the book. She also set out a luscious platter of bread, tomatoes and salami, cheeses and fruit like the picnic Cosmo put together and served to Olivia when they were on the boat in Ibiza.'

'Don't tell me she chilled the wine by hanging the bottles in a sink full of cold salt water as if it was the Mediterranean Sea.' They'd whiled away several evenings reading and discussing the book together.

'She didn't go quite that far.' Melissa eased away from the door and stepped closer, reaching up to stroke her soft, warm fingers down his cheek. 'You haven't answered my question.'

He struggled to remember what it'd been. 'I was thinking.' He cleared his throat. 'About us. Our next step.'

'What a coincidence. The girls had something to say about that tonight too.'

Nathan's heart thudded in his chest. 'Tell me you're joking.' The colour leached from her face. She hadn't been kidding.

'I didn't bring it up. Josie thought—'

'Josie thought? What's it to do with her?' His voice reverberated around the room. 'We haven't even discussed it ourselves yet, but you thought it was okay to bandy around our private business to your half-drunk gossipy friends?' She flinched as if he'd hit her.

'They wanted to help. That's all,' Melissa whispered. 'I'm sorry. I never meant . . . It might've got a little out of hand.'

'You think so? Go on then, tell me what gems of wisdom the Penworthal coven came up with.'

Heat flared in her cheeks. 'They said you needed a push so I should take the initiative.'

'So, you're here to seduce me down the aisle?'

'No!' The idea clearly horrified her. 'I told them to butt out because we're taking it slow and don't need other people pushing us into things we're not ready for.'

His heart sank. She'd made her view perfectly clear. Perhaps he should have been relieved, but oddly enough he felt the exact opposite. A sudden flash of perception hit and he realized he was acting like a spoiled toddler. A more mature man would make fun of the situation instead of forcing the woman he loved to defend her friends. Nathan took a few quiet breaths to get a handle on his emotions then held out his hands. She hesitated for a second before placing hers on his palms, resting them there so his fingers could curl around, binding them together.

'I'm sorry. I spoke out of turn. I don't want to be that man. The one who flies off the handle rather than talking things through reasonably.' Nathan cleared his throat. 'You know I struggle to express myself sometimes, so I need your help.' Her eyes filled with tears. 'For God's sake don't cry. Please. I love you so much, Melissa. All I want is for us to make a life together.' He managed a wan smile. 'I'm pretty sure we've established that Robin wouldn't object.'

'What exactly are you asking?' Her voice trembled.

'Well, before I answer, I need to know if you meant that part about us needing to take things slow? Words, my darling, this is the time for them. If you're honest about how you really feel, I promise I'll be the same.'

'Okay.' Her pulse fluttered under his fingers. 'Right now I'm not in a hurry to make another trip down the aisle, but in the future, maybe? I'd love it though if we moved in together.' An impish smile broke through. 'Josie and Harry reckon it saves them a whole bunch of time instead of going backwards and forwards.'

'I'd be good with that. More than good. So where would you prefer to live? Yours, mine . . . or somewhere different?' Nathan hurried on. 'It can be as different as America, if that's what you want. I'm sure I could get a job there and—'

'You are a honey, but I love it far too much here to drag us back across the Atlantic Ocean.' Heat flared up her neck. 'Not to live, anyway.' A long rambling story about the phone call she'd had with her mother earlier tumbled out. 'I don't want you to feel pressured in any way. You probably go to Catherine's for the holidays and—'

'Catherine invites me but I rarely go. I'd love to meet your family and experience Christmas in Tennessee.'

'Great, that's settled then.' She beamed. 'As for where to live, I adore this house and would be happy to share it with you. It doesn't hold the memories that *Gwartha an Dre* does.'

A momentary punch of guilt hit.

'Don't apologize or get all noble on me,' Melissa warned. 'That's me being selfish enough to want a fresh start.'

He loosened his hands and slipped them around her waist to tug her close. 'I am too. My life's a thousand times better with you in it.'

'Only a thousand?' She pulled her mouth down in a pout.

Nathan pretended to think. 'It might be ten thousand on a particularly good day.'

'When I show you the purple silk lingerie hiding under these clothes, do you think that might crank it up a few degrees?' Wickedness sneaked into her voice.

'Perhaps.' Nathan shifted his aroused body, letting it speak for itself, and watched her eyes flare. 'I vote we take this to my bedroom so I can give a more considered verdict.'

'You sure know how to win a girl over.'

'We aim to please. I'm pretty sure we've done enough talking for now.'

'Actions instead of words, Professor Kellow?'

With a laugh he swept her into his arms and headed for the stairs.

* * *

Something tickled the back of her neck and she glanced over her shoulder to meet her lover's sleepy blue eyes. 'Are those stroking fingers the Kellow version of an alarm clock?' A delightful shiver ran over her skin as his hand shifted, caressing the sensitive hollow at the base of her spine. Melissa smiled at the puddle of purple shimmering silk on the floor. Her abandoned lingerie told its own story.

'Don't you think it's an improvement on harsh beeps or jangling music?' Searing, searching kisses heated her skin until she groaned. 'I'll take that as a yes.'

'I'm pretty sure I can't say no to you.' That feeble effort to sound put-out made him chuckle.

'Good.' He continued his lazy explorations. 'One thought struck me last night.'

'Only one? By my recollection you were full of them and followed through on most — not that I'm complaining.'

'Didn't think so.' Nathan turned her to face him. 'What about Chloe? I can't turf her out, but we don't need my niece around 24/7.'

'Well, when I move in here with you I don't plan on selling my house — at least not immediately. I hate the idea of leaving it standing empty but I'm not keen on the idea of renting it out and possibly getting stuck with nightmare tenants.' She needed to skew the truth slightly now and present the next suggestion as her own. 'Last night Tamara asked if any of us knew of a flat or house suitable for Toby and Chloe. It seems they're keen to move in together too. They'd prefer to stay in the village but so far they can't find anything suitable they can afford. I could let them have my house at a low rent so it'd leave this lovely place all for us.' The group had tossed around all sorts of ideas — from the eminently sensible to the wild and crazy in their efforts to help Melissa out. Tamara had come up with the solution Melissa had just suggested as her own.

'That's a great plan.' A frown wrinkled his brow. 'I'm not sure how thrilled Catherine will be. I suspect it'll shift me a few more steps down the favourite brother ladder. Deep down she still blames me for Chloe's refusal to go back to Oxford, and for her attack.'

'That's totally unfair.'

'Maybe, but Catherine's used to bossing me around and me not standing up to her. This is new territory for us. I doubt she'll be over the moon when you move in here either.'

She held back on saying that his sister had never been "over the moon" about her so that'd be nothing new. Perhaps with time Catherine would come to see Melissa as a positive addition to her brother's life rather than a negative one. Until then, she'd live with it — and him — and to heck with her.

'Let's not talk about my family any longer.' A sexy smile inched over his face. 'The special Nathan alarm clock earlier was for a very good reason.'

'Oh yeah, and what might that be?' Her efforts to sound wide-eyed and innocent failed when she stroked his chest then stepped her fingers inch by tantalizing inch down his body.

'If you keep this up we might need to put a blindfold on my sensitive Victorian house so it doesn't die of shock.'

'It'll have to learn to handle it.'

Nathan flipped her on her back. 'Last night you told me you wanted actions instead of words. I've a good memory.'

CHAPTER THIRTY-SEVEN

Six months later — early spring

'For heaven's sake, Josie, sit still or I'll poke this mascara wand in your eye!' Melissa remonstrated.

'Is he there?'

'For the third time — yes. Harry is in the garden waiting patiently for you.' She stood back to study her make-up job. 'Stand up. Turn around and let me check you over.'

'You've become very bossy.'

So much for her friend's determined assertion last autumn that she and Harry had no intention of getting married. His surprise Valentine's Day proposal had led to them all gathering today, a mere six weeks later, for a simple ceremony in Josie's garden. Thankfully the Cornish weather was close to perfect, with only a few puffy white clouds dotting the sky and temperatures mild enough that no one would shiver. Melissa smoothed out an invisible crease in the marshmallow-pink silk dress draping flatteringly around Josie's curves before falling softly to the floor. Next she tweaked one of the antique pearl slides holding back the bride's freshly dyed strawberry-blonde hair, a much more toned-down shade than her usual bright red. 'You ready to do this?'

'Very ready. I'd thank you for everything, but—'

'We'd both cry and ruin all my hard work.' Brisk was the only way to hold back the tears.

They made their way downstairs and stepped out the back door.

'Oh,' Josie gasped.

The Back of Beyond Book Club girls were waiting for them. They'd chosen their own dresses in complementary shades of pinks and purples and, like them, each one was unique and very different. On the elegant end of the spectrum was Evelyn's subtle pale lilac lace sheath, while Amy's was the complete opposite, a slinky purple satin hardly-there mini dress baring more tanned skin than most people risked on the beach.

"Marry Me" by Train started to play, courtesy of Nathan's old CD player. Melissa gulped back a rush of emotion as the detective, broad-shouldered and handsome in a grey suit, looked stunned as his bride walked towards him. She couldn't help smiling at his bright pink silk tie, a totally un-Harry selection that Josie had chosen to match her dress. Now the small gathering of friends and family turned for a glimpse of the bride.

'Off you go, and don't worry, the girlfriend posse will be right behind you.' Josie had coined that name for them. She'd insisted that the word bridesmaids was outdated, and matrons of honour — as most of them would officially be termed — a hundred times worse.

The brief ceremony was conducted by a nursing colleague of Josie's who moonlighted as a wedding and funeral celebrant. When she declared them man and wife, Harry gleefully swept his new bride into his arms and shamelessly kissed her for far longer than usual. Melissa reached for Nathan's hand but he continued to stare straight in front of him, as though his mind was elsewhere. Having lived together for months now she'd become more attuned to his moods but couldn't pin down what was wrong with him today. Tomorrow, her parents were arriving to spend the next ten days with them over Nathan's spring break. She couldn't imagine why that would be bothering him because they'd all got on famously over Christmas. In fact, when they left Tennessee her mother had pulled her to one side to say how much they loved Nathan, tentatively adding how much better suited they were than she and Robin.

She became aware that everyone else in the girlfriend posse was standing up again and hurried to join them. They'd let Harry in on their plan but Josie looked totally baffled as Laura grabbed an armful of books from under her chair and passed them one each. Melissa slipped into her allotted place between Tamara and Becky. Laura, Evelyn and Amy made a neat line opposite them. On a nod from their de facto leader, they lifted the books in the air to form a guard-of-honour.

'They're all Hercule Poirot stories,' Melissa explained to Josie. 'We know you've got a massive crush on the little man with the extraordinary moustache and only hope Harry knows you've married him as a poor substitute.'

'You're awful, the lot of you.' Josie's laughter hitched on a sob.

'Hurry up and walk through before our arms get tired,' Laura begged.

The happy couple headed down the makeshift aisle, a narrow grassy path between the rows of chairs, decorated by Mother Nature in a drift of fragrant pink blossoms from the two cherry trees flanking Josie's small patio.

Spring was such a hopeful time of year, Melissa thought, and it'd been "officially" that season in Cornwall for a good month now since the end of February. It'd amused her when Nathan explained that spring was declared in the county when the gardeners in charge of certain magnolia trees at six of the great Cornish gardens declared that each had reached at least fifty blooms.

Her friends had pulled up a circle of chairs on the lawn, appropriating bottles of champagne and glasses to get the party started.

'Where's the handsome professor?' Becky teased.

'I'm not sure. Maybe he needed the loo?'

'Sausage rolls or stuffed mushrooms anyone?' Chloe waved a silver platter in front of their noses. Nathan's niece and Toby had been pressed into service by Pixie, who was in charge of the simple catering needs for the low-key reception. 'We need to keep our landlady happy, don't we, Melissa!' The girl was back to her vibrant self these days, thanks partly to her caving in on seeing an excellent counsellor who'd helped her put her knife attack into perspective. She rarely had time for a breather between college, her shifts in the village shop and a full social life. The young couple were taking good care of her house too, and sounded on the same page when they talked about the future. 'Where's Uncle Nat?'

She almost told Chloe, and anyone else who was interested, that she wasn't his keeper. They lived together but weren't joined at the hip. If he chose not to hang around her and her chatty friends right now, that was fine. Except it wasn't. He'd barely made any comment when she put on her Grecian-style rose-pink chiffon dress that morning, or said a word when they drove through the village to the wedding. Through a taut smile she trotted out a repeat of the answer she'd given Becky. She determined to put Nathan out of her mind and throw herself into enjoying the afternoon.

By five o'clock she was dragging but rallied to join in the cheers when they gave Josie and Harry a rousing send-off.

'I've got a message from Uncle Nat.' Chloe joined her. 'He says to tell you he's got a headache and he's gone home.'

Headache? She'd give him headache.

'Toby's happy to run you down in his car so you don't break your neck in those heels.'

'That would be great.' The high-heeled silver sandals were rubbing tender feet more used to tennis shoes or flip-flops and she could hardly wait to kick them off. 'He's a good guy.'

'Yeah, he is.' Chloe blushed. 'I'm lucky.'

'So is he. I'll go find him.' She said goodbye to everyone and hurried away, spotting her nominated chauffeur in the middle of picking up empty glasses. 'I hear you're my designated driver.'

'Yep, and don't worry, I haven't been sampling the champagne. Strictly water for me.'

Thoughtful, kind, smart and good-humoured young men were thin on the ground and Melissa hoped Chloe would learn from her own mistake. "Exciting" wasn't all it was cracked up to be — in her case it had landed her with an easily bored husband. Nathan was like Toby, steadfast and decent. There must be a reason behind his strange behaviour today, and it was time to discover it.

* * *

Nathan turned over the small turquoise box in his hands. He'd registered a definite hint of wistfulness in Melissa's face when Josie and Harry announced their engagement. No one else would've noticed it, but after six months of sharing their lives he'd learned to decipher her emotions. Her father, Bill, a bluff, jovial man, was amused when Nathan phoned a couple of weeks ago to ask for his blessing. Clearly, he hadn't expected such a thing regarding his widowed, forty-year-old daughter. Now Nathan was afraid he'd got it terribly wrong.

'Is the dark helping your headache, sweetheart?' Melissa's voice was laced with suspicion and he turned to see her standing by the study door. 'In case you're interested, Toby gave me a lift so I didn't fall over in these killer shoes.'

His face burned, making him grateful for the dim light.

'You gonna tell me what got into you today or shall I take a wild guess?' She strolled across the room as the last burst of light from the setting sun shot in through the tall, narrow window. The rich rose-pink of her dress was a perfect foil for her silver hair. 'You've got it stuck in your head that I want what Josie and Harry have, is that it?'

If he agreed and was wrong, she'd be dismayed, but if he disagreed he'd be heading down a rabbit hole of dishonesty. 'I did think so, but I've talked myself out of being sure of how you feel and it's tearing me apart. *I* desperately want all of that with you,' Nathan rasped. Shock swept over her face. He set the box on the small inlaid wood table next to his chair and caught her gaze zeroing in on it. Rising to his feet, he held out his hands. In a repeat of the momentous day last September when they'd agreed to move in together, Melissa placed her palms on his upturned ones and he curled his fingers around hers. 'I've never proposed to a woman before and I'm scared stiff. There, now you have it. Mr Coward at your service.'

'Oh, Nathan, you silly, silly man.' A glorious smile wreathed her face. 'Trust your first instincts. Go on.'

'Go on, what?'

'Say what you've planned but please don't bother with the down on one knee rigmarole.' Melissa shuddered. He guessed she might be remembering Robin's proposal — a romantic extravaganza made at the top of the Empire State Building.

'In that case I'll keep it simple. I love you, and if you'll let me I want to spend the rest of my life proving it. Will you marry me?' Relief swept through him that he'd got the words out without making a complete idiot of himself.

'In the same spirit of simplicity I'll keep my answer short and sweet.'

Beads of sweat popped out on his forehead.

'Yes.'

'Yes?'

'Yes.' She grinned. 'I assume it's a yes or no answer? There isn't really a third option.'

Nathan let her hands drop and scrambled to pick up the box from the table. In his nervousness it slipped from his fingers and Melissa caught it in mid-air. She proffered the box to him with a broad grin.

'Yours, I believe.'

His shaking fingers almost defeated his efforts to prise the lid open. 'If you don't like it we can—'

'Oh God, Nathan, it's absolutely stunning. May I take it out? Say yes, please, please, please.' As soon as he nodded, she removed the ring and turned on the lamp to examine it closer. 'I've never seen a design like this before.'

'Well, I've never seen anything to compare to you so I had to search for something equally unique.'

'Professor Kellow, you are such a wordsmith sometimes.' She ran a finger over the irregularly shaped gold ring with a myriad of tiny diamonds set into the deepest of the crevices.

'They're made by a local jeweller who casts them in moulds filled with sand. That creates the pitted texture. This one is from sand collected at Lamorna Cove.'

Melissa's hand flew to her mouth and tears brimmed in her eyes. 'Oh my goodness, I couldn't say no to that, could I? Not that I want to.' The haste with which she raced to say the last sentence made him grin. Now she thrust the ring at him and held out her left hand. 'Go on then, and hope to God it fits.'

The ring slipped on as if it was made for her. Which it had been, but he'd keep that to himself.

'OMG, Josie will be totally amazed to hear this bit of news when they get back from Portugal.' She fell silent, then threw him a knowing look. 'Ah, but she won't be surprised in the least, will she?'

Nathan fought against blushing but his skin betrayed him.

'You conniving things. Was anyone else in on this?'

'I suppose she might've told Harry,' he mumbled.

'And the rest of the book club girls?'

He shrugged. Who knew how tight-lipped Josie had been.

'My folks will be knocked for six when I flash this around tomorrow.' When he didn't respond she shook her head. 'Not them as well?'

When he confessed to calling her father, she burst out laughing.

'That must've shocked the heck out of him.'

'He *was* mildly surprised.'

'I bet. Tell me you didn't announce it in the Rusty Anchor too?'

'Of course not!' After a few drinks one night he'd been on the brink of sharing his plan with Paul, but came to his senses at the last minute.

'And please tell me you haven't copied that dreadful reality show where the groom and his cohorts plan a surprise wedding? It's always hideous and the bride either throws a fit and tells him where he can go or bursts into tears and lies about how wonderful it all is.'

'My God, no!'

'Good, because I'm not dressing up as Ross and Demelza and getting hitched at the bottom of a derelict tin mine.'

Nathan pretended to consider the suggestion. 'Mmm, not a bad idea.'

'Yeah, it's not a bad idea — it's an appalling one.' She wagged a finger in his face. 'It'll be very quiet. Something like today's do. Midsummer in your garden will be perfect.'

Now he was the one laughing. 'You've had this planned for bloody ever, haven't you?'

'Not "forever".'

'Liar.'

Melissa's chin jutted in the air. 'Since about October, I suppose, if we're being pedantic.'

'Which we always are — words being our thing. So a month after you moved in was long enough to decide I was a keeper?'

Her eyes turned smoky. 'My heart knew that a long time ago, but it took a while for my head to catch up.'

'Mine too.' Nathan wrapped his arms around her.

'We can't change the past but you've sure said everything right now.'

It'd be a foolish man who kept talking at this point, and where Melissa was concerned, he refused to be one of those a moment longer.

EPILOGUE

Melissa stroked her brand-new wedding ring absent-mindedly as it glinted in the early evening sunshine. Glancing up, she caught Josie's blatant smirk. 'So I'm happy, is that okay?'

'It's more than okay, you daft creature.' Josie picked up the bottle of prosecco and topped up their glasses. 'There won't be any left for the girls if we're not careful.'

Tonight's July book club meeting was at Melissa's house. Or, to be strictly accurate, Dr and Mrs Nathan Kellow's house. It had been that for the last couple of weeks since their beautiful intimate wedding ceremony right here in the back garden.

'Don't worry, I've plenty more in the fridge. We've lots to celebrate . . .' Melissa's words trailed off. 'I was so down when I came back to Cornwall. It's hard to believe that was only just over a year ago. We're definitely poster girls for not being foolish enough to say "never again" on the romantic front. Do you think Evelyn's ready to agree with us?'

'I still can't get my head around her dating again.'

Melissa couldn't hide her satisfaction. 'I must say that introducing Evelyn to Professor Quinten Moore was a genius suggestion on the part of my brilliant husband.' Her cheeks heated. The novelty of calling Nathan that still made her tingle in all the best places.

'Quinten definitely isn't "dusty".'

They both burst into giggles. Melissa had been dubious when Nathan suggested his former English literature professor, a widower who'd recently moved to Cornwall, as a possible companion for Evelyn. He'd promised Melissa there was nothing stuffy or dull about the man, but she hadn't been convinced until Quinten came for dinner. The good-looking silver-haired man with his twinkling blue eyes, brilliant mind and youthful manner had entertained them with witty stories until long after midnight. By the time he left, Melissa was determined to get him and Evelyn together if it killed her. It'd been an epic undertaking to convince Evelyn to meet Quinten for a coffee, but it wasn't an exaggeration to say the couple clicked immediately.

Josie grabbed a handful of roast chicken crisps and crammed them in her mouth. 'Our whole group's grown so much closer,' she mused. 'We went through some tough times there for a while but I feel we've come out the other side stronger than ever.'

'We sure have,' Melissa enthusiastically agreed. She was so thankful Nathan understood that the important role her friends played in her life didn't take away from their own relationship.

Josie picked up her book and flipped through the pages. 'Tell me you'll have chocolate on offer tonight.'

'Is the Pope Catholic? How could we read a book called *Chocolat* centred around a chocolate shop and not eat some?' This month's read was the Joanne Harris classic set in a small French town. 'No one's dieting seriously at the moment so I've made wickedly fudgy brownies and a devil's food cake, and I've bought truffles from the fancy shop in Truro.' She smirked. 'Plus there are chocolate martinis!'

'Your idea of reading food-related fiction this year was a great one.'

'I'm not gonna argue with you there! Mind you, I felt a little pressure tonight on the refreshments front after Amy did such a good job in June with the yummy gingerbread recipe from Ruth Reichl's *Delicious!*

'And what about those awesome rose petal scones and lavender bread that Tamara made when we discussed *Garden Spells* the month before?' Josie said.

'Yeah, they're definitely high up the list. I loved the book that month. Sarah Addison Allen is a great writer.' She gave a warm chuckle. 'We can't forget the real purpose of the club.'

'Come on, we both know the book discussions are fine in their own way, but it's the friendship and companionship that mean the most — and thrashing *Proper Choughed* at quiz night, of course!' They laughed, but as Josie continued, both had tears in their eyes at her words. 'Friends who are there for you no matter what, and always have your back.'

'You won't believe what I heard in the pub today!' Tamara's yell broke through the moment, and next thing she scurried around the corner, her cheeks pink with excitement.

'Save it until we're all here,' Melissa said indulgently.

The rest of the group trooped in over the next few minutes and the usual round of good-natured gossip started, fuelled by the tray of chocolate martinis Melissa had hurried inside to fetch.

Melissa caught Josie's eye. This was everything.

THE END

THE CHOC LIT STORY

Established in 2009, Choc Lit is an independent, award-winning publisher dedicated to creating a delicious selection of quality women's fiction.

We have won 18 awards, including Publisher of the Year and the Romantic Novel of the Year, and have been shortlisted for countless others. In 2023, we were shortlisted for Publisher of the Year by the Romantic Novelists' Association.

All our novels are selected by genuine readers. We are proud to publish talented first-time authors, as well as established writers whose books we love introducing to a new generation of readers.

In 2023, we became a Joffe Books company. Best known for publishing a wide range of commercial fiction, Joffe Books has its roots in women's fiction. Today it is one of the largest independent publishers in the UK.

We love to hear from you, so please email us about absolutely anything bookish at choc-lit@joffebooks.com

If you want to hear about all our bargain new releases, join our mailing list: www.choc-lit.com/contact

ALSO BY ANGELA BRITNELL

LITTLE PENHAVEN
Book 1: ONE SUMMER IN LITTLE PENHAVEN
Book 2: CHRISTMAS IN LITTLE PENHAVEN

PEAR TREE FARM
Book 1: A CORNISH SUMMER AT PEAR TREE FARM
Book 2: A CORNISH CHRISTMAS AT PEAR TREE FARM

CORNISH CONNECTIONS
Book 1: A CORNISH SUMMER AT CLIFF HOUSE
Book 2: A CORNISH ESCAPE TO ST AGNES
Book 3: A CORNISH WEDDING RETREAT
Book 4: A CORNISH GETAWAY TO HERRING BAY
Book 5: A CORNISH SUMMER AT SEASPRAY COTTAGE

STANDALONE
A LITTLE CHRISTMAS PANTO
SPRING ON RENDEZVOUS LANE
CHRISTMAS AT MOONSHINE HOLLOW
NEW YEAR, NEW GUY
CHRISTMAS AT BLACK CHERRY RETREAT
THE BACK OF BEYOND BOOK CLUB

Milton Keynes UK
Ingram Content Group UK Ltd.
UKHW031041020824
446373UK00004B/188